Acclaim for Caridad Piñeiro's first South Beach Chicas novel

SEX AND THE SOUTH BEACH CHICAS

"A tart and tasty tale of South Beach chicas on a quest for love, lust and laughter. And not always in that order."
—Eloisa James, *New York Times* bestselling author

"You'll laugh and cry and cheer on these fun, gutsy and very real friends! Caridad's South Beach is so real I could smell the Cuban coffee. I wanted more!"
—Berta Platas, author of *Cinderella Lopez*

"A zesty, sexy read about real single women today—dealing with love, family, careers—struggling to balance all the things that matter to them and yet be true to themselves. I couldn't put it down. *Sex and the South Beach Chicas* is fun, sassy, sexy, and honest."
—Jennifer Greene, *USA Today* bestselling author of *Blame It on Chocolate*

"Caridad Piñeiro presents us with several delicious slices of life bonded together in strong female friendships. I found myself in one of the chicas. Read it, love it. You'll find yourself there too."
—Shirley Hailstock, bestselling author of *The Secret*

ALSO BY CARIDAD PIÑEIRO

Sex and the South Beach Chicas

South Beach Chicas Catch Their Man

Caridad Piñeiro

New York London Toronto Sydney

An *Original* Publication of POCKET BOOKS

 DOWNTOWN PRESS, published by Pocket Books
1230 Avenue of the Americas
New York, NY 10020

Library of Congress Cataloging-in-Publication Data
Scordato, Caridad, 1958—
    South Beach chicas catch their man / by Caridad Pineiro.—Downtown
Press trade pbk. ed.
      p. cm.
    ISBN-13: 978-1-4165-1489-3
    ISBN-10: 1-4165-1489-9
      1. Hispanic American women—Fiction.   2. Female friendship—Fiction.
3. Women journalists—Fiction.   4. Miami (Fla.)—Fiction.   I. Title.
PR9240.9.S36S68   2007
813'.6—dc22

                                                    2007002438

This Downtown Press trade paperback edition September 2007

10   9   8   7   6   5   4   3   2   1

DOWNTOWN PRESS and colophon are
trademarks of Simon & Schuster, Inc.

Manufactured in the United States of America

For information regarding special discounts for bulk purchases,
please contact Simon & Schuster Special Sales at 1-800-456-6798
or business@simonandschuster.com.

To my father, Gonzalo, who kept La Cubanidad alive for his children and grandchildren. Gracias, papi.

South Beach Chicas Catch Their Man

1

Sylvia Amenabar's life was anything but ordinary, thanks to three sex-crazed friends, her mother, who was a witch, and the undercover detective with whom she had yet to get under the covers.

But Sylvia loved her less-than-fairy-tale life and wouldn't change anything about it—except possibly the part about not being beneath the covers with Carlos, the Bad Boy detective who had turned out to be a Prince. Come to think of it, on top of the covers or on the floor or even on the kitchen counter would do.

In reality, anywhere would do, since all Sylvia could think about was having wild monkey sex with Carlos once he got out of the hospital. Of course, Carlos might interpret the having-sex part as meaning more than just having sex, which complicated things.

Sylvia wasn't sure that she was ready for anything more . . . involved. Her friends—all three having recently experienced the throes of committed relationships—would say Sylvia had intimacy issues, and they would be totally right.

She didn't trust men. In fact, as far as she was concerned men were dogs. She would allow, however, for a few rare exceptions. The problem was that she didn't know enough about Carlos to be able to decide if he was one of those exceptions, which was the reason why she wasn't ready for anything hinting at a Happily-Ever-After kind of ending. But she was ready for sex with him. More than ready for it.

As her mother had warned her months earlier, Sylvia had met a man who had started an itch. Maybe sex with Carlos would satisfy that itch, although her mama, witch that she was for putting such a curse on her, would argue that with some men not even sex was enough.

Not that her mama was any kind of expert on that, Sylvia thought as she walked out of the elevator in Miami's Jackson Memorial Hospital and toward Carlos's room.

Thirty years earlier, her mama had picked the absolutely wrong man. One who had impregnated her and then skipped out on most of his fatherly duties. Sylvia should be grateful that her father had at least provided for her financially, but that hadn't made up for the missing dad on birthdays, holidays, and on those days when life wore you down and you needed someone to hold on to.

Her mama had always been that someone and, of course, Sylvia's friends. They had been there for her nearly a month earlier when Carlos had been shot protecting her.

Which added guilt with a capital G to the list of reasons why she wasn't necessarily ready for anything more serious with Carlos. Her first investigative report on drug dealing in the South Beach hot spots had nearly gotten Carlos killed as he threw his body in front of hers when the drug dealers had opened fire. They had been angry that her article in a glossy monthly magazine had called attention to their activities, almost immediately creating increased scrutiny on them and a drop in business.

Carlos, she thought, pausing at his door and taking a deep breath. *Prince or a Bad Boy Frog?* she asked herself yet again, but told herself she didn't have to make that decision right at that moment.

She still had a little time.

She knocked and entered the room after his muffled "Come in."

He had been reading a magazine but smiled and tossed it aside as he saw her. The smile inched upward and lit up his eyes with their amazing mix of dark blue flecked with bits of teal and green. His hair hadn't been trimmed in the month he'd been in the hospital and the dark sable locks were tousled around his face, highlighting his eyes. Rough evening stubble darkened his cheeks and the strong edge of his jaw, all of it combining to make him decidedly and dangerously sexy.

"Querida," he said, the tones of his voice low. "I didn't think you'd make it tonight."

Visiting hours would be over in less than fifteen minutes, but Sylvia's afternoon assignment for the magazine had run longer than expected. She hadn't wanted to miss seeing him, maybe even cuddling close and sharing some physical intimacy the way they had the last couple of weeks. She'd come to need that sharing with him, something she didn't want to consider too intently for fear of what it would mean.

She walked over to the bed, sat on the edge, and considered him. A hint of his usual devil-may-care attitude glittered more brightly in his gaze tonight and she wondered why.

"You're awfully chipper," she said, leaning toward him and kissing him, but what started as a chaste hello kiss quickly morphed into something more intense as Carlos opened his mouth and moved his hand to her waist to possessively bring her closer.

"I'm finally going home," he somehow managed to get out between kisses and the slide of his tongue through the seam of her mouth.

"Mmm. Home," she said and laid a hand on his muscled chest over the fiftyish-style cotton pajamas his mother had insisted on bringing for him to wear. "I'm sure you'll be glad to be free of this getup," she said and playfully tugged on the pajama shirt.

He covered her hand with his and stroked it. "I recall you freeing me of these quite nicely on a couple of occasions," he said, grinning. His eyes had dilated to a deeper blue, and when she eased her hand from beneath his and undid the first button on the serviceable cotton pajamas, his eyes darkened a bit more.

"Like this, you mean?" she teased and snuck her hand beneath the fabric to caress his taut pectoral muscle. Beneath her palm, his nipple tightened and she shifted her thumb, dragged it across the heard peak, earning a muffled protest.

"*Querida*," he began, but she stopped him with a kiss and a tweak of the tight button of his nipple.

When they came up for air, she reminded him, "We still have time before they toss me out."

"Definitely," he said, and with his free hand, he lowered the hospital bed until it was flat and she could climb in and snuggle up against him.

They kissed again and Carlos slipped his hand beneath the hem of her knit cotton sweater and upward to cup her breast. Her nipple beaded instantly with his touch. He took it between his thumb and forefinger, gently rotated it, yanking a gasp of pleasure from her.

Her delight was short-lived as the door to his room flew open with a slam.

She scrambled out of his arms and off the bed to find his mother and sister at the door, the looks on their faces a combination of shock and displeasure. Sylvia hastily rearranged her top as Carlos fumbled with the blankets to hide his erection.

"*Mami*, I wasn't expecting you," he said as he raised the bed and shot Sylvia a look of dread from the corner of his eye.

The apprehension filling Carlos's amazing blue-green eyes surprised her. She had thought that there was very little that could scare her big brave cop. Sneaking a glance at the source of that terror—his *mami* and *hermanita*—it occurred to her that they didn't seem all that fear-inspiring.

"We came as soon as we heard that the doctors plan to release you tomorrow. We wanted to make plans for you coming home," his *mami* said. Without acknowledging Sylvia's presence, she walked right to the edge of the bed and seated herself there, leaving Sylvia cornered in the small private room.

His sister likewise ignored Sylvia as she approached and took a position on a chair on the other side of Carlos's bed.

"I appreciate your concern, but I'm headed home to my sailboat," Carlos corrected politely, determination replacing the earlier dread.

"*Mi'jo*, you can't live on that leaky old boat." His mother rose from the bed to plump the pillows behind his back, her elbow jabbing Sylvia in the side as she did so.

"She's not leaky, *Mami*. *Abuelito* and I made sure of it," he said with growing impatience.

"*Ay, mi'jo.* You and that *promesa* to your *abuelito*. Just because it got us here from Mariel doesn't mean you have to hang on to that old tub," his mother admonished, and his sister, Veronica, chimed in with, "Don't you think it's time you got a real home?"

"She's not leaky, and living there helps me save money," Carlos replied.

"Besides, she's actually rather yar," Sylvia jumped in, hoping that she could help Carlos out or at least deflect his mother and sister's attention.

It worked a little too well. The two women looked at her with annoyance. They were clones of each other with the same dark hair and blue eyes as Carlos. Beautiful Latinas with to-die-for *café-con-leche* skin who in unison said, "Yar?"

"It's a sailing term, *Mami*," Carlos explained. It occurred to her that this conversation might soon become like a tag team wrestling match, with each of them trading off in order to fend off his mother and sister.

"So you sail a lot, Sylvia?" Veronica asked, one dark brow flying upward to stress the doubt behind her question.

Sylvia shot a nervous glance at Carlos, who grasped her hand. *Tag, I'm "It,"* she thought. "Actually, no. I've only sailed with Carlos."

"Oh." Again in unison. Accompanied this time by some rather scrutinizing glances before Carlos's *mami* said, "You're coming home with me."

"And if not *Mami*, then me," his sister tacked on. "The *niños* will love having their *tío* around."

"How many kids do you have, Veronica?" Sylvia asked, her tones saccharine sweet.

Veronica tilted her head a bit defensively. "I have four wonderful children. They all love their *tío*."

She imagined that they did. She also imagined that

four children would leave Uncle Carlos little time to rest. Not to mention that they would possibly bump his injured leg or play with him a little too roughly, maybe aggravating his other wounds. As she met Carlos's gaze, it was clear he felt the same way, only this time, he defended himself.

"I appreciate the offer, but you both have enough to handle. *Mi amigo*, Riley, has offered—"

"You can't go with Riley," Sylvia blurted out, so forcefully that it shocked everyone in the room. "Riley's a little busy right now. He may not even be home all that often, and it would be nice for you to have someone around in case you needed help."

Carlos smiled and with a sexy wink said, "*Comprendo*. Riley's been spending a lot of time with your friend Adriana."

His mother clasped her hands and rose. "Well then, that settles it. You'll come home—"

"With me," Sylvia said, stunning everyone in the room again, including herself. It probably had been her guilt that made her actually say it, but now that she had, she was glad. For a couple of weeks, ever since it became apparent that Carlos was getting strong enough to leave the hospital, the idea of having him stay with her while he recuperated had firmly set its hooks in her brain and refused to let go.

"With you?" Carlos asked, his look dubious. He tightened his hold on her hand, as if that might keep her from retracting the offer.

Sylvia did in fact reconsider—for about a millisecond—but then she imagined Carlos in her apartment. Sitting at her table. Lounging on her couch. Sleeping in her bed. Any and all reasons why this might be a bad idea flew out of her head with the last image.

What better way to scratch her itch than having the source of it right in her bed!

"Yes, with me. My condo is big enough and has an elevator. It's a block from the park and gym, so you can exercise and get some fresh air. I'll be around, but not all the time, so you'll get to rest."

Veronica immediately went on the offensive. "Were you helping him *rest* when we came in?"

"Ronnie," Carlos warned as bright color swept across his cheeks.

Straightening her shoulders and facing his mother and sister head-on, Sylvia said, "Carlos will get the rest and attention he needs, plus I have plenty of room at my place."

"*Mi'ja*, that's very nice of you, only my son, Carlos—"

"Is going with Sylvia. It's what makes the most sense," Carlos said emphatically, a broad grin on his face.

Actually, it might not be sensible, but then again, playing it safe had never been her credo in life. Although as his mother and sister glared her way, she realized she would have to make sure Carlos's recuperation didn't hit any bumps. These two would take a piece of her hide if anything went wrong with their precious boy.

"I'll take good care of him."

"Like you did when you got him shot?" Veronica attacked once again, ice dripping from her words. She crossed her arms in a challenging stance as she awaited Sylvia's reply.

That ice did its job as a chill settled on the room. Sylvia knew Carlos felt it, since he rubbed her hand with his. When he spoke, his voice was tight and angry. "What happened on my assignment had nothing to do with Sylvia."

"*Mi'jo*—" his mother began, but he stopped her with a sharp slash of his hand.

"This discussion is over. *Mañana* I go home with Sylvia."

Tomorrow, she thought. Tomorrow she would have him sitting at her table, lounging on her sofa, and sleeping in her bed.

The last brought a curl of warmth that drove away the earlier chill of guilt. "Yes, definitely. Tomorrow you come home with me."

And yet after she confirmed it and his family reluctantly accepted the decision and left the room, it occurred to her that despite her thoughts that it was time to scratch her itch, sometimes scratching wasn't a good thing. Chicken pox, poison ivy, and mosquito bites all made you itch, but scratching too hard could leave scars.

But the thought of having Carlos in her bed brought a delicious blast of desire in her body that she was hard-pressed to deny.

"Having second thoughts?"

She realized that she was holding on to his hand with a death grip. Because their relationship had started with less than honesty between them, she wanted to continue whatever was going on between them on the right foot. "Mixed thoughts."

He leaned forward and cradled her cheek. "Don't be afraid of trusting your heart."

She wondered if it was some kind of cop thing that allowed him to read her so well. "I'm attracted to you, but . . . We need time to really explore what's going on between us."

He nodded and rubbed his thumb across her lips, his gaze hot as it settled on her lips. "If you lock the door, we can avoid any more surprises and maybe start that exploration."

The spiral of warmth that had started earlier ignited with his touch. His look. Those words.

She did as he asked, walking to the door and locking it before returning to his side. He had shifted on the narrow bed, leaving space for her, and lowered the bed once again. He patted the empty spot beside him, and she lay down as she had done a half dozen or more times before over the course of his hospital stay.

At first, she had just offered the comfort of her body to drive away the loneliness of his being trapped in the hospital. The last few times, however . . .

"I'm glad you're ready to leave here." She raised her hand and placed it over the cotton pajama top he wore. Beneath her hand the beat of his heart was strong and steady. So unlike the way it had been the night he had been shot.

"Don't think about that," he urged, reading her mind, and brought his lips to hers.

"How did you know?"

He smoothed a finger across the ridge of her brow. "You get a small furrow. Right here." For emphasis, he stroked that place, the pad of his finger rough against her skin. Awakening the thought of how that finger might feel elsewhere.

"And you get tense. Your eyes grow cold."

"Cold? Tense?" She shifted so that their bodies were almost touching, reached up and cradled the back of his head. "So maybe you should help me warm up. Relax."

He did, bringing his lips to hers, kissing her. His lips were hot and pliant. Wet. *Delicious,* she thought as she opened her mouth against his, sucking his full lower lip into her mouth. He groaned and she chuckled. "Like that?"

"*Sí,* as much as you like this," he whispered, cradling

her breast and rubbing his thumb against her nipple, which immediately peaked at his touch.

She let out a little mew of pleasure as he tweaked the tip, and she kissed him again. Tongued the outline of his lips and then slipped past his lips to taste him. Sucked on his tongue and after, shifted to drop kiss after kiss on his face. Along the strong line of his jaw to the spot between his neck and shoulder, where she gently bit him.

He groaned again. "*Dios,* if this is just the start—"

It *was* just the start, and she didn't think she could take it slowly after the months of waiting and wondering. Of wanting him like she hadn't ever wanted another man.

That thought was like an icy bucket of water being tossed over her. She was afraid of wanting him so much. She had to play it safe before she scratched so hard that it left a scar.

She slipped from the bed and stood beside it, arms wrapped around her midsection. "Maybe this isn't such a good idea."

"Really?" he said with a look in his eyes that said he wasn't buying it. He moved to sit up but grimaced and grabbed his side as he did so.

"Are you okay?" she said as she immediately went to help him, but he shrugged off her attempt to help.

"I'm not a sick puppy, okay? I'm a man. I can handle this."

Pricked by his tone, she fought back. "So you're a man? Duh, I hadn't noticed."

"Sylvia," he warned, but she charged on.

"Big brave man, right? Not afraid of bullets or knives. But your *mami* and sister . . . Oooh, you're right. They're scary. Downright frightening."

Carlos chuckled. She plopped down on the bed beside him. He cupped her cheek and offered up an apology.

"*Perdoname.* I'm just suffering from a bad case of cabin fever."

"I understand." She couldn't imagine being trapped in a hospital for nearly a month, especially over the holidays. No parade of people could make up for not being home during those times.

"Do you?" he asked, but the tone in his voice dared her. As she met his gaze, she realized he was asking her to try and understand about more than his injuries. He was asking her to try and understand the complex man he was. To accept the attraction that had been there between them from the moment they had first laid eyes on each other. An attraction they hadn't really had a chance to let grow.

He was asking her to take that chance now.

Because she didn't want to be like her mama, wondering thirty years later about what might have been, she nodded. "The offer to come home with me is still good. You better accept it before I change my mind."

"It will give us time to explore what we feel for each other."

"That sounds good," she said, but as his deep blue-eyed gaze deepened to an almost sapphire color, she knew he was imagining just how delightful their explorations might be.

And she couldn't help wondering about it herself.

2

The drive from the hospital back to South Beach wasn't that long. She still had time to meet her friends for their regular Monday night gathering. It had been a month since they had started them up again after their major falling-out over Tori's surprise elopement.

That elopement had rocked the foundations of their lifelong friendship. At one point, they hadn't spoken to one another for weeks. It had taken a series of unrelated but life-altering events for all of them to realize just how valuable their friendship was and how they couldn't abandon it so easily.

Sylvia was glad that they had gotten back into their normal routine of workouts and dinners, especially with the holidays having just finished.

Since her main task at the magazine was still being the After Dark and Gossip reporter, the seasonal festivities had necessitated her covering parties at all the Miami hot spots, not to mention visits with her friends and their families, and her own mother's annual Christmas bash for her real estate agency employees and clients.

After Sylvia drove down Ocean Drive past the former Versace mansion and turned on Thirteenth by the Cardozo Hotel, she lucked out and was able to park her car right by her apartment close to Collins. Grabbing her bag with her workout clothes, she walked up the street toward the gym, but at the corner, she caught a glimpse of herself in the gleaming metal and glass facade of a newly opened clothing store.

Was the elegant winter white suit she wore a little tight around her hips? she thought as she glanced at her reflection, smoothing the fabric over the rounded curves of her bottom. The jacket barely closed over her breasts where the cotton knit sweater she wore clung lovingly.

Damn, her hips felt and looked about a hundred pounds heavier, Sylvia thought with a grimace, tossing back her long blond hair. She hurried to the gym. She didn't want to be late to meet her friends.

The January air was crisp by Miami standards—a chilly sixty-five degrees with a strong breeze blowing in from the ocean that made her shiver. She pulled her light wool blazer tightly around her and rounded the block where a few patrons waited at David's Cafeteria's corner counter, ordering *café con leches* and Cuban sandwiches to go.

As she walked by, the waitress behind the counter picked up her head and called out, "*Hola, Sylvita.* How's Carlos?"

At the young woman's greeting, the patrons turned to look at her and also added their well wishes. Carlos was the equivalent of a local celebrity in South Beach, especially among the Cubans.

"Missing your Cuban sandwiches, but he'll be out soon," she tossed back as she paused for only a second.

"*Prebecito*. Tell him I'll have his favorites waiting for him. We'll need to get some meat back on his bones after all that hospital food."

Sylvia nodded and waved, then continued up Thirteenth toward the gym. Just a half block ahead between Collins and Washington, the South Beach Fitness Association had been just a local joint when it first opened, but had somehow caught the attention of the rich and infamous who liked its "authentic" feel. For years now, an assortment of celebs and wannabes had flocked there to keep their bodies buff after the excesses of life in Miami. Too much food, drink, and drugs needed to be cleansed from the system by a good clean sweat.

Sometimes the stream of celebrities grew tiresome, but most of the locals stuck with the gym, knowing that in South Beach fads came and went as quickly as a category 5 hurricane.

Sylvia had just opened her locker when her friends Adriana and Juliana arrived. They were co-owners of Casa Criolla, one of the trendiest hotel/restaurants on the Ocean Drive strip. As the chef, Juliana provided the soul of the kitchen, while Adriana's sharp business skills kept things running smoothly behind the scene.

"That tamale pie was a big hit, although I think I need to go a little spicier with the sauce," Juli said.

Adriana, ever the businesswoman, saw the dollar signs instead. "Lots of orders for it. Especially with the chill we've had this week—"

"So maybe we should add an old-fashioned *caldo gallego*," Juli suggested, but as both women realized Sylvia was waiting for them to take a breath, they stopped to greet her.

"Good to see everything's back to normal," Sylvia said. Adriana and Juli had clearly dealt with the fallout from their fight before the holidays and if anything, they seemed to have a newfound balance and equality in their relationship.

"Better than ever," Juli answered and they all exchanged exuberant hugs.

They changed into their workout clothes. Sylvia eased on a FILA sweat suit while Adriana donned her usual tight-fitting cropped baby tee and capri pants. The clothes accented the voluptuous curves on Adriana's petite physique, so unlike Sylvia's own long and relatively lean body, holiday pounds not withstanding. With a quick little flip and turn of her auburn shoulder-length hair, Adriana secured it into a fashionable twist at the back of her head.

Juliana still hid behind the door of her locker, partially obscuring her view, but she seemed less bashful than before. In the past, Juli would have slipped into a loose gray fleece sweat suit that hid her ample attributes. But no longer. In fact, as Juli changed into more stylish Reebok togs, it occurred to Sylvia that her friend looked rather fine. The new cut of her thick coffee brown hair accented her stunning almond-shaped eyes and cheekbones. She had also slimmed down, but still had those dangerous Latina curves men loved.

"Juli. You look amazing. What's the secret?"

"Sex," Juli replied without hesitation, shocking Sylvia so much that her mouth dropped open.

"Sex?" she stammered.

"*Sí*. You should know, *verdad*," Juli said with a wink as she walked to her locker to put away her street clothes.

"Sex?" Sylvia repeated again, her comment close to a croak, and shot a glance at Adriana, who shook her head and chuckled.

"Girl, you do get it, don't you?" Adriana teased and nudged her with one rounded hip.

When Sylvia shook her head, clearly confused, her friend continued. "You really are in a bad way if you can't tell that Juli's teasing." After a moment's hesitation, Adriana whipped around to face her partner and asked, "You are teasing, right? Are you dating someone?"

Juli chuckled and secured the sleek thick locks of her hair with a utilitarian scrunchy before admonishing her business partner. "*Sí, como no.* You know I'm between *novios* right now, although Vince has been calling again. Unlike Sylvia who—"

"Doesn't want to discuss this." She raised her hand to stop Juli from prying about Carlos.

Luckily, she was spared from further discussion about her sex life as Tori arrived in a hurry, dressed in a conservative black suit and crisp white shirt that just screamed "Lawyer!"

"Tough day?" Sylvia asked since it looked like her friend had just come from her office.

As Tori slipped off her blazer, she mumbled, "Not really. It's just that Gil and I . . . Well, we had a brief to work on."

It took but a second for Sylvia to notice that Tori's shirt was misbuttoned and even less time for her to see that her friend's long brown hair was mussed in a way that told her just what she and her new husband had been working on. "So, Tori, was the brief a nice tighty-whitey or boxers?"

"No way, Sylvita. You are not going to get any vicarious smoochies from my life," Tori responded and started in on the buttons of her shirt. As she realized they were off, she mumbled a curse and a becoming blush blossomed across her face.

Adriana eased over to Tori and laid a hand on her shoulder. "Don't let Sylvia rattle you. She's just a little jealous," Adriana said, but her words lacked their prefallout sting.

Deciding to avoid any response, which might prompt scrutiny of her nonexistent love life, Sylvia rose and inclined her head in the direction of the gym. "We came here to work out, didn't we?"

"We did, *amiga*. But that doesn't mean you can't spill the *frijoles* about Carlos," Juli said as she wrapped an arm around Sylvia's waist and walked with her out to the gym.

Sylvia playfully nudged her much shorter friend. "What's there to tell? He's in the hospital—"

"But getting out tomorrow according to Riley," Adriana chimed in from behind her.

Which would have been the perfect time to tell them that Carlos was coming home with her, only she wanted to keep it to herself for just a moment longer. Wanted to let the idea firmly establish itself, because she didn't know how they would react to the news and worried they would misinterpret it as being something more than it was—just a friend helping out a friend.

Or at least that's what she was trying to convince herself it was because emotionally she couldn't handle anything else.

As Adriana took a spot on the bench press, Sylvia spotted her while Tori slipped onto a second bench-press machine. When Adriana grabbed the handles, she said, "Riley's worried about Carlos going back to that damn boat. He doesn't think Carlos can manage, as injured as he is."

Needing to turn the focus on anyone but Carlos right now, Sylvia asked, "So how are things between you and Riley?"

With a quick hoot and a nudge, Juli supplied the answer. "It's a wonder she can walk, *amiga*." To emphasize the point, she took a few bowlegged little steps.

They all laughed, and she considered her boisterous friends as both Adriana and Tori began their reps. "So, I gather you three are now *locas* in love. Am I right?"

Tori and Adriana didn't say a word, while Juli fanned her hand to deny it. "In between *novios,* remember. Not that I'd pass up Señor Right, or even Señor Maybe, if he came along. So *que pasa* with you and Carlos?"

So much for diverting attention. Especially when both Adriana and Tori stopped their reps and added their undivided attention to Juli's determined gaze.

"What? Is this true confession time?" With a flick of her wrist, Sylvia urged Adriana to finish her reps.

Her friend did as she asked, as did Tori. But once they had switched places, the conversation resumed.

"So, Sylvita," Tori began. "You were involved with Carlos for months before he was shot. Now he's getting out of the hospital—"

"And going home," Sylvia advised, still in avoidance mode.

"Girl, come on. Going home to his sailboat? With a bum leg and other assorted injuries?" Adriana pressed, her tone slightly sharper and more condemning.

Sylvia excused the tone because of all of them, Adriana possibly understood what it was to be involved with a cop. When Riley and Carlos had been shot several years earlier, Adriana's now boyfriend Riley had opted to leave the force, but the scars had reopened, thanks to his ex-partner's more recent wounding. It had been Adriana who had been at Sylvia's side in the hospital, waiting with her and Riley to find out if Carlos would survive.

Trying to stop her friend's dogged questioning, Sylvia

dropped her weights with a clang and sat up. "And again, what is this? The Spanish Inquisition?"

Juli stopped her reps and leaned toward her. "*Mira.* You were always the first to say that you shouldn't feel guilty about the whole sex thing. Take him home and have your way with him."

At Juli's words, heat erupted across her face. She stammered, since the words stuck in her throat at first, but she finally managed to get them out. Barely. "Who said anything about taking him home? Or about having sex with him?"

"It makes sense, even to lil' ol' married me," Tori chimed in and leaned against the metal of the weight machine.

With an emphatic nod, Adriana echoed that opinion. "More sense than him going home with his *mami, hermanita,* or Riley. Especially not Riley."

Sylvia sighed heavily and dragged back a lock of hair that had come loose during her workout. "What if Carlos came home with me? Don't you think it would really complicate things?"

Juli jumped into the fray first. "If Carlos did go home with you, it would make the whole sex thing—"

Sylvia waved both her hands in the air to stop them. "*Locas.* You are all absolutely certifiably insane, since no one has even mentioned the whole sex thing."

Silence greeted her before her three friends exchanged worried glances. Knowing that she would never get any rest if she didn't explain, she started. "We . . . I didn't . . . There hasn't been any . . . you know . . ."

"*Amiga,* forgive us. We forgot he's been hurt. So it's probably been like in one of those mushy Lifetime movies, all slow mo and fuzzily tender. *Verdad?*" Juli looped her arm around her shoulders and gave a reassuring squeeze, but Sylvia shrugged it off.

While there had been a few romantic overtures recently—all that the narrow hospital bed would allow—she wanted a break from the whole her-and-Carlos discussion. Trying to change the subject yet again, she asked, "You watch Lifetime?" At the same time, Juli exclaimed, "You've never slept with him!?"

Silence reigned again at the workout equipment for long moments as they all peered at one another, but when it became apparent that Juli's statement was correct, Adriana laid a hand on her shoulder and patted it consolingly. "I don't understand, Sylvia. That day in the hospital, when we were waiting—"

"I said I had feelings for him in the heat of the moment," Sylvia admitted and then plowed on. "There's definitely mutual attraction there. But maybe that's all there is."

She slipped from the bench press to the next piece of equipment. As her friends followed her, Tori swapped places with Adriana and spotted her at the leg press. Tori's concerned gaze was intense as Sylvia began her reps. So intense that Sylvia knew she had no choice but to finish the conversation.

"I offered to bring him to my condo to recuperate, okay? He accepted. Will that satisfy all of you?"

"But you haven't . . . you know . . . ," Adriana continued, but faltered.

At that hesitation, Juli said, "*Amiga*. Considering what you and Riley have been up to, you should be able to say it. Sylvia hasn't had sex with Carlos."

Sylvia cringed, unsure that she liked Juli's new forthrightness. She scrutinized everyone else in the gym to see if they had heard, then shot a withering glance in Juli's direction. "Juli, please. It's complicated."

"It wasn't complicated when you thought he might

die," Adriana challenged, clearly annoyed with Sylvia's in-decision.

Tori, ever the mediator, jumped in. "Cut her some slack, Adriana. It's been a rough few weeks, and she's bound to be feeling confused."

Sylvia thought about those first few hours in the hospital when she hadn't known whether Carlos would die and the week after that, when he'd barely clung to life. Rough was an understatement.

"I'm the one who caused all the pain he's in," she reminded them.

"You didn't shoot him, Sylvita," Tori said gently and laid her arm over Sylvia's shoulders, trying to offer comfort.

"I might as well have. If it hadn't been for me—"

"It would have been on account of someone else. He saved Riley four years ago, remember. He's a Save-the-World kind of guy," Adriana added in an attempt to make up for her earlier attack and defuse some of Sylvia's guilt.

Her guilt being one of the dozens of reasons why she didn't know where to go with Carlos. "He *is* Mr. Save the World," she said softly and clasped her hands tightly on the handles of the leg press. "I wonder if I'm just another damsel in distress that he thinks he has to save?" she considered out loud.

Tori reassuringly squeezed her shoulder. "The last thing anyone would think about you is that you need to be saved. You're too strong, but . . . Don't guilt yourself into doing something you don't want to do."

"*Mira*, I'm probably the last one to be giving advice. *Pero* his coming home with you is a good thing, *sabes*. It will give you the time to get to know each other so you can get over whatever commitment issues you have," Juli said.

"You are so totally right," Adriana joined in, but then immediately added, "but don't take as much time as Riley and me because you don't have twenty years to waste."

Sylvia couldn't help but laugh at that. Adriana had had a crush on Riley since the age of nine, when she had first met him. The feelings had apparently been mutual, but the two had only recently gotten around to doing something about it. Which for some reason brought her mother to mind, since Sylvia suspected that for her mama, there hadn't really been a man in her life in the thirty years since she had met Sylvia's Argentine polo-playing playboy of a father. The father who had taken her mama's heart with him when he left.

"A few months ago, my mama said that one day I'd meet a man who I wouldn't be able to get out of my system. I guess my mama should know."

"*Por que?*" Juli asked.

She faced her friend directly. "Because mama's had a thirty-year itch for my daddy, only she hasn't scratched it."

"Which is a humongous mistake," Tori responded.

"Girl, don't I know it," Adriana offered, which prompted chuckles from all of them. "So tell me, Syl. What do you plan on doing about your Carlos itch?"

Her mama had never scratched until relief came, making it impossible for her to get Pablo out of her system and find someone else. As much as she loved and respected her mother, Sylvia had no intention of making the same mistake.

"I plan to scratch."

3

In anticipation of having Carlos move in with her, Sylvia borrowed the key to his sailboat and dropped by to pick up some of his things so they would be waiting for him at her condo.

As she undid the lock on the railing and swung it open, she hesitated about going on board. It was just one little step, she told herself as she grabbed hold of the metal railings on either side of the opening. The railing was gritty, the metal a bit dull. Not in the condition it would be in with Carlos living on the boat. He kept everything gleaming and shipshape, much like he seemed to keep everything in his life in order.

So unlike her with her hectic and erratic life. Between her dysfunctional family situation and her job as a reporter, nothing was ever orderly, which just increased her doubts about the wisdom of what she was doing. She and Carlos were total opposites in every way she could think of, but inside her heart, something told her that maybe in some of the important things they were very similar. That made her grasp the railings more tightly and boost herself up and over onto the smooth teak deck of the boat.

Just one small step at a time, she told herself, but the annoying voice in her head added, *One giant leap for Sylvia.*

Like the railing, the deck had been washed down, but not carefully. In the many hours she had kept Carlos company, she had gotten to know just how special this boat was to him, although she had known it even before he had told her the story about his family's trip from Mariel on the boat. The care he gave the craft spoke volumes.

His mother had called the boat a *promesa,* and it was true. Carlos had promised his grandfather that he would one day sail the boat back to a free Cuba.

Carlos intended to honor that promise, and as she unlocked the cockpit and went below, she considered the kind of man he was and the kind of woman she wasn't— one who could commit to something as important as that promise.

Below deck it was musty, but not overly so. His best friend, Riley—Adriana's Riley—had been coming by to air out the boat every now and then. Everything below deck was diligently tidy the way Carlos had left it.

She walked toward the bow and the stateroom there. Searching through a small chest of drawers, she located some shirts and underclothing for him, grabbed some jeans from a small closet as well as a duffel to stuff everything into.

She lingered for a bit, sitting on the large bed taking up most of the space in the stateroom and remembered the one night they had spent there. A night just holding each other. Talking until they drifted to sleep.

Was that what they would do tonight? she thought as she finally forced herself to move.

Carlos was waiting for her at the hospital, and the longer she delayed, the greater the possibility became that she might change her mind.

Just one small step at a time, she reminded herself.

Because she couldn't imagine Carlos prying himself into her small and rather low Bimmer convertible, she had borrowed Tori's husband's Jeep that morning. A wise decision she realized as Carlos carefully eased onto the seat of the SUV barely a couple of hours after she had picked up his things from the boat. Carlos settled himself into the passenger seat and stretched out his injured leg with a grateful sigh.

As she started the short drive from Jackson Memorial to her condo, she shot a glance at him. Beneath the wonderful light caramel color of his skin, he seemed pale. His full lips were pressed into a thin grim line, and although he had tried to hide it, she had noticed his limp and the way he favored one side—the side where he had been shot—as he walked the short distance from the hospital door to the Jeep.

"You okay?" She laid a hand on his thigh as she drove, wishing she could ease the pain he was so stoicly trying to hide.

"I'm okay, it's just . . . Those small little strolls in the corridor didn't prepare me for much," he grudgingly admitted.

With a nod, she stopped at a light and met his gaze. "Once you start to really move around—"

"It'll get better. I know. I guess I'm just impatient to be a hundred percent again."

She totally understood. A man like Carlos didn't like relying on anyone, and in that way, they were a lot alike. "I wouldn't like being dependent on anyone either."

He cradled her cheek, shifted his thumb and rubbed it across her lips. "*Amorcito*, I think both of us are going to have to learn to lean on each other little."

A honk from behind them pulled her attention away and they were silent for the remainder of the ride to her condo. The block was full, and although she would normally then pull into the public lot a few blocks away rather than trying to find parking on the street, she didn't think Carlos could manage it. Instead, she kept on going around the block and lucked out as someone finally pulled out just a few spaces down from the front door of her building.

She struggled with the larger-size Jeep, but after a few awkward moves—and a slight case of parking by touch—she managed to fit into the tight spot.

With a glance in his direction, she said, "Ready?"

He nodded and opened his door while she grabbed the small bag that contained all the stuff he'd had with him in the hospital. As she stepped to the curb, she watched him struggle out of the car and then lean heavily on the fender as he made his way to the front of the Jeep to wait for her. At the curb, he did an awkward little hop-skip to get up onto the sidewalk.

He teetered for a moment, and she rushed to his side and helped support him.

"*Gracias.*"

"No problema," she said, and between the two of them, they slowly walked to her building and took the elevator up to her floor. Once inside, she sneaked a peek at him.

He had grown even paler. Beads of sweat had popped out on his upper lip. "Let's get you settled in bed."

That he didn't argue—or offer any comment drenched with sexual innuendo—was a testament to his pain. They shuffled to her bed and she helped him sit.

"I'm sorry," she said as she gazed down at him, unable to ignore his discomfort.

Carlos raised his hand to stop her. "Don't go there. It's not your fault."

She kneeled before him and cupped his cheek. "I try to tell myself that it wasn't. That you're Mr. Save the World and it was part of your regular job."

"It *was* just part of my job." He laid his hand over hers, then twined his fingers with hers. He applied gentle pressure until she rose up on her knees. Thanks to her height, her lips were almost level with his, and he took advantage of that, leaning forward to place a kiss on her lips. Not one of desire, but of thanks. Of caring.

It humbled her, something that wasn't easily done. Possibly had never been done.

Sinking back onto her buttocks, she laid her hands on his thighs, rubbed them back and forth there nervously, but lightly, conscious of the wound to his one leg. "I got some clothes and stuff from the boat. This way you can be more comfortable. Feel more at home."

He half-turned and glanced at the large expanse of the king-size bed. "I will definitely be comfortable here. There's more than enough room for us—"

"I'll be sleeping on the couch," she said, her earlier doubts surging and making her rethink how nice it would be to sleep with him tonight. "Why don't you lie down and get some rest. I'll be back in a couple of hours."

He masked the surprise and dismay on his face for all of a second before he said, "You can only run for so long, *amor.*"

Because she wasn't normally the kind to back down, she leaned close and whispered, "I think a fast shuffle will suffice for right now."

He chuckled. "Well, you've just given me even more incentive to get better soon."

It dragged a reluctant laugh from her. "There's nothing that scares you, is there?"

With a shrug of his too broad shoulders, he said, "Just one thing, actually."

She considered him carefully but couldn't figure it out. "What?" she asked, but wasn't prepared for his answer. "You."

She'd had one short afternoon assignment for the magazine. Luckily, the fashion show at the Delano was done well before dinnertime, and her next assignment wasn't until eight, giving her a few free hours. It occurred to her on the way home that she had nothing to feed Carlos. She was used to shopping for one. Actually, who was she kidding? She rarely shopped, living off the goodies offered at the assorted parties she had to attend and dinners out with her friends. Occasionally takeout if she was going to be home at night, which wasn't that often.

Which made her consider that Carlos might have been better off going to his *mami*'s or sister's house. It wasn't like she was suddenly going to go all domestic and become the next Martha Stewart or do the whole Daisy Cooks! routine.

But then again, being a single man, Carlos probably knew how to fend for himself. All she had to do was have some food on hand so that he could whip up something when she wasn't around.

She stopped at the market on the way home. Wondered what a man like Carlos would like. Meat came to mind. Lots and lots of red meat. Probably the kind of thing he needed anyway to rebuild his strength.

Heading to the meat aisle, she grabbed an assortment of steaks and, for good measure, some pork chops. She added potatoes and some plantains—because she knew her friends regularly ate them. Her American mama had stuck to potatoes as the main side dish.

She wondered what he would drink and decided that there would be no diet stuff for him. Which meant he might want chips and salty things, she thought.

By the time she got to the register, the cart was piled high. The bill was even higher, and she was thankful for the salary increase she had gotten after the story she did on the designer drugs. Her boss, Harry, had been pleased with the investigative report on the new pharmaceuticals available at the South Beach clubs and the people behind the trade.

The piece had brought both Sylvia and the magazine a great deal of attention, but the story had also gotten Carlos shot.

So the high grocery bill was karma, she realized. Having to house him and feed him was payback for nearly getting Carlos killed.

By the time she unloaded the car and unpacked everything, Carlos was awake. He shuffled into the kitchen, rubbing sleep from his eyes and raking back the thick, unruly strands of his dark brown hair. "What's up?"

"Did some food shopping." She opened the door to the fridge and his eyes widened in shock.

"Planning to feed an army?"

Peeking in, she realized her once empty fridge was now packed, mostly with meat. "Too much?"

He chuckled, walked over to her, and cupped her cheek. "What if I'm vegan?"

"Oh no," exploded from her lips, but then she recalled the many times they had eaten together. "You're kidding."

"Definitely kidding. But you don't have to cook on my account."

"Thank god, because I'm not very domestic. I mean, I know how to cook, but I'm usually not around for dinner and I really can't change my schedule all that much, so maybe you should have gone—"

"Stop, *por favor.* I don't expect you to be domestic. Or change your life in any way. It's enough that you offered to let me stay here until I can manage a little better," he said, and when she would have begun another rambling protest, he slipped his thumb over her lips to stop her.

"Let's just take this one step at a time," he said, eerily echoing her earlier thoughts.

She nodded. "At eight I have to be at the opening of a new restaurant on Lincoln Road. After that, there's an event at the Tides."

"Will you be very late?"

Normally, she had no reason to rush home, but with this being his first night and all . . .

"I won't be very late. Plus we have a couple of hours before I have to head out. We can have dinner early, if you don't mind."

"I thought you weren't into being domestic?" he teased, tracing the outline of her lips with his thumb.

She looked up and met his gaze, which twinkled with amusement. "Don't think this is going to become a habit. I don't do dinner or dishes or—"

He silenced her this time by bending down and kissing her until she was clinging to him. When he finally eased away, he said, "I get it, Sylvia. Don't worry. I know how to cook and clean. But for right now, I was thinking a walk might be nice."

"Do you feel up to it?" She looked him up and down, trying to decide if he seemed any steadier on his feet.

"A short one. If you don't mind my leaning on you a bit."

A simple enough request. Just someone to lean on. It occurred to her that what he was asking was possibly about more than just the physical leaning.

He was asking if she would be there for other things, and guilt rose up, but she remembered what Tori had said about not being guilted into doing anything she didn't want to do only . . .

It was just a walk. A short time together to talk. Get to know each other. Wasn't that one of the benefits of his moving in until he was better?

With a nod, she said, "Let's go."

He smiled and held his hand out in the direction of the door. "After you."

Once in the lobby, they exited onto Thirteenth and slowly walked side by side down toward Ocean Drive. The Cardozo Hotel was on the corner, and to the right, most of the Ocean Drive strip of Art Deco hotels and restaurants, but Carlos motioned across the street to Lummus Park.

Carlos slipped his arm around her waist and guided her to one of the paths that would take them close to the seawall along the beach.

"Need to lean already?" she asked, although she hadn't seen any sign of a limp yet.

He bent from his greater height and nuzzled the side of her face as he said, "Needed to touch you. You've seemed too distant today."

Distant. More like terrified, not that anyone would believe that she could be, but she was. Letting him into her home brought the risk of letting him into her heart. She wasn't ready for that yet.

With a shrug, she replied, "Just a little worried you won't be comfortable. I want you to get better soon."

"So you can get rid of me sooner?"

They had reached the seawall, and she stopped, faced him. "Is that what you think? That I want to get rid of you already?"

Carlos looked away from her and blew out an exasperated sigh as he gazed out over the beach and ocean beyond the low cement seawall. When he met her gaze once again, he said, "Tell me guilt wasn't the main reason you asked me to come stay with you?"

Guilt certainly had been one of the reasons she was giving him her home, food, and bed. However, she wouldn't add having sex to that list of guilt-inspired acts, because she had wanted to do that since the first day she had laid eyes on him. Nope, having sex with him was definitely not going to be about guilt.

Just satisfaction.

She inched up her chin and defiantly answered. "Sure guilt was one of the reasons. But so was wanting to get to know you better and jumping your bones and not necessarily in that order."

Carlos chuckled and shook his head. He took a step closer to her, slipped his arm around her waist once again, and as they started to walk again, he said, "*Querida*. I suspect that spending time with you will never be dull."

"Never."

4

What do you wear to meet a hero? Virginia Cooke considered as she flipped through one outfit after another as she contemplated her upcoming surprise visit to her daughter.

Sylvia apparently couldn't make it to their usual Sunday gathering. Her daughter had been vague as to the reason why she couldn't make it, but rumor had it that earlier in the week Carlos had come home with her from the hospital. Carlos, the man Virginia hadn't heard anything about until her daughter's tearful visit nearly a month earlier.

Even now the memory of that night still sent a chill through her. The late-night buzz on the intercom and opening the door to find Sylvia there, her tear-stained face cut and bruised. The expensive designer gown she wore bloodstained and torn in spots.

She had opened her arms and taken her in, held her as Sylvia had cried for nearly an hour, explaining about what had happened and how she had nearly gotten a man

killed. But not just any man, Virginia had known immediately. A man for whom Sylvia seemed to have some
affection, not that her daughter would admit to such an
emotion.

Which was why Virginia now intended to surprise her
daughter with this visit. Although she was glad that Sylvia
might finally allow someone into her heart and stop being alone, she was perplexed. First that her daughter had
suddenly decided to take him in—Sylvia had never been
the nurturing type. For too much of her adult life, Sylvia
had run away from any kind of emotional involvement
with men. Not that Virginia would mind her daughter finally falling in love. She wanted what was best for Sylvia,
which was yet another reason why she intended to visit.

She wanted to know for herself whether this man was
the right one. The one who might finally make Sylvia
happy.

Pulling out a dark blue suit, Virginia held it up against
her body and examined herself in the full-length mirror
along the back wall of the walk-in closet. *So sorry for your
loss,* she thought, since the suit was fine for either a business meeting or a funeral—which sometimes were not all
that different.

Definitely not what to wear to meet Sylvia's new man.
She didn't want her daughter thinking that she was regretting Carlos's presence in her daughter's home.

She slipped the suit back into the section of dark blues
and blacks and moved to the next area. After scanning
several more outfits, she pulled out a dress in a fire engine
red and again perused herself in the mirror. *Hello, good
lookin'. I'm Sylvia's hoochie mama.*

She really should give this one away to the Salva-
tion Army, it occurred to her and tossed the too-revealing
outfit from Frederick's of Hollywood into a corner of the

closet. She had bought the dress during a Valentine's Day moment of vulnerability. She normally wasn't one to get overly sentimental or worse—remotely depressed—over the state of her love life. But for some reason it had hit her stronger than ever a few years back that besides Sylvia, no one was special enough in her life to rate a valentine. There hadn't been anyone since . . .

She drove that thought away because it had produced a horrendous fashion disaster, namely a dress sure to make the wrong kind of man—well, at least make certain parts of the wrong kind of man—sit up and take notice.

Which was the last thing she wanted today, when she was finally going to meet the man who had not only saved her daughter's life, but had somehow also tamed Sylvia's shrew. That made him a hero in her book not once, but twice.

She rushed to select an outfit and be on her way because Virginia couldn't wait to meet the man who Sylvia thought of as "nice." Coming from Sylvia, that adjective was a sure sign of . . .

Trouble, Virginia thought as she swept out the door of her condo to head to her daughter's South Beach home.

Virginia knocked sharply on the door to Sylvia's condo, aware that she was unexpected and Sylvia might not hear the knock. It took a few telling minutes for her daughter to open the door. Shock filled Sylvia's features, and in a hissed whisper she said, "Mama, what are you doing here?"

"Since you couldn't make it for brunch, I decided to come for a visit." She grinned and craned her head to look through the open doorway as she heard someone call out from inside, "Who is it?"

Sylvia motioned for silence with a wave of her hand

and stepped into the hall, closing the door behind her to avoid any additional snooping.

"Mama, this really isn't a good time," she said, obviously squirming, eager for her mother to leave.

Virginia considered Sylvia carefully, trying to get a read on her. She was dressed casually, in faded low-rise jeans and a cropped T-shirt that showed off her sculpted midriff. She yanked at the hem of the T-shirt guiltily, since it was slightly askew. Her long highlighted blond hair was loose and hung in carefree waves that were in slight disarray, making her look younger than her close to thirty years of age.

There was no denying Sylvia had her father's face, Virginia thought. No matter that people often said the two of them looked like sisters, she could still see Pablo in the arch of Sylvia's brow and the fullness of her lips; in the color of her eyes, much more like Pablo's green ones than her own hazel ones.

She met that worried green-eyed gaze directly and said, "Is something wrong with my visiting? I thought you said I was always welcome—"

She didn't get to finish as the door opened behind Sylvia and he stood there—Sylvia's new young man.

Nice? she thought. Sunsets were nice. So were lazy swims in the pool. A man handsome enough to curl your toes should never ever be described as just "nice." Which made her examine her daughter's face even as her new man friend laid a hand on her shoulder and said, "You must be Sylvia's mom. Why don't you come in?"

Sylvia shot him a murderous glare, but Carlos didn't back down, and so her daughter reluctantly ushered Virginia into the apartment.

Carlos held out his hand and said, "Carlos Ramirez."

His voice was deep and rich. His eyes an amazing

shade of blue, and his body—he had that kind of rangy muscular build that told her he was a man used to physical activity. As she shook his hand, the roughness of his palm confirmed her speculation.

But there was something else about him. Something reckless and adventurous and dangerous to a woman's control. She recognized it well, for Sylvia's father had possessed It.

Like mother, like daughter.

"I'm pleased to meet you," she said and shot a quick glance at her daughter's face. Gone was the anger and instead there was a different look—one that said her daughter was totally and thoroughly in lust with this man, which made Virginia wonder about the whole "nice" comment again and whether her daughter was sleeping with Carlos. Maybe that accounted for Sylvia's slightly disheveled look and the minutes it had taken for her to answer the door.

"Now that you're here, why don't I get us some drinks," Sylvia suggested.

She hurried from the room, leaving Carlos and Virginia standing there awkwardly, until she noticed the fine beads of sweat on Carlos's upper lip, as if just standing there was taxing him. "I'm sorry, Mr. Ramirez. Please, sit down."

"Carlos, please, Mrs. Amenabar," he said and invited her to take a seat first.

At least his mama had raised him right, but she was quick to correct his mistake after she sat down on the sofa. "Ms. Cooke, or better yet, Virginia. Sylvia's father and I . . ."

She hesitated, slightly uncomfortable for a moment, and yet she knew that if this man was in the least bit interested in Sylvia, he deserved a little family history. Especially since Virginia suspected that a lot of Sylvia's hang-ups about men had to do with that dysfunctional family background.

Once Carlos had taken a seat beside her, she finally finished her earlier statement. "Sylvia's father and I . . . I didn't take his last name."

"I'm sorry. I didn't know," he replied and shifted uncomfortably on the cushions of the couch.

"It's okay, really. And your family? Were you born in Miami?" she asked.

"Cuba. We came here during the Mariel boatlift," he explained.

"And you met Sylvia—"

"While I was working undercover and she was working on an assignment for her magazine."

Virginia eyed him, wondering why he hadn't mentioned something as momentous as the shooting, which actually brought him up a notch in her estimation.

"I admire what you do, Carlos. Being an undercover detective must be quite difficult."

"It's really not that—"

Carlos didn't get a chance to answer as Sylvia walked in with a tray holding three drinks. She handed her mother a glass and then offered one to Carlos. "Those are virgin ones," she clarified as she sat down in a chair beside him.

Although she didn't say it, Virginia knew Sylvia's drink was full strength, as if she thought she would need the Dutch courage if Virginia decided to linger for dinner. Which she in fact planned to do.

"So, Carlos. You were telling me—"

"About my sailboat. My family used it to come here from Cuba. You should come out with Sylvia and me for a spin one day," he said, and his gaze seemed to plead with her to not return to the earlier topic in their conversation.

Interesting. A man who didn't want to bring attention to himself? Carlos was truly beginning to intrigue her.

"I will definitely do that. Where do you live, Carlos?"

"Mama, there's no need for the third degree, you know," Sylvia jumped in and nervously rattled the drink in her hand before she took a sip.

"Don't worry, *amor*. Your *mami* and I shared all kinds of interesting things while you were gone. She even showed me all the shots of you bare-assed in the tub, so it's only fair I answer some questions," Carlos teased, bringing a flush of color to Sylvia's cheeks and dragging an uncertain chuckle from her.

"Actually, the photo of Sylvia with the mumps is really the best, but I don't have that one with me," she added, pleased by Carlos's perceptive attempt to ease Sylvia's discomfort.

"Maybe next time, Virginia," Carlos began, but Sylvia immediately tensed up once again.

Virginia held her breath. It was a stance she recognized all too well—Sylvia's defensive posture.

"Assuming there's a next time," Sylvia said, a warning in her tone that she was none too pleased with their apparent bonding.

Carlos snapped his fingers. "Ño. I forgot that you don't do the whole domestic thing."

"Right, I don't," Sylvia reminded, but as she looked at him heat filled her gaze, even with Virginia sitting right there.

The look Carlos shot her was equally intense, but as he caught Virginia's earnest perusal, he reined in his apparent desire. "Maybe when I'm better I can pack a Sunday brunch and take you both for that ride on the sailboat."

With a reassuring touch of his hand on her thigh, Sylvia's apparent pique evaporated.

Virginia had to admit she was impressed. That Carlos had somehow managed to get past all her daughter's obstacles in the first place was interesting. That he could also hang in there when Sylvia put up barriers was a testament to his character and possibly to the strength of what he felt for her daughter.

Virginia realized then that as patient as Carlos seemed, Sylvia was bound to push him away if she couldn't help Sylvia deal with her perception of men, which possibly stemmed from the mess that had been their family life.

As difficult as it might be for her, she suspected there was only one way to fix that problem.

5

"Can't sleep?"

Carlos stood in the hallway leading to her room, light limning the silhouette of his lean body.

There was no sense denying it, so she sat up on the couch. "Thinking about . . . work and things. How about you?"

He walked toward her, the limp in his gait less noticeable than it had been a few days earlier when he had moved in. He had improved a lot in a short time, even though she had noticed after their walk that morning that he had taxed himself. He had been tired and in pain when they had returned, although her attempts to ease his discomfort had turned into a rather nice interlude—until her mother had arrived for her surprise visit. But even then Carlos had toughed it out for her during the afternoon and the early dinner they had shared.

Despite this morning's seeming setback, she could

already notice not just his increased mobility, but also that he seemed to have more strength. Even his color was better. Afternoons spent lazing in Lummus Park and the morning walks they were able to occasionally take had added a nice healthy glow to his skin and replaced the hospital pallor.

"Can't sleep. Too much noise coming from in here." He sat on the couch beside her, and it creaked loudly. He met her guilty gaze. "There's no reason that we both can't get some sleep if you come to bed."

"Come to bed? I was worried I might disturb your rest." Feeling decidedly exposed, although the Victoria's Secret cotton pajamas she wore were rather tame, she pulled up the comforter to just below her neck.

Carlos dragged a hand through his hair and sank back against the couch, prompting another squeak. "Sí. In bed. With me. This way I can finally rest because I won't be awake listening to you toss and turn and maybe you'll even be able to get some sleep."

She hadn't realized she was keeping him up. "I'm sorry. I thought you were comfortable."

"I am. But I'd be better if you just stopped being . . ."

"Pigheaded?" she offered when he hesitated.

"Okay, if pigheaded is the way you're feeling. And what does that mean anyway? Pigheaded? How stupid a way is that to describe your stubbornness."

"Stubbornness? How about understanding that I'm trying to be considerate," she shot back, anger flaring to life at his annoyance.

"Considerate? The bed's big enough for an army. What's so considerate about—"

"Leaving you alone to sleep? Do you think we would get much rest if I got into bed with you?" she said, because she wanted him more than she cared to admit but was smart enough to know that she also possibly wanted . . . more than something physical.

He sighed harshly and faced her. He wore a white muscle shirt and dark-colored sweats. The shirt did nothing to hide the immense breadth of his shoulders or his well-defined muscles. The sight of them reawakened the desire to feel those strong arms around her and just confirmed to her that getting in bed with him might lead to nothing but trouble.

"Do you think you're that irresistible?" he said, surprising her.

"Huh? Me? You think this is about me?" she nearly yelled.

"*Sí.* Do you think I can't resist you?"

Well, that was a big ouch in the ego column. "You're right. You're a big boy. No reason to think you can't keep your hands off me," she said as she regally rose from the couch and wrapped the comforter around herself.

"If that's what you want, *amorcito,*" he said, and even in the dark, she could see the twinkle in his blue-green eyes. *She had been played.*

"What I want? I don't know what I want. Maybe that's the reason I've tried to be sensible and grown-up about this," she finally admitted.

Carlos shook his head. "Sensible? Grown-up?"

He stood slowly, a bit of a hitch in the action as his leg protested the rise from her low-slung sofa, but then he stood before her. Leaned impossibly close and in a low, sexy tone said, "I think I like you better when you're less sensible. When you follow your heart."

He didn't wait for her reply and headed for her bedroom, leaving her to stand there and think about what her heart wanted. About her giving in to her itch and finally doing all those things she had only just thought about for months now. Thought about every minute for the five days he'd been in her home.

As she walked toward her bedroom, she reminded herself that scratching too hard wasn't a good thing. That if she maybe waited a bit, the itch might just go away.

But as she saw him waiting for her, his gaze hot as he tracked her flight to the far edge of the bed, she realized just how hard it was going to be to resist him.

She walked to the bed, tossed aside her comforter, and got beneath the covers. He eased in on the opposite side, and then they lay there, on their backs. He had his fingers laced together and behind his head while she dug hers into the mattress at her side.

Rest? she thought, but then he muttered a curse and said, "Roll over."

She did, shifting on the side she favored for sleep and a second later he was spooned against her back, his one arm tossed around her waist.

"That's better," he mumbled, the warmth of his breath stirring the wisps of hair by her forehead. "Relax," he said as he noticed the stiffness in her body.

She took a deep breath and smelled him. Holding the inhalation within her, she slowly released it, allowing it to take the tension from her body. She laid her arm over his, twined her fingers with his.

"Good night, *amor*," he whispered into her ear.

"Good night," she said, grateful that he wasn't pressing the issue, but also battling the desire to raise his hand to her breast and get something started.

With a shaky breath, she reined in her desire and reminded herself, *One small step at a time.*

The rasp of evening beard.

Warmth along her entire body.

His lean muscled arm tight around her waist, holding her close.

The hard jut of his morning erection against the small of her back.

Those sensations brought the memory of the one night they had spent together nearly two months earlier. A night filled with talk, but also with cuddling and kissing. Touching and caressing. Waking much as she was now, surrounded by him.

Not an unpleasant way to wake, she thought and snuggled tighter to the hard length of his body.

"Buenos días," he said, his voice sleep-husky and his breath warm against the shell of her ear.

"Morning," she replied.

He splayed his fingers across her midsection, and she twined her fingers with his once again. When he nuzzled the side of her face with his nose, she scrunched up her shoulders. "Stop. Just a few more minutes."

"Lazybones," he teased but sleepily settled against her. They lay there together for a few minutes before he said, "Do you have to be anywhere this morning?"

"Not until ten. What time is it?" she asked, her eyes still closed because opening them might ruin the moment.

"Not even eight. That means we have time for—"

"Breakfast," she filled in for him to avoid it going anywhere dangerous. Or maybe she should say more dangerous as he shifted his hips against the small of her back and murmured, "I am hungry."

"Me too. How about News Cafe?" She let go of his hand and sat up, turned to look at him as he lay back and pillowed his head against his hands, his look intense as he considered her suggestion.

"I guess I'm game," he said, although as he slid out of

the bed, she clearly realized he'd had other ideas in mind for their morning and quite honestly, so had she. Her night had been filled with dreams of what they might do to make that big bed not so big anymore.

They took turns cleaning and dressing. It seemed to Sylvia that they were trying to establish some kind of balance for the days to come before Carlos would go . . .

She didn't finish that thought because she didn't want to think about his leaving.

Carlos came out of the bathroom, hair damp from a quick shower. He had put on loose jeans and a black T-shirt that hugged every bulge of muscle and made his dark brown hair seem even darker.

"Ready?" he asked, and for a moment she was tempted to say, no, but instead nodded.

They headed out of the apartment and once on Thirteenth, walked down to Ocean, where they strolled along the restaurant side of the strip. Since it was a Monday and relatively early, only a few tourists were out in the restaurants, along with the workers, who were busy clearing away the debris from a weekend in South Beach.

Hand in hand, they ambled past the former Versace mansion, which was being renovated into luxury hotel accommodations. They passed the Clevelander Bar and Edison Hotel, walking in amiable silence until they reached the News Cafe on Eighth, where a number of people sat at the outdoor tables, having breakfast and people watching.

They were quickly seated at a table close to the sidewalk, providing them a clear view of Ocean Drive and Lummus Park. In the park there was a little more activity as people in-line skated or jogged along the winding path close to the low seawall. At one of the playgrounds, a bodybuilder used the metal frame of a swing set to do pull-ups.

Sylvia noticed that Carlos's attention had settled on the man. "Do you know him?"

With a shrug, he said, "He was trying to work his way into the Reaper's gang."

She looked over at the young man and shivered. His thick squat body reminded her too much of the Reaper and his sidekicks—they had been killed during the shoot-out with Carlos. "What will he do now?"

"Look for another crew," he said matter-of-factly, troubling her. He picked up his menu and perused it. When he put it down, she asked, "What will you do when he does?"

"Stop him."

Again delivered too calmly and coldly for her peace of mind. "Is that what you'll do once you're better? Go back to work as if everything's normal?"

The waiter came over at that moment, and they quickly placed their orders for some of the News Cafe's breakfast specials, huge plates laden with eggs, home fries, and bacon. The waiter poured them mugs of coffee and then stepped away to fill their orders.

Sylvia immediately asked Carlos again. "So? Will you go back to the police force when you're healed?"

Carlos met her gaze directly. "It's what I do."

"I guess you like it," she said, trying to understand him. Trying to get an idea on how he could deal so calmly with nearly losing his life not once, but twice.

Again he shrugged, and as he spoke, he looked out toward the playground again. The young thug had left and been replaced by a mother with a child of about four. She was pushing the child on the swing where the thug had been working out just moments earlier. With his index finger, Carlos pointed to the mother and child. "I like making the streets safe for people like that, but maybe there's a way to do that without being undercover. And you?"

"Me?" she asked and picked up her mug, blew on the hot coffee before taking a sip.

"Sí. You're back to working the party beat. Is that what you really want to do?"

She took another sip before shaking her head. "No. I'd like to do another investigative report."

Carlos cradled his coffee mug in his big hands. "So what's stopping you?"

The waiter came by at that moment to place the plates mounded with food before them, along with a basket of breads and small muffins. Carlos motioned for her to begin eating, and she forked up some of her omelet, but after she swallowed, she finally provided him with her answer.

"The holiday season was busy, and I didn't have much free time." She didn't say that he was part of her reason for the lack of time and instead plowed on. "I've suggested some stories to my boss—"

"Harry?" he questioned and snagged a piece of buttered toast from the basket between them.

"Yes, my boss, Harry. If I don't hear from him soon, I'm going to press him."

A pedestrian passed by them, loud music blaring from his earphones. Carlos watched the young man's passage, seemingly alert to something she hadn't noticed, but then he returned his attention to her. "What will you do if you don't get a story you want?"

"I'll see about finding a job elsewhere," she answered quickly. Even though her first and only investigative report had ended with Carlos in the hospital, the story had called attention to the growing designer drug problem in the clubs. She hoped that she had accomplished some good by doing that. She hoped to do more with other similar stories.

"It means that much to you?" he asked, chewing on the piece of bread thoughtfully as he considered her.

His intense perusal unnerved her, maybe because he was asking that she reveal more than she was prepared to. But if this time together was about anything, wasn't it supposed to be about getting to know each other? Because of that, she answered.

"I want to be a real reporter, not just little Miss Fluff and Stuff. I want it more than anything."

"I hope you get what you want."

The emotion that tinged his words befuddled her for a moment until she realized what it was—regret. Maybe because he recognized, as did she, that their wants might take them on very different paths in life.

It saddened her more than she had expected, and she laid a hand over his as it rested on the tabletop. "It's not the only thing I want," she admitted.

A slow sexy grin spread across his full lips. "Really? Dare I hope?"

The warmth and playfulness of his smile transferred itself to her, pulling an answering grin from her. "Hope away. Who knows? You might just get lucky one day."

6

Sylvia hadn't expected it would happen so soon.

Carlos had only been with her a week. A week of spending time together and sharing a bed. A bed where it had become increasingly more difficult to just lie there together without doing more. The tender kisses and touches from the hospital had returned on the second night they had shared the bed and become increasingly torrid each night. As she had told her friends just a few days ago during their regular Monday night meeting, she didn't think she could resist him much longer. Being in his arms felt too damned good.

Which was why when she returned home from an afternoon assignment on Thursday and Carlos sat on the couch, reading a book, she didn't hesitate to walk over and crawl into his lap.

Carlos seemed surprised at first, but then he tossed aside the novel, leaned back into the sofa cushions, and took her with him, cradling her body on his. Gently passing his hands up and down her sides. Keeping her close, not that she planned on going anywhere at that moment.

It felt too right.

She leaned forward and kissed him. Her hands fisted in his hair as she opened her mouth and accepted the welcoming thrust of his tongue. Imagined other parts of him moving in her. Hot. Hard. Slick.

She wanted the whole wild monkey sex she had been thinking about now for months and sat up, which in turn had her straddling him and feeling his hard swell dead center. Way dead center, she thought and shifted her hips, pulling a deep groan from him.

That rough sound tightened her insides with need. She ground herself down, slowly dragged her center over him again and again, which—given that she was incredibly horny—nearly made her come right there and then. A harsh breath escaped her lips, and Carlos brought his hands to her hips, kept her from moving.

"*Amor*, I'm not sure—"

"I am. I'm sure—"

"That I can wait any longer."

She moaned then, because she couldn't wait either. She whipped out of her suit jacket, then quickly pulled off her silk knit shirt. Her bra followed hastily, leaving her half-naked in his arms.

Carlos sat up a bit more, which brought her face-to-face and groin to groin with him. She was about to draw herself along him again, but he said, "Don't."

"Don't?" she said but couldn't find a breath for another word as he trailed his thumb over the tip of her nipple and held her breast in the rough palm of his hand.

She brought her hands up and draped her arms over his shoulders, giving him an all-access pass, and Carlos didn't hesitate. First with his hands and then with his mouth, until she couldn't keep from pressing herself into him as he grew even harder and larger between her legs.

His breathing was rough, and when he raised his head from her breasts for a kiss, she mimicked what she wanted with her tongue, slipping between his lips and inviting him into her mouth.

A groan exploded past his lips and he bucked up against her. "*Dios*, Sylvia. Touch me," he said and whipped his T-shirt from his body.

In the light of day, the sight of the two fresh-looking scars on his torso were like a bucket of icy cold water, drenching her desire. She was responsible for those wounds. She was the reason he had almost died.

Guilt had her ready to bolt, but he took hold of her arms and softly said, "Don't run. *Por favor*, don't."

"I'm sorry," she said and met his gaze.

"I hope that's a 'sorry that you got hurt' and not a 'sorry I can't go through with this,'" he said, but as he examined her face, he realized it was the latter.

She didn't know how it happened, but she was suddenly sitting on the sofa, and he was slipping his T-shirt back on. "I think it's time I left."

"Left?" She somehow managed to get out the word, since her brain didn't seem to be working. It was too caught up in the confusion of how something that had felt so right had suddenly turned so totally wrong.

Jumping to her feet, she chased after him as he strode to her bedroom. When he opened one of the drawers she had emptied for him and started pulling out his clothes, she grabbed hold of his arm. With a yank, she turned him around. "Left? As in 'I'm leaving' left?"

"I think that would make sense. You keep on using

your guilt to avoid dealing with what's happening with us. To run away from what you're really feeling," he said, a grim look on his face.

She wanted to tell him it made no sense. That there was no way they would ever be able to settle things between them if he ran, but then again, she had been running from him all along. Maybe not physically, but definitely emotionally. So she didn't challenge him, knowing it would be unfair. Knowing he had been right with his assertion. The real reason she was running was her fear of commitment, not guilt.

"Fine. Let me drive you and . . ."

Shit, she thought as she realized she was still half-naked. "I'll get dressed and drive you."

"I can get a cab," he said and turned away to the dresser to continue pulling his clothes from there.

"No, I'll drive you. It's the least—"

He whirled then and angrily slashed his hand. "I don't need any more of your pity."

With an abrupt nod, she walked away and back into the living room where she picked up her clothes and slipped them back on. She wrapped her arms around her midsection and dropped down onto the leather couch to wait for him.

He came out a few minutes later, bags in hand. Something white stuck in the zipper of one. He nervously gripped the handles of the bags and shifted his weight from foot to foot for a second before he asked, "Is that offer of a ride still there?"

She wanted to say no. Wanted to protest his leaving just when they were . . .

Going nowhere fast, thanks to her. She rose and nodded. "Yes."

*   *   *

Even with the slight cold from having the top of her BMW convertible down, the sun was brilliant, heating everything with its warmth as they drove to Coconut Grove and Carlos's boat.

Besides, as tall and big as Carlos was, the interior of her Bimmer might be cramped with the top up.

The ride was silent except for the rushing sound of the wind as she picked up speed and the noise from the cars and passersby around them. Once she pulled off the highway to Coconut Grove, it was quieter as they passed the homes, seaside restaurants, and businesses leading to the marina. When she eased into a parking spot and killed the engine, the slap-slap-slap of water against the docks and hulls of the boats, along with the screech of seagulls replaced the earlier street noises.

They sat there, ill at ease, staring straight ahead at the docks before Carlos turned slightly and said, "Well, I guess this is it."

She was still gripping the leather steering wheel tightly and flexed her hands on it for a moment before she said, "Why don't I help you get settled?"

When she looked at him, he seemed to be considering her offer, trying to decide what to make of it. But then he nodded before gingerly getting out of the low-slung car.

She popped the trunk and put up the top to protect the leather from the intense rays of the Miami sun. Once the top had locked into place, she stepped out of the car. He was waiting on her side, by the front bumper. When she shut the door, he turned and attempted to quickly walk away, leaving her to chase after him.

Luckily for her, although clearly not for him, he pulled up short, muttered a curse beneath his breath, and grabbed at his leg. In his haste to end his time with her, he had clearly exceeded his current physical capabilities. Without saying a word, she took hold of the smaller of the bags and slipped beneath his arm, providing some support.

"*Gracias,*" he muttered as they began a slow walk to the slip for his sailboat. Little by little, the stiffness seemed to leave his gait, so that by the time they stepped up to his boat, the limp was gone.

Extracting a key chain from his jeans pocket, he unlocked the railing of the boat and opened it. He tossed one bag over the edge, and it landed on the teak deck of the boat with a thud. He grabbed hold of the railings and gingerly slipped over the edge and down onto the deck. Turning, he offered his hand to help her up and over, since she was still wearing her heels, which made for precarious footing.

Once she was on the teak deck, she kicked off the Fendi shoes and waited for him to unlock and open the doors leading down from the cockpit to the living area below. As he had before, he tossed the bag down, grabbed the banister along the stairs, and slowly went below.

Sylvia didn't wait for him now that she was barefoot, and she rushed down the stairs with the bag she was carrying.

When she reached the lower level, Carlos was already heading toward the large stateroom at the front of the sailboat. She placed the bag on one of the banks of benches along the side of the galley and took a deep breath. It wasn't musty, although it was a little warm.

She walked to the side, opened one of the portholes, and then went to the opposite side, did the same. A cross breeze quickly brought fresh air blowing into the galley. The air was flavored with the tang of salt from the ocean.

"Thanks for opening it up," he said as he returned, stopped a few feet away from her, and shoved his hands into the pockets of his jeans.

"It's not too stuffy," she confessed, and he nodded.

"Riley's been coming by to check on things. He must have recently aired it out for me."

Which only confirmed to her that on some level, Carlos had known that he would eventually leave her and come back here. Like her, he too had been running before they had even gotten started.

"It's not like that," Carlos said, clearly aware of her thoughts, and immediately moved to stand before her.

"You knew you wouldn't be staying with me for long." Tartness colored her tone.

He shrugged those broad shoulders, hung his head down, as if he couldn't meet her gaze. Her big, brave cop was afraid . . . of her.

Sylvia stepped to him, cupped his cheek, and applied gentle pressure to urge his head upward. "Carlos?"

"*Sí*, I knew," he confessed, his amazing blue eyes darkening with emotion. "I knew this . . ."—he raised his hand and motioned between them—"was complicated."

Complicated. *A good euphemism for all screwed up*, she thought. All screwed up because she was messed up about men. About what they wanted. About the fact that men were dogs and couldn't be trusted.

Which was the one thing the man standing before her had asked of her—that she trust him.

On some level, she did trust him. She had to. He had saved her life.

She closed the distance between them and wrapped her arms around him, needing his stability. He embraced her, and she lost herself in his arms. Permitted herself the comfort of having him surround her with his strength.

Looking upward, she met his gaze and noticed the flecks of green and teal in his dark blue eyes. She realized he was searching her face for a sign. So she raised herself on tiptoes until her lips barely brushed his.

"I don't want this to be complicated."

"So shut up and kiss me."

He closed the final distance and opened his mouth to hers. Warm. The edges of his lips hard, but his tongue smooth and moist as he licked her lips, begging for entry.

She opened her mouth, accepting the thrust of his tongue, pressing herself against his hard body.

He eased his hands to her waist and pulled her shirt from her pants. Moved his hands beneath to her skin. The heat and roughness of his palms against her damp skin undid her.

"Please, Carlos," she begged against his mouth.

"*Dios, amor.* I hope you don't plan to stop."

She smiled and cradled his cheek. Ran her thumb along the full outline of his lips as she said, "Do you remember what I promised you the first time we met?"

He groaned and his hands tightened at her waist. "You said that you would fuck me so slow, I'd beg for you to stop—"

"And that when I did, you'd beg for more. Well, I'm here to keep that promise." She kissed him, placed her hands on his chest, and applied slight pressure to move him back until he bumped the edge of the large bed in the middle of the stateroom.

"No running this time?" He stroked the bare skin at her waist and tentatively slipped his hand upward beneath her silk knit shirt until he cradled her breast.

A shiver worked through her body at that touch, awakening the passion that had been simmering since their interlude at the apartment. Reminding her that it had been way too long since any man had roused such feelings in her. She didn't want to stop this time.

"I'm sorry about what happened before. It was just—"

"A shock. Believe me, it's as much of a shock to me."
He leaned forward, placed a kiss in the middle of her
forehead while strumming his thumb across her rock hard
nipple.

It feels so good, she thought, urging him on with the rub
of her body against his and the soft moan that escaped her
lips. She raised her head and kissed him, murmuring, "We
just need to take it slow."

His grin erupted against her lips. "That's a good speed
to start."

He sat on the edge of the bed and ripped off his T-
shirt.

As she approached him, Sylvia teased, "That's not
slow at all, *amor.*"

Carlos chuckled, laid his big hands on her waist and,
with a smile, said, "No, but this will be."

He eased his hands beneath the shoulders of her blazer
and urged it off. Slipping his hands beneath the hem of
her knit shirt, he did the same, pulling it up and over her
head until she stood there in just her pants and bra.

He placed his hands at her waist again and with gentle
pressure, urged her closer. His movements were languid,
tender as he ran the back of his hand against the skin at
her midsection, exploring every inch of her. Creating heat
everywhere he touched.

She placed her hands on his shoulders, running them
along the muscled width and then down his arms. His
body was hard beneath her hands and hot. Slightly damp
from heat and their passion.

As her gaze grazed his, she realized the color of his
eyes had deepened to nearly a sapphire blue with arousal,
but his gaze immediately shifted upward to her breasts.
She couldn't wait for him to touch her again.

Reaching upward, she undid the front clasp of her bra.

Her breasts spilled free, and with a shrug, she let the bra slip off.

His seated position gave him a prime seat, and she didn't protest as he craned his head to suck her nipples and bring them to tighter peaks.

He was gifted with his mouth and hands, alternating gentle caresses with a rougher demand that soon had her shaking in his arms and drenched. He calmed her with a soft murmur and the drift of his hand downward, to the waistband of her slacks.

Swiftly he undid the button and then the zipper, eased his hand down beneath the edge of her panties. With sure fingers he found the center of her and stroked his fingers across her clitoris.

She nearly came from that sure loving touch, but held on, grasping his shoulders for support as her knees threatened to buckle from the pleasure he was bringing her with his mouth and hands.

But she didn't want to make the journey alone. Not after waiting so long for him.

She inched her hand downward to the thick muscles of his chest and stroked him. His hair tickled the palm of her hand, and his nipple beaded into a hard bud beneath her fingers. He murmured a satisfied sigh as she caressed it, and that sigh tightened something inside of her, dragging her to the edge of pleasure.

She stepped away from him, earning a ragged complaint until he realized her intent.

Leaning backward on the bed, Carlos watched as she undid his jeans and dragged them down. He was naked beneath the denim and erect. *Magnificently so,* she thought as she encircled him with her palm.

"Sylvia, I—"

"Ssshh," she whispered, urging him on with sure

strokes until he reared up, brought his hands to her pants, and made short work of removing them and her panties, leaving her totally naked before him.

There would be no slow this time, she realized. They both wanted this too much.

As he moved into the center of the bed and lay down, she followed. Before he could protest, Sylvia positioned herself above him.

He brought his hands to her waist as she hesitated, the tip of him barely breaching her slick and wet entry. Waiting for his possession.

"Are you sure, *querida?*" he asked.

Sylvia was sure of one thing and one thing only. She wanted him. More than any other man ever.

With a nod, she thrust down and completed their union.

He filled her completely. Perfectly.

She didn't want to move and risk shattering the beauty of the moment, which far surpassed anything she could have imagined in all the months she'd been dreaming about him.

He seemed to understand, since he didn't move. He just stroked her thighs, the palm of his hand rough against that skin before he levered himself up on one arm and kissed her lips once again. He whispered, "I feel like I've been waiting for this moment all my life."

She shuddered, almost undone by his words, but she couldn't respond. She was unable to confess to what was in her heart. Instead, she showed him with a tender caress of her hand across his jaw as she deepened the kiss. Slid her tongue into his mouth.

He opened his mouth and took her in. Devoured her with his mouth and lips. She could feel him thicken inside her. A little gasp escaped her as he brought his other hand up and caressed her nipple before a slow upward flex of his hips had her shuddering in his arms.

With his greater size and strength, he easily reversed their positions, bringing her beneath him, driving her on with the sure, powerful thrusts of his hips and gentle, nurturing kisses.

The climax built within her. Demanding. Wild after so much wanting.

When he slipped his hand downward and found her clitoris, caressing it with his fingers, Sylvia came, calling out her release with a loud shout of his name.

7

*Heat surrounded her.*
Smooth muscle against her back.
Wet as he trailed his mouth along her neck to the crook of her shoulder.

Hard. Sweet Lord, so so hard easing into the center of her. Pressing deep and drawing a strangled gasp from her.

"*Mi amor,* don't move," he urged in soft tones close to her ear.

Sylvia wanted to move. Just a shift and she knew she would come, but she kept still. Imprisoned by the strength of his arms wrapped around her and his one thigh, thrown over hers. Trapped by her need.

He moved his one hand to touch her breasts, tender still from a night of lovemaking. From his mouth and hands and teeth. He brought his other hand down over her ribs and past her navel. Drifting lightly over her abs before parting her curls and finding the nub between her legs. With just the touch of his finger there, Sylvia came, crying out her completion with the rough call of his name.

"I'm here, *amor.* Always here," he whispered and finally moved, shifting out and then upward again, so deeply that her pleasure rose up again.

When it was over and they both lay shaking, roughly breathing as they tried to regain reality, Sylvia suddenly wanted to blurt out that this had been about more than sex. More than just scratching an itch, but instead, she curbed her tongue and her emotions. It was too scary to think she might actually be feeling something for him other than lust. Way too scary.

Carlos must have sensed her withdrawing from him, since he said, "Are you going?"

She sat up and looked at him over her shoulder. He was as beautiful as she remembered, and this time, not even the sight of his scars could diminish the need she had for him. Turning, she laid her hand on one rough mark and then the other before she said, "Friday's always a busy day. I need to go and see if any of today's assignments have changed."

Carlos nodded but reached up and stroked the side of her face. "Will you be back later?"

She made a quick mental list of everything she already knew she had to do, including at least one event that night which might last until early morning. "I'm not sure."

He ran his thumb across the line of her cheekbone and forced a smile. "I understand. Come by though, if you're free."

"I will," she said and slipped from the bed, quickly gathering up her clothes, and dressed.

When she was ready, she faced him.

He too had slipped from bed and put on some

clothes—a T-shirt and sweats. His hair was still disheveled from the night before, and the scruff of his morning beard shadowed the strong line of his jaw.

She stepped over and smoothed the errant locks of his dark brown hair and met his gaze. "I *will* call you. I'll come by if I can."

"I know," he said, but she could tell that he was doubting her. She said nothing else. Offered up no kiss or other entreaty. Certainly no apology, since they had both enjoyed themselves during the course of the afternoon, night, and morning.

She just walked to the stairs leading above, up the short flight of steps to the deck, keeping her pace slow so that he could keep up with her. Her Fendis had been sitting on the deck all night, and she slipped them on. At the railing, he helped her up onto the dock, and she faced him for only a brief second to whisper her thanks.

Then she was off, nearly racing up the ramp to the cement wharf and her car, telling herself the whole time not to look back. That if she did he might misread the whole thing. That such a gesture might be too much like one of those lame lovesick-woman-finds-true-love movies on Lifetime.

But as she walked to the door of her car, she felt compelled to look back toward his sailboat, only he was no longer on the deck.

She didn't know why that bothered her so much, but it did. She had expected . . . more of him.

The little nasty voice in her head warned that maybe the issue wasn't with Carlos.

Maybe she had expected more of herself.

She didn't return to Carlos's boat that night. She told herself it was because it had been too late after the last event—a fund-raiser for the Miami City Ballet that had somehow managed to run until well past two.

Surprisingly, she was wide awake early the next morning. During the nearly two weeks that Carlos had been with her, she had gotten used to getting up earlier, in part because he rarely slept past eight. It had not been easy the first few days, but then she had come to enjoy the benefits of rising with him. The slow wake-up kisses and caresses. The easy and revealing breakfast dates at News Cafe as they talked about themselves or just sat and people watched.

This morning she stretched out her hand, but his side of the bed was cold. Still neat and untouched. Empty. Too too empty.

Which was so not good. She shouldn't be feeling his absence so quickly and so strongly. She shouldn't want so badly to go to his sailboat and crawl into bed with him. Make love with him again and tell him that . . .

What? she asked herself, still reluctant to consider that he had touched her heart. That he was the kind of man who could make her forget that trusting men was a big mistake. But then the little voice in her head warned that it might be an even bigger mistake to not trust him. To not go back to him and explore what could happen between them.

Confusion reigned as she lay there, the sounds of the ocean and some passing cars drifting through the open window of her bedroom.

South Beach was already coming alive, and while she had a busy weekend ahead, she had to consider whether she would go see Carlos.

She ran through all the pros and cons in her head, but by the time she finished, she was no closer to an answer than when she had begun, which meant there was only one thing to do. Rolling over, she grabbed her cell phone from her nightstand and dialed Tori.

When her friend answered, her voice groggy with sleep, Sylvia said, "I need to call an emergency meeting. Can you make it this morning?"

"This morning as in—"

"Is in an hour too soon?" she asked, and across the phone line, an annoyed male voice grumbled something unintelligible a second before Tori said, "Sure. Of course. Adriana and Juli will be busy. Maybe we can meet them at their restaurant?"

Of course, Saturday would be busy for her friends. As early as it was for her, they had likely already been at work for hours, prepping for one of their busiest days. She hesitated, reconsidering her request, but then Tori said, "Don't worry, Sylvita. It won't be a problem for them. I'll call to let them know. Maybe we'll luck out and Juli will make us breakfast."

Her stomach grumbled at the thought of one of Juli's delicious creations, and any doubts she had about imposing on her friends flew out the window with that thought. "I'll see you there in an hour."

Casa Criolla—Adriana and Juli's restaurant with the small luxury hotel above it—wasn't open for breakfast, but as Sylvia walked up to the open-air portion of the restaurant, the staff was already at work prepping for the lunch and dinner crowds. She once again hesitated and was about to leave when Tori came bounding up to her, clearly dressed for a day of recreation. Her long brown hair was pulled back up and off her face, and she wore a loose tank top that revealed the straps of the bathing suit beneath. Stylish board shorts and flip-flops completed the outfit. On her hand, glittering in the morning sun, the wedding band and diamond engagement ring Sylvia still couldn't get used to.

"Going somewhere later?" Sylvia asked after Tori had hugged her.

"Gil and I were going to get in some windsurfing, since it's so warm today," Tori said, slipping her arm through Sylvia's and leading her up the stairs to the covered veranda of the restaurant. At the door to the main portion of the restaurant, one of the restaurant's hostesses greeted them. She smiled and immediately led them to a table at the back of the restaurant.

It had been set for four. The young woman indicated that she would get some coffee.

Sylvia didn't sit, however, as she waited for her two friends who came out from the restaurant's kitchen barely moments later. Adriana was dressed casually in low-rise jeans and a knit cotton shirt that exposed a slice of flat belly. Juli was wearing chef's clothing and had her hair neatly secured in a ponytail.

The four women embraced and sat down. Almost instantly the hostess came by with the coffee, followed by a waiter who placed plates laden with golden brown slices of French toast beside eggs scrambled together with bits of spicy chorizo sausage.

Sylvia's stomach grumbled and Juli chuckled. "*Amiga*. I know you wanted to talk, but how about just satisfying your *ganas* first."

Sylvia smiled and motioned to the food. "It definitely will satisfy one craving. It looks delicious and smells even better, but . . . What if food isn't what I've got a craving for?"

Her friends all paused at her pronouncement. Adriana—coffee addict that she was—with her nearly drained cup of espresso halfway to her lips. Juli stilled in the act of cutting a piece of the French toast, and Tori placed down her fork and said, "I hope you're talking about more than just physical satisfaction."

With a nod, she said, "Maybe that's my problem. Carlos and I . . ."

At her hesitation, all her friends knew at least part of what had happened.

Juli let out a quick hoot of delight. "*Comprendo.* You and Carlos finally—"

"Sweet Lord, we did," Sylvia admitted playfully and dug into her eggs, groaning as the flavor exploded in her mouth. "These are delicious."

"And Carlos? Was he delicious?" Adriana asked. Her voice pitched a tone lower and her eyebrows wiggled as she leaned closer.

From beside her, Tori issued a dubious admonishment. "Come on, Adriana. You can't expect Sylvita to kiss and tell." Tori glanced her way and with humor said, "But a little bit of info would help us get a better idea of why you needed to talk to us."

"Carlos was . . . amazing. As delicious as Juli's food."

A shocked laugh erupted from Juli. "*No me diga.* It was that good?"

"Better," she said and cut off a piece of the French toast with her fork. She jabbed it, brought it to her mouth, and as she ate the piece said, "It was . . . hot. Sweet. Wonderfully tiring."

"And this happened last night and now you're here with us instead of with him and getting some more?" Adriana asked, a furrow of disbelief marring her forehead.

"Is that why you were late this morning, *amiga?* Did Riley keep you busy?" Juli teased, earning a playful nudge from her partner.

"Juli, *vamos chica.* This isn't about me, it's about Sylvia, who finally slept with Carlos."

"I did finally sleep with him on Thursday afternoon and Thursday night and early Friday morning." She ate yet more of the eggs and chorizo and took a sip of the hot coffee, but Tori immediately jumped in with, "But you didn't sleep with him last night or this morning?"

Leave it to Tori with her lawyerly mind to always be looking for inconsistencies. Because Sylvia had brought them together to discuss not the sex part with Carlos but the what-to-do afterward, she confessed to all that had happened. "I didn't sleep with him this morning because he moved back into his boat on Thursday afternoon."

Shocked silence followed her announcement, but then the words sank in and her friends reacted.

"*Que pena.* I thought it would last longer than this," Juli said.

Adriana echoed that sentiment, shaking her head and muttering, "Barely two weeks. Riley and I had thought it would take at least a month."

She glanced at Tori and waited. As their gazes met, she realized that Tori seemed to understand better than the other two. "You're not sure you did the right thing by letting him leave."

"I'm not sure. He left because . . . we had a fight about how I was always pushing him away," she confessed and with shaky hands, picked up her mug and took a bracing sip of the hot, slightly bitter liquid. *Bitter.* A good word to describe her future if she couldn't somehow figure out what she wanted with her life.

Well, her romantic life anyway. She knew what she wanted from her career—to become the kind of journalist who actually accomplished something with her stories. To be known for the quality of her work and not the celebrities she knew or the parties she got invited to.

"When did you fight?" Tori asked as she too sipped on her coffee.

"Thursday—"

"Before or after the hot, sweaty, and tiring part?" Adriana challenged and waved her hand for Sylvia to continue when she hesitated.

"Before."

Once again all her friends took a moment to digest the news, and it was the new and surprisingly direct Juli who spoke up first. "So I guess you couldn't have been that upset with each other if you made love."

"Had sex," she corrected.

"There's the real root of the problem, isn't it? Even now you're pushing him away," Adriana said and shook her head with dismay.

Sylvia put down her mug and splayed her hands on the smooth fabric of the tablecloth. She flexed them nervously, searching for the answer, but then Tori took her hand in hers. "It's okay to be confused, Sylvita. Love isn't a simple thing."

She shot a quick look at Tori before inspecting the faces of her other two friends. Nothing but compassion and caring was present there. She knew then she had made a wise choice in asking them to get together this morning. "It isn't simple and I'm not even sure it's love."

Adriana began to blurt out something, but then she bit her tongue and laughed harshly. "Who am I to question why you're confused? It took me nearly twenty years to wake up and realize what I could have with Riley."

"*Pero* you woke up," Juli said, but immediately tacked on, "at least Sylvia is finally thinking that there might be more to this thing with Carlos. That is what you're thinking, *verdad?*"

When she hesitated, Tori squeezed her hand reassuringly. "You do have feelings for him."

"I have . . . feelings for him. Maybe more than I thought I could ever have for a man."

"Men are dogs, *sabes.* But not all men," Juli said and shot a glance at Adriana.

"Not all. Especially not Carlos. He's honorable. A hero. Steady and dependable," Adriana said, pleading on his behalf maybe because, in part, Carlos was much like Riley, and in her heart, Adriana wanted to believe it as well.

Turning her gaze to Tori, ever reasonable and sensible Tori, she asked, "What do you think?"

"I think that sometimes you have to take a gamble and risk your heart because if you do, the reward can be more fulfilling than anything you ever imagined."

Sylvia wasn't made of dreams and hopeless romanticism. Her life had been too grounded in reality up until now, including the reality of her mother's own unhappy past. But as she examined the faces of all of her friends, her very smart, independent, and thoughtful friends, she realized that they all believed in those dreams for her. That they all thought it was possible that Carlos and she were a good thing. A forever kind of thing.

With a nod, she told herself that she had to consider that they might be right. That it might be worth the gamble. After all, they were her friends.

Who else could she trust with her heart?

8

It *was another sunny*, hot, and humid Sunday afternoon, much like any other in Palm Beach. Much like the afternoon a few months ago when curiosity had gotten the better of Virginia and she had driven up to catch one of the polo matches. One where Pablo would be playing. Binoculars in hand, floppy-brimmed hat tucked tightly on her head, she had slipped on her Chanel sunglasses and eased into her seat to watch the match.

Time hadn't changed him much. He still had the same lean athletic body. On or off a horse, he moved with a grace and strength that turned many a head. His face, or what she had seen of it from beneath his helmet, was a bit more weathered, with a few extra lines here and there. Or at least, that's how he had seemed to her from her position up in the stands. She had kept her distance.

Maintaining a safe distance from Pablo having been the number one . . . maybe make that the number two goal for that day. Number one had obviously been seeing

Pablo. *Seeing Pablo,* she thought to herself as she wheeled her Cadillac XLR convertible into the parking lot of the polo club.

She'd gone, she'd seen, and she'd run, Virginia recalled. But today, there would be no running. No avoiding the one and only man who had ever made her feel anything. Everything. Love. Hate. Ecstasy and abject pain. Pablo had been capable of filling her life with one and all for the nearly three years they had been involved.

Which made her wonder yet again as she parked her car, *Why was she even considering seeing him?* But the answer came instantly—Sylvia. She was here for her daughter, since there wasn't anything she wouldn't do to make her happy, including doing something about Pablo.

Virginia believed with all her heart that what had happened between her and Pablo was responsible for the way Sylvia felt about Carlos. Or rather, the way Sylvia couldn't believe in Carlos or any other man for that matter.

Her daughter had looked confused yesterday when Virginia had come by her condo unexpectedly. It wasn't like she didn't regularly see Sylvia. In addition to their Sunday get-togethers, they went out for dinner or lunch during the week at least a few times a month.

But from the moment Sylvia had entered the condo early Saturday evening, Virginia had known something was worrying her normally unflappable daughter.

Sylvia had been dressed for a night out in a stunning silk gown in a coffee-brown that had highlighted her hazel-green eyes. The gown had been demure by her daughter's usual standards, with a collar that went all around her neck to hold up the front bodice.

With her motherly eye, however, she had seen the slight bruise just above the edge of the collar. The kind of bruise that told her that she and Carlos had been rather busy, but the troubled look in her daughter's eyes said that there was definitely more to the story.

Sylvia eventually confessed her plight, not just about her night with Carlos, but also about the fight before-hand and the Saturday morning discussion with her friends.

Having given her body to the detective—and if Virginia was any judge, possibly her heart as well—Sylvia was doubting the wisdom of the choices she had made. Worried that if she had been wrong, her life would never be the same.

Just as mine has never been the same, Virginia thought. For too many years Sylvia had questioned the wisdom of what her mother and Pablo had done so long ago. Wondered if it had been a wise choice or one that had doomed her to forever compare every man she met to Pablo. The problem was that Sylvia was possibly right. Every man she had met had invariably come up short.

Like mother, like daughter, she thought yet again, and it occurred to her that maybe her own doubt about the choices she had made was also part of the reason why she was here at the polo match. Maybe by finally exorcising the ghost of Pablo's memories, she would be free to find someone else.

She was still young after all. Still capable of enjoying the pleasures life had to offer.

She walked with the crowd toward the entrance of the polo club. She had checked the schedule, and Pablo's team was slated to play shortly. After handing over her ticket, she headed toward the edge of the lawn where Pablo was sure to be, prepping for the match.

Much as she had expected, there he was, rubbing down one of his ponies. She stopped short, unable to believe that after nearly thirty years, he stood just yards away.

Pablo tossed the brush to a young man, turned, and faced the crowd. That was when he saw her and abruptly froze in place.

Virginia held her breath. Sweet Lord, but the years hadn't made him any less attractive. If anything, they had added maturity and muscle to the young man's body she had so eagerly loved long ago.

His caramel-colored hair was tousled from his helmet, but still thick and with barely any gray. A slight shadow of beard covered the strong sharp lines of his face. He'd always had a thick beard. It had used to rasp her face raw when they . . .

She stopped and met his gaze. That marvelous green-eyed gaze that hadn't changed except for a few wrinkles at the corners of his eyes.

In the movies, this would be the point where the director called for the soft music to play romantically as the hero and heroine gazed at each other longingly before running into each other's arms.

But there was no music, just the noise of the crowd. The thud and jangle of horses and bridles as players warmed up. No running; if anything, it was a rather hesitant if not almost staggering step forward on both their parts. One unsteady step at a time until they stood about a foot from each other.

This is a big mistake, she thought as she stood there, the hot Florida sun making her sweat. She felt unnerved by the too intense look that Pablo shot her during the entire agonizing walk toward her. But then he smiled, and that smile was as brilliant and warming as the sun beating down on her.

"*Hola,* GinGin," he said, using his pet nickname for her.

This is definitely a big mistake, she thought again as they closed that final short distance between them and stepped into each other's arms.

His body was hard. Harder even than it had been as a young man. *Or maybe it was her imagination,* she thought as she eased out of his embrace and awkwardly juggled the binoculars and hat in her hands.

"Pablo. It's good to see you again," she said softly, for she was experiencing a breathlessness that was so not good.

"I . . . I hadn't expected . . ." He faltered and shook his head, as if chastising himself. "It's good to see you, *también.*"

"Right," she said and rocked back and forth on her flat-heeled sensible shoes. They made her inches shorter than his six-something height. She wished that she had worn her Blahniks, which would have evened up the playing field by placing her eye to eye with him.

"This is . . . awkward, isn't it?" he said, almost as if thinking out loud.

"It is," she admitted. "I mean, especially since . . . it's been a long time."

"It has."

"So what do you do when it's been like . . . thirty years?" she asked, and he surprised her by smiling yet again.

"Thirty years, which makes me wonder what you're doing here after all this time."

"I was hoping we could talk," she said and tightly grabbed hold of the binoculars and floppy hat, almost mangling the brim of the hat as she did so. She took a quick look around and inclined her head in the direction of the polo field. "But I think the match is going to start shortly. It may be best if you and I discussed this afterward."

"If something is wrong, I can excuse myself from the match," he said, laying his hand on her arm.

She appreciated his offer. It was more than she maybe had a right to, after so many years away from him. She shook her head and said, "It's nothing urgent. It can wait until after."

"Later, then." With a gallant nod, he walked away from her. A familiar sight and one that still stirred a myriad of emotions. Pain, because he had walked away too many times already, and lust, since even at fifty-three, he still had a hell of a nice ass.

Hurrying from the field, she located a spot up in the stands and settled in to watch the match in its entirety. Last time, she had lasted only until the end of the first chukker—all of six minutes. She had been afraid of lingering too long.

Today, she had every intention of staying until Pablo agreed to do what she wanted—for him to come and meet his daughter.

Putting on the hat to shade the intense Florida sun, which was quite strong even in the later afternoon winter hours, she slipped on her sunglasses and opened the program for the match. As she skimmed the names of the players on the teams, she noted the ten handicap next to Pablo's name. The highest ranking a player could get.

When they had first met, that had been his dream, much like hers had been to get to college and flee the small Virginia town that had been a prison for most of her life.

Funny how dreams sometimes came to pass in the most unexpected of ways, she considered as she settled in to watch the match.

It was a tight match for the first few chukkers, with Pablo managing to keep his team ahead by a couple of goals with his play in the number one position. At the end of each chukker, he returned to the side of the field and picked up a fresh pony, as did many of the other players.

She was enjoying the game except for the constant attentions of the gentleman beside her, who had decided she needed not only champagne to loosen her up, but also a never-ending prattle about the game and the players. By the closing minutes of the third chukker, she wished she had chosen one of the lawn seats rather than the pricier ones up in the stands. At least down on the lawn she could have worn her jeans and packed a picnic lunch.

The third chukker was nearly over, and with it came the announcement that all were invited down to the field for the traditional stomping of the divots. Although a number of spectators ran down to help replace the pieces of turf dug up by the horses' hooves, she remained in the stands. She was almost sorry she did as she noticed a young woman who raced to Pablo's side and glued herself to him during the entire divot stomp.

Not that he seemed to mind. Virginia experienced a spike of unwelcome jealousy and tamped it down. Pablo and she hadn't been an item for quite some time. She expected that he had become involved with other women. Of course, it would have been nice if the women were older than his daughter, but then again, men were dogs.

She cringed as she heard the echo of her daughter's voice in that thought. It was the reason she was here now, hoping to change that perception in Sylvia. Maybe even hoping she could change it within herself.

Returning her full glass of champagne to the overly friendly man next to her—she hadn't had a drink since her one reckless night with Pablo, blaming excess libations in part for her abandon with Pablo—she settled in for the rest of the match, intending to approach Pablo once again at the end of the event.

Pablo's team ended up winning handily, in large part due to his play. Just as Virginia left the stands and headed to where Pablo was turning his horse over to an assistant, the very young and very attractive woman who had plastered herself to Pablo during the stomping of the divots reappeared at his side. She was quite obviously throwing herself at him.

It wasn't jealousy she felt, Virginia told herself again. It was just annoyance at the youngster who was creating an obstacle to her being able to talk to Pablo. When she reached him, he was intently listening to the young woman, but with a slight scowl. As he noticed her, he looked up and smiled warmly, creating a little flutter in her stomach.

"Would you excuse me?" he said to his nubile companion and walked toward Virginia.

Being no slouch in the stalker department, the young woman followed Pablo and slipped her arm through Pablo's as he approached. "Pablo, you didn't tell me you had friends coming to the match today," the girl cooed.

So he knows her? Virginia thought and held out her hand, about to introduce herself, but Pablo grabbed hold of it. He deftly switched positions so that he was now at her side, his arm through hers and facing the stunned young woman. "Tiffany, I'd like you to meet my wife, Virginia."

Shock erupted on Tiffany's face. It took the greatest amount of her control for Virginia to school her own surprise and paste a bright smile on her face. "If you'll excuse us. Pablo and I have something private to discuss," she said, and with gentle pressure on his arm, she led him away from the shell-shocked woman.

They walked together back to where Pablo's ponies were waiting. It was then she turned on him, anger finally getting the better of her. "What the hell was that? Your wife? I have not been your wife in some time and I will never again—get that, buster—*never* again be your wife," she said, poking her finger into the hard planes of his chest.

As if to infuriate her more, he said, "Never say never, GinGin."

Count to ten, she told herself.

One.

Two.

Three.

"What the hell were you thinking?" she nearly screamed, losing her control. Once again, she jabbed her index finger into his chest to emphasize her point.

He grabbed her finger in midpoke. "I was thinking that the only semisure way of ridding myself of Tiffany and others like her until the end of the season in April is to make it clear I am unavailable. Besides, Tiffany's young enough to be my daughter."

When she spoke, her words were softer in volume, but intended to cut him down. "You mean *my daughter,* don't you? Because in nearly thirty years, Sylvia hasn't been a part of your life."

His face hardened, and with that change, he seemed older. More remote. Those vibrant green eyes of his grew cold, which never ceased to amaze her. Green was the color of life and warmth. That his could evoke such opposites could still surprise her, even after all this time. "Not because I didn't try, Virginia. Not because I didn't care."

No, not because of you, she agreed silently. It had just gotten too hard for them to see each other after Sylvia's birth. "I know. Maybe it's time to remedy that."

A ripple seemed to move over his body. One of shock mingled with expectation. "Sylvia wants to meet me?"

It pained her to even think about denying it, since

despite all that had happened between them, she cared for Pablo on some level. She hated that weakness she had for him, but she couldn't hurt him to make herself feel better. "Could we discuss this somewhere more private?"

"*Sí*, somewhere quieter would be good," he said with a polite nod of his head. A respectful and reserved kind of nod, so much like the one he had first given her so long ago. He was putting up his defenses, and that was fine.

Virginia suspected he was going to need them if he decided to meet Sylvia. With a genteel incline of her head, she gave him the name and address of a restaurant on Ocean Drive. "My daughter's . . . Our daughter's friends run the place. I like to support them when I can."

Pablo gave her a puzzled look. "You're not worried about Sylvia's friends seeing you with me?"

She laughed and passed a hand over his face in a gesture meant to soothe. "Honey, I'm a grown girl. I think I can handle it."

He smiled then, and a vibrant light returned to his eyes. "I never doubted that you could handle anything you wanted to, GinGin. Tonight, then. At eight?"

"At eight," she replied with a teasing lilt to her voice and walked away, but as she did so, she took a deep breath, wondering if she hadn't just made the second biggest mistake of her life.

9

Pablo waited for her by the steps of the restaurant, devastatingly handsome in a dark charcoal gray suit that emphasized the long lean lines of his body. It occurred to her he was much like one of his ponies, strong and lithe. Nervous, as he almost seemed to paw the ground with his foot as he watched her approach.

Heat filled his gaze again as it had earlier that day, causing her steps to falter for a second, but then she forced herself forward.

"Pablo," she said and he leaned forward, kissed both her cheeks in that Latin way.

She answered that kiss with just one of her own, right by the edge of his mouth, where if she truly dared, only a slight shift would have brought their lips together. If only she would dare, she thought.

He still understood her too well for he smiled and warned, "Don't play with fire, GinGin."

She realized how right he was—the fire was still there

after thirty years. The itch still strong and needing scratching, much as she had warned Sylvia months earlier.

Sylvia, she reminded herself. Tonight was only about Sylvia and nothing else, because well, there was nothing else between her and Pablo. They had both decided on that long ago.

Slipping her arm through his, she led him to the podium where the young hostess, who recognized her, immediately led her to one of their prime tables next to the windows along the open-air veranda. The glass protected them from the slightly chilly breeze that had sprung up as well as the noise of a South Beach night—the music from the cars passing along the street, the murmurs of the crowd on the street and veranda.

"Very nice," Pablo said as he held out her chair.

She sat down and he joined her, taking not the seat across the way, but the one adjacent to her. Too close, but as their eyes met, she realized he was waiting for her challenge. Testing her much as he had when they had been younger.

But she wasn't as hot tempered as she had been in her youth. Too much needed to be discussed for her to get angry so early in the evening.

"The ambience is wonderful, but the food is even better," she said as a busboy discreetly placed a basket of bread and a small dish with rich olive oil before them.

He picked up the basket and offered her a piece. She took a small roll, tore a small piece off, and watched as he did the same.

A mistake. She had always loved his hands. The gentle strength in those long fingers. The shape of them. Broad. Manly. A scar here and there a testament to the dangers of what he did.

She dragged her eyes off his hands and finally got to

the matter requiring attention. "I wanted to talk to you about Sylvia."

"I saw her article in the magazine last month. It was wonderful," he said, surprising her. She hadn't known that he paid that much attention to what their daughter did.

"Then you must know what happened after?" She dunked her bread into the oil and popped the piece in her mouth, chewing slowly as she examined his face. His eyebrows drew together and his gaze grew turbulent.

"Yes, I know about the shooting. I understand she wasn't hurt." With a curt motion of his hand, he signaled a waiter over.

When the young man brought over their menus, he said, "Bottle of merlot. House wine will do. And you?"

Virginia passed on the wine. "Iced tea, please. Sweetened if you have it."

"She wasn't hurt, but the detective was seriously injured. She's involved with him. Or at least I think she is."

"He hasn't hurt her, has he?" As the waiter placed the bottle and a glass before him, he poured some and after, took a big bracing gulp. When he put the glass down, he flexed his hands, not that he had ever been the kind quick to anger or violence. On the contrary, he had always been one of the gentlest men she knew.

Because of that, she had no hesitation in placing her hand over his as she said, "No, he hasn't."

A muscle ticked along his jaw as he replied, "That's good, because I'm not sure I could do the whole fatherly vengeance thing."

"Good, because that's not why I asked you here," she said, but couldn't continue as the waiter came over. They hadn't really looked at the menus and she was about to wave him off, when Pablo said, "You must know what's good here. Why don't you order for both of us?"

She hoped his haste was due to his desire to continue the conversation. The restaurant had its staple signature dishes, and so she ordered them, beginning with a sampling platter of appetizers and a paella that took an extra twenty minutes to prepare. She hoped that Pablo was still too much of a gentleman to run out in the midst of a meal, no matter how upset he might become with their conversation.

His chuckle, confirming that he had seen through her machinations, amused her as well. "Am I that obvious?"

He leaned forward, cradled her jaw, and ran a thumb along the flush of color that had sprung up on her cheeks. "You never had a poker face, GinGin. So tell me what's happening with our daughter."

And so she did, detailing what she could without giving away any of Sylvia's confidences. He listened patiently, considering her comments while they shared the appetizers and after, waited and then ate the paella.

When he leaned back in his chair, he had the look of a well-satisfied man on his face. A look she remembered all too well and which brought an awakening of desire between her legs.

"So, what I'm gathering is that you think that my meeting our daughter and getting to know her will somehow help her get over her commitment issues."

"Basically, yes."

He leaned his elbows on the table, steepled his hands before him, and considered her. "It's not that simple, *sabes*. And it may take some time."

"You're here until April right? The end of the polo season?" she said, slightly unnerved by the intensity of his gaze as it travelled over her features.

"You think that in three months I can—"

"We can," she said, motioning to the two of them.

"We caused this problem together and maybe together we can fix it."

She had tried to make it sound simple, but even to her own ears, it seemed lame. How could you make such a drastic change in so short a time? But then again, hadn't their lives changed in that short a time thirty years earlier? Hadn't it taken only a few weeks to set them on a course that would irrevocably alter the rest of their lives?

"Well?" she asked at his continued perusal, which bothered her more than she cared to admit.

"I want Sylvia to be happy. So if this is what you think will make that happen, I'll do it."

With a nod, she said, "I think it will help Sylvia be happy."

She buried in her heart the possibility that she might also find a way to finally be happy.

As Sylvia sat in Harry's office for the early Monday morning meeting he had called without warning, she considered that she had been blinded by the knight. Carlos Ramirez, aka Mr. Save the World, resplendent in his shining armor when he had rushed in to slay the dragons, was maybe much closer to being the dragon than she had thought. Facing the man beside her, she examined his features as she said, "Could we go over this again, Mr. Davis?"

Randy Davis's gaze skittered uneasily between her and her boss, Harry. "I already told you everything I know. What more is there to say?"

"Why don't you start at the beginning again?" She had been so flummoxed by his accusations that something inside of her had shut down. She wanted to hear the entire story again so that she could process it the way she should. So that she could determine for herself whether Randy Davis was credible.

"My younger brother, Simon, was killed four years ago along with two drug dealers. Two other undercover officers were shot during the same stakeout," Randy said, his arms braced loosely on the arms of the chair. His demeanor tense, but not as aggressive as before.

"Simon was undercover?" Sylvia asked.

Randy nodded. "Yes. Simon was undercover with Carlos Ramirez and Riley Evans."

Carlos and Riley, Sylvia thought yet again, but forced herself to write their names down anyway on the pad of paper where she had earlier tried to take some notes but had managed only unintelligible scribbles. With a quick glance at Randy, she said, "And you think these two detectives were involved—"

"Not just involved. I think they killed my brother."

She shot a quick look at her boss, then back to Randy. "Why are you telling us and not the police? And why now?"

A rough shrug shifted across Randy's thin shoulders. "I told the cops something wasn't right four years ago. Simon had been antsy. Not himself. They wouldn't listen. As for why come to you now—the article you did. You got it all wrong in your article."

"The article was about designer drugs," Sylvia reminded him.

"You mentioned an undercover detective. Made him out to be a hero, but I know who he is and he's a killer." Randy jabbed an angry finger in her direction with each word.

"You think the officer I mentioned—"

"Is Carlos Ramirez. Can you deny it?" he challenged.

She wasn't about to be baited or let him become the interrogator. "When you went to the police, what did they say?"

"That this was an internal investigation. You know how they close ranks around their own, but my brother was one of their own as well," Randy said and grew increasingly agitated.

Sylvia raised her hands and urged him to calm down. "Why do you think these two officers killed your brother?"

"Simon and I had a drink hours before he died. He was upset. He said there was something he had to do, but he didn't want to do it." Tears came to Randy's eyes, and he looked up at the ceiling. She had no doubt about the sincerity of his emotions.

Sylvia leaned forward and laid a hand on Randy's arm. "What didn't he want to do?"

Randy slowly lowered his gaze until it met hers. "He told me he had to go to IAD. That something was wrong and he had to do something about it. That night he was killed. What would you think?"

She would think what she didn't want to think. What she couldn't imagine believing—that Carlos and Riley had played a part in Simon Davis's death.

After Randy Davis left, Harry assigned her another investigative piece—to discover the truth behind Davis's allegations. Harry was convinced that if the story was true, it would garner as much attention as her earlier exposé.

She should have advised Harry of her conflict of interest, since she was involved with Carlos, but she needed to get to the truth. She needed to know if Carlos was not what he seemed. If she had made a mistake in believing in him. Plus she agreed with her boss that if there was any truth to Randy Davis's accusations, it would make a hell of a story.

She headed to the library to read through the old newspaper archives.

The story was there in black and white, seemingly complete. But beneath what was written was another story. One that suddenly didn't seem as improbable as it had seemed earlier that morning.

Despite that, Sylvia still didn't want to believe Randy. To her Carlos and Riley were heroes. Cops who had almost lost their lives doing their jobs four years ago. Carlos had almost lost his life again a month ago while saving her from . . .

One of his drug dealer pals? she thought as she rewound the microfilm and started reading the article again from the beginning. Hoping that as she did so, the pieces wouldn't fall into place in a way that made Randy's accusations almost believable.

But by the time she finished it, she couldn't deny that Randy's claims could be substantiated by the facts in the story. As she rewound that microfilm and set up a second reel for review, she considered that there were many parts to a story. That while the details might seem the same at first, the actual facts behind them could be different.

Again it came to her that she couldn't let her feelings for Carlos blind her to what he really was. That by doing so, her journalistic integrity was at risk and that there was only one thing to do.

She had to find out what had really happened on the night that Simon Davis had been killed. She had to do it because that was her job as a reporter.

As for her personal reasons—she wanted to believe in Carlos. She wanted to think he was the real deal. That what she was feeling for him was real. That *he* was real.

She bit her bottom lip, wondering if she even had what it took to know what was real and what wasn't anymore.

To know whether Carlos was a dog, like most men. She worried that she might be ready to believe Randy Davis's story because it gave her an easy out. An easy way to avoid acknowledging her feelings for Carlos.

Not that she was in love with Carlos. It was too soon for the *L* word. Especially now, when it was possible that Carlos was . . .

Dirty. Dishonest. Character traits that weren't just limited to when he was being a cop. How would she know? Sylvia wondered as she advanced through the second microfilm, but then it came to her.

Trust your gut and not your heart.

10

"To life, love, and always being *amigas,"* Tori said, raising her mojito high in the air as they began their regular Monday night after-workout dinner.

They had opted to extend their workout by making the longer walk to a Cuban restaurant on Lincoln Road instead of one of their usual haunts on Ocean Drive. They strolled together up Washington, pausing to look at some shop windows before heading farther north on the avenue. Then they went past Sylvia's magazine's offices on Española Way and continued onward to Lincoln Road, where they turned into the pedestrian mall.

They were quickly seated at a table in the restaurant, close enough to the windows to be able to watch the flow of pedestrians along the wide width of Lincoln Road. As in South Beach, the restaurant had some tables outdoors, but it was quiet on a Monday night and the open-air dining area remained empty.

Sylvia toasted along with Juli and Adriana, but her

mind was on her meeting with Randy Davis and the research she had done for the better part of the afternoon. Research that had only created confusion and doubt.

"Hello, Sylvia," Adriana said, waving a hand in front of her face. "Earth to Sylvia."

She shook her head free of distracting thoughts and turned her attention to her friends. "I'm sorry. I was thinking about—"

"Hopefully not Carlos with that sour look. Speaking of Carlos, I saw him down at the beach today when Gil and I went out for lunch. He looked well," Tori said and sipped her mojito.

Sylvia recalled him in bed in his sailboat stateroom, his skin boasting a new tan instead of hospital pallor. The muscles of his arms and chest flexed as he pillowed his head on his hands. The feel of all that muscle against her and the heat of his sleep-warm skin. It had only been a few days, but she missed seeing him. Which only confused her more, given all that had happened today.

"*Pero ahora* you are definitely thinking about him. You have 'the Look,'" Juli said, teasing and wagging a finger at her playfully.

"The Look?" she asked and took a bracing swig of her own icy cold mojito.

"Like this." Tori mimicked a faraway, adoring, puppy-dog kind of expression.

She chuckled and nudged her friend playfully. "I know that Look. It's the one you get when you think about Gil."

"It's the kind of look your *mami* had last night," Juli piped in.

"What? Why would my mama have 'the Look'?"

"She came by the restaurant with a man," Adriana explained and buried her nose in the menu, but not before adding, "a very handsome man."

"You're sure it was my mama?" Sylvia asked as she put down her mojito and perused the menu. Rice. Beans. Roast pork. Her mouth watered, but the temptation was tempered by the thought that the one Cuban thing she was truly craving might not be on the menu. She told herself she had to be on a Carlos-free diet until she figured out what had really happened four years ago with Simon Davis.

Adriana nodded emphatically and motioned for the waiter, who came by and took their orders. After he had gone, Adriana said, "Definitely your mother, since I dropped by the table at the end of the night to make sure everything was fine."

Her mama being with a man was nothing out of the ordinary. Virginia had a small stable of male friends who accompanied her to various outings, not to mention assorted male business associates. "And you say this man was—"

"Drop-dead gorgeous. Dangerously . . . interesting," Adriana said and shot a look at Juli. "Right? You saw him as well, Juli."

Juli nodded emphatically. "*Verdad.* A *primo papi chulo* even for an older man. Well built. Gorgeous green eyes and thick hair the color of *dulce de leche.* There was definitely something going on. Something like . . ." Juli's hands fluttered in the air as she tried to find the right word.

Adriana helped out her partner and friend. "Tension. Sexual tension."

Sylvia considered Adriana's and Juli's comments, and finally, shock settled in. "You think Mama is interested in a man? That maybe she's finally found another man who makes her itch?"

Shrugging, Adriana said, "*No se* 'cause . . . Something

was happening. They weren't really touchy-feely. Yet. But you could see they wanted to."

"Wanted to what?" she asked with some annoyance at her friend's semicryptic statement.

"Wanted to touch. Wanted to get lucky. You could just feel it," Adriana clarified.

"Okay, you're grossing me out," she said and waved her hands to urge Adriana to stop.

"Why?" Tori asked. "I mean, sixty's the new forty, right? So your *mami* is—"

"Almost forty-seven. So if sixty's the new forty, is forty the new twenty?" she quipped, but was unprepared for her friends' answers.

"Your *mami*'s a young and attractive woman," Adriana replied after taking another sip of her mojito.

"She's in her sexual prime," Tori chimed in.

She shook her head emphatically and waved off their suggestions. "And to that I say, 'Eeww.'"

Adriana held her hands up in question. "Sylvia, I can't believe you're being so dense about this."

"*Sí.* I think it's great that after all this time, your *mami* seems to be interested in someone," Juli said as the waiter finally placed the appetizers they had ordered in the middle of the table. Juli reached out, took a small piece of tamale from the plate of assorted *antojitos*.

Sylvia considered all that her *amigas* had said and with a shake of her head, commented, "Well, then there's only one thing to do."

"And that is?" Tori wondered, her forkful of empanada stilled in midair.

"I've got to meet this man and find out what his intentions are toward my mama."

After all, if her mama was going to . . . Well, she wanted to make sure her mama wasn't making another mistake like the one she had made with Pablo. Her mama deserved a good man. A Prince, if there was such a thing, instead of Pablo the Frog, who had broken her heart.

Maybe by helping her mama out, she would even figure out just what to do about Carlos, because she was missing him just way too much for it to be healthy. Especially with what was happening in her professional life. She couldn't let down her defenses until she was more sure of Carlos. Her mama had done that once and look at what happened.

As Sylvia sipped on her mojito and listened to her friends, who had switched to a different topic, she decided she had to make sure her mama didn't make the same mistake again.

It was two in the morning on a Friday night, but Sylvia wasn't ready for sleep, although she was finally in bed after a night filled with visits to at least five different locations.

The first two had been to cover assignments for the magazine's After Dark and Gossip section. Typical Miami fare—a party for the opening of a show at the Jackie Gleason Theater and an out-of-control *quinceañera* at the Ritz-Carlton South Beach hotel.

The last three locations had come courtesy of the copy of the police file she had gotten midweek after numerous requests.

Sylvia leaned over and shuffled the copies from the file she had laid out on one side of her bed. Sad replacements for the man who had been there oh so recently.

She pored over the papers for what seemed like the hundredth time, going over every detail from Carlos's and Riley's statements to those of the police officers who had first responded to the call that officers were down. The crime scene photos captured the area where the shooting had occurred. The bullet holes in the walls of the buildings and nearby cars reminded Sylvia of her own recent experience. The bodies of the two drug dealers, awkwardly sprawled on the sidewalk, sent a shiver along her spine as she remembered Carlos lying in the alley bleeding.

In the crime scene photos, Simon Davis's body lay barely ten feet away from the dead drug dealers. Someone had made a notation on the photo to indicate where Carlos and Riley had been found by the first officers responding to the scene.

In her mind, she replayed the most likely scenario based on the information from the file.

Simon Davis approached the drug dealers.

Simon shot one dead before the dealer had a chance to act.

The second dealer opened fire, hitting all three police officers in a barrage of bullets from his Tec-9.

Simon Davis lay bleeding to death on the sidewalk, feet from where Carlos and Riley also lay injured.

As the drug dealer continued shooting at them, Carlos pulled Riley into a safe location and fired his gun.

Second drug dealer dead.

After, Carlos had gone to Simon's side to help him but had passed out from his own loss of blood.

Even without Randy Davis's accusations, the explanation of what had happened that night didn't seem airtight. Certainly not wrapped up nice and pretty the way the police report tried to make it appear.

Why had Simon dropped the first drug dealer? The M.E.'s report made it clear that the man had died from a single gunshot wound to the chest, but like his partner, he'd had an automatic weapon beneath his jacket. He would have pulled it and opened fire if he had found Simon threatening in any way.

Clearly Simon's actions had surprised the first man. *Why?* she wondered.

As for Carlos and Riley, why had they hung back when Simon first approached the drug dealers?

It occurred to her then that maybe it hadn't been Carlos and Riley who had set up Simon. Maybe it had been the other way around. Maybe Simon had had a reason for eliminating the other two officers on the assignment with him.

She needed more information. Information she wasn't going to get from the police reports or newspaper articles or the people hanging out in South Beach's assorted hot spots.

She needed to speak to Simon Davis's widow, to the sole eyewitness identified on the police report, and to the other cops with whom Carlos and Riley had worked. Possibly even those who had first arrived on the scene.

As she gathered up the papers strewn over the surface of her bed and walked them over to her desk, Sylvia considered whether she might finally share that bed with Carlos once this investigation was over.

But only when I've discovered the truth, she reminded herself. No matter how much she wanted to be with Carlos after their very pleasant interlude on his boat, she had to maintain her distance.

Sylvia told herself to think of her itch for him as poison ivy. She forced herself to remember that if she scratched too hard, she would only succeed in leaving a scar.

It took a few phone calls on Saturday to track down Simon Davis's widow. When Phyllis Davis had first answered, she had not wanted to discuss anything, but Sylvia wouldn't take no for an answer. Phyllis finally relented, sensing that Sylvia would keep on calling until she got what she wanted.

By late afternoon, Sylvia was on her way to the Davis home, and the only thing it had cost her was a promise to bring dinner—McDonald's for Phyllis's boys and some Cuban sandwiches for Phyllis.

She knew she would hit a McDonald's somewhere along her drive but made a point of stopping in Little Havana for the Cuban sandwiches. She would have brought Phyllis a thick Cuban *batido* as well, but with the heat, the shake would be warm and runny by the time she got there.

That didn't stop her from grabbing a mango shake for her road trip, since she hadn't had a chance to eat anything for either breakfast or lunch.

She rode Calle Ocho southward, through Little Havana and past the airport, out of the city until the spaces between the homes and businesses got wider and the signs for the Indian reservation casinos nestled in the Everglades became more numerous and prominent.

She was about ten minutes away from her destination when she noticed the familiar golden arches up ahead. She pulled through the drive-through window and ordered a few Happy Meals. Back on the road, the wind whipped up the smell of the greasy fries and burgers, overpowering the subtler smells of the pork and ham in the Cuban sandwiches sitting in a paper bag on her front seat.

After barely two miles, she noted the small stucco structure squatting in front of a small canal. The rusty mailbox tilted toward the road and bore the number for which she was looking.

Sylvia pulled up into the gravel driveway next to an

older Dodge Caravan. She remembered from Davis's file that he had children, so the minivan was a necessity. Another recollection came as well—that the youngest had not yet been born when Simon had been killed. That would make the smallest child still a toddler. One who would never know his dad.

You didn't either and you still came out all right.

The door opened as Sylvia walked up the cracked cement path along the front of the house. The toddler she had been wondering about was balanced on his mother's hip, wailing.

"Sorry, but Billy hasn't been feeling well. He just got up from a nap," the woman said and pushed open the screen door, which gave a metallic groan in protest.

As Sylvia walked in, she took note of a number of things. The home was older, but tidy. The furniture was dated and slightly worn, but clean. Not stylish by any stretch of the imagination, much like the woman who stood before her, pushing back unruly brown hair from the crying child's face.

Phyllis wore tight jeans that hugged ample curves and a T-shirt that proclaimed THESE COLORS DON'T RUN together with an American flag. The T-shirt likewise was a bit too tight, as if all the clothes had been from a thinner time in her life. Her hair was a flat brown badly in need of a touch-up, since her part showed a very noticeable line of gray.

"Thanks for agreeing to speak with me. I brought dinner." Sylvia held out the bags and the child immediately quieted as he noticed the familiar McDonald's colors and logo.

"You are such a man," Phyllis said to the toddler. "A full belly always make them quiet," she told Sylvia and kissed the youngster on the cheek. "Come on back to the kitchen."

Phyllis called out to her other children, and from another room came the squeak and pound of sneakered feet on the linoleum floor.

The two kids who raced into the kitchen quickly battled over chairs for themselves while Phyllis secured the youngest in a high chair. With a wave, Phyllis motioned Sylvia to a free chair at the head of the table—what had probably been Simon's place—and after getting drinks for everyone, she took a seat to Sylvia's right.

As the three boys tackled their burgers with gusto, Phyllis murmured her approval of the Cuban sandwich. Sylvia ate her own sandwich slowly as she watched the dynamics of the mother and children during the meal.

The elder boys looked like their dad. Or at least the photo of their dad from the police report she had reviewed so many times it was as good as memorized. As Sylvia examined Phyllis, she wondered how the woman handled seeing her husband in those faces every day. Or maybe that made it easier, knowing that while Simon was gone he lived on through their children.

The youngest boy looked nothing like the others. His hair was a mousy brown and he had hazel eyes, not the light blue his brothers possessed. In fact, his face was fuller, with a thin sharp nose. His two brothers had small pug noses.

The boys finished their food quickly and politely asked to leave the table, but they complained when their mother asked them to take their younger brother with them. When they finally scampered out of the room, dragging the youngest behind them, peace settled over the kitchen.

"They're good kids," Phyllis said, almost as if she expected some kind of condemnation.

"They seem like it. I'm just not used to kids."

"Not married?"

"Not married and not likely to be ever," Sylvia answered honestly.

Phyllis eyed her over the top of her glass of iced tea. "Guess you're one of those career women." She said it as if it was a curse, and after taking a long swig of her drink, she motioned with her glass. "So what do you want to know about my Simon?"

"I have an informant—"

"Probably his crazy-ass brother, Randy. Randy and his mother always thought Simon was a saint, but he was just a man. A good man, but human and not above temptation."

She'd have to be blind not to see that all had not been good between Phyllis and Simon. As for temptation, the image of Simon's youngest son painted a picture that spoke volumes. "Your youngest boy—"

"Things had been bad for a while. That temptation I mentioned—I think Simon was seeing someone else. One night I needed some attention myself . . . Well, it just kind of happened."

Regret colored her words, so painfully that Sylvia put down the last little bit of her sandwich and laid a hand over the other woman's. "Did he know you'd had an affair?"

Phyllis shrugged. "Maybe. After he was killed, I asked myself if his mind wasn't totally on what he was doing that night. That maybe he was thinking of leaving me."

"Why do you say that?"

Another tired shrug of her plump shoulders came before Phyllis said, "A couple of months after Simon died, I finally went through his things. I found a bankbook. One just in his name with lots of money."

A nest egg for a new life, Sylvia thought, but it could

also have been something else. "How do you think Simon got all that money?"

Phyllis pulled her hand away. "Simon wasn't dirty. He might have been a lot of things, but he loved being a cop. It was the one thing that made him truly happy."

Phyllis didn't make him happy, Sylvia thought. But cops didn't make "lots of money," which left her wondering how Simon had amassed so much cash in a separate account. Phyllis must have known what she was thinking since she quickly piped up. "Simon had been working a lot of overtime. When he wasn't on duty, he had a second job as a bouncer. Things were always tough."

"And now?"

"We manage. There's the police widow's benefits and Social Security." She picked up her hands and motioned to the house. "My mom and dad passed about a year ago and left me this. It's all paid up, so I can actually make ends meet now."

Sylvia hesitated, uncomfortable with what she was about to ask, but knowing that she had to. "What about the money in that other account?"

"It's still there. Keeping it for the kids and college."

"College?" The words slipped from her before she could control herself. "Must be a nice amount if you're keeping it for college."

Phyllis leaned her hands on the table and pushed herself up. "I think it's time you left, Ms. A-me-na-bar," she said, unduly stressing the syllables, as if they were distasteful to her.

Sylvia rose but asked again, "Was it a lot, Phyllis? More than possible with just Simon's overtime and a second job?"

Phyllis seemed to recognize, much as she had initially over the phone, that Sylvia wouldn't let up until she answered. So she shrugged once again and said, "I don't know how Simon got the money, but I do know who might be able to tell you."

"Who?"

"A cop named Carlos Ramirez. He and Simon used to spend a lot of time together down at the Port O'Call. It's a dive near the precinct."

Sylvia's blood ran cold, and she braced herself for what might come next. "Why do you think he might know?" she asked casually as Phyllis ushered her to the front door.

"Because if there's one cop who's dirty, it's Carlos Ramirez."

11

Virginia wheeled her XLR convertible into the underground parking garage for the offices of her real estate company. Friday afternoon traffic on Brickell had been heavy all the way through downtown Miami. She parked her car in her reserved spot and hurried to the elevator, checking her gold and diamond Movado. She cursed under her breath as she realized how late she was.

She would barely have time to prep the rundown on all the new premiere listings she wanted to present at the staff meeting in less than an hour. In addition, she had to prepare for a dinner meeting with a developer who was considering whether to allow her agency to assemble the financial backers to build some new luxury condos that the agency would later be responsible for selling. The developer thought the project needed her special attention. *Special attention* being the buzz words that had made her real estate agency one of Miami's elite real estate companies.

Tapping her high-heeled foot impatiently, Virginia

wished for the elevator to be an express, and amazingly it complied, depositing her on the twentieth floor in record time. With a smile and a wave at the receptionist, she headed to her corner office, intending to review the new listings and possibly order a quick bite to stave off hunger until her dinner meeting later that night.

As she blasted by the anteroom to her office, her administrative assistant popped up from her chair and waved at her to stop.

"Yes, Celeste?" she said, tapping her briefcase against her leg in annoyance.

"I'm sorry, Ms. Cooke, but there's a gentleman who insists on seeing you. He says he wants to buy a house," the young woman advised.

"Celeste, you know I don't handle routine sales anymore. Get one of the—"

Celested motioned behind her as she said, "I'm sorry, but he refuses to consider anyone else. He says only you can help him."

Virginia turned in time to see Pablo rise from the couch in her anteroom. He strolled toward her, and she could see her assistant staring at him and another one of her female agents pausing to watch his undeniably sexy swagger. Her irritation grew by leaps and bounds. Virginia swept into her office, not caring whether or not he followed.

"*Buenos días,* GinGin," he said as he approached her, arms open wide, as if to embrace her. She kept her position on the opposite side of the desk and held up her hand to stop him.

"Not a good day, Pablo. How did you know where to find me?"

He shrugged. "It wasn't difficult. You've made quite a name for yourself in Miami business circles."

"Is there some reason why you came to the office? I have a rather busy schedule—"

"Don't tell me you've become a hard-hearted business-woman, GinGin," he said, a hurt look on his handsome face. "I was hoping you would have the time to help me find a house."

She shook her head in puzzlement. "A house? Here? In Miami?"

"I'm tired of living in hotels during the polo season."

Virginia didn't buy it. "Correct me if I'm wrong, but haven't you been living in hotels during the season for what? Almost thirty years now?"

His shoulders shifted elegantly below the fine fabric of his dark blue suit. "I thought that if I was going to meet Sylvia, I might stay beyond the end of the winter season to have the time to really get to know her."

As she met his gaze, it was plain to see there was more there. More than she wanted to consider right now. "This is not a good idea."

"I thought that you wanted me to get to know Sylvia," Pablo quickly responded. Obviously in no mood to leave, he settled himself into the chair positioned before her large mahogany desk.

Refusing to let him push her buttons the way he had thirty years earlier, Virginia took a deep breath and calmly sat down. "Real estate in Miami has gotten to be quite expensive. What with the downturn in the Argentine economy a few years back—"

"I diversified long ago and am well able to buy any piece of property you could show me," he said, his face hardening before he continued. "Let's just get to the real reason for your . . . hesitation. Despite your supposed desire that I meet *our* daughter—"

"It's not a 'supposed desire,' Pablo. I really think it's

important that you get to know each other," she jumped in, annoyed at his doubting her intentions.

"You want her to be happy, as do I." He crossed his legs, and then twined his fingers together and placed them in his lap. He was the picture of refinement and calm.

She hated that she wasn't. That he could make her feel like the poor backwater stable hand she had been when they had first met. She realized she was sitting there tensely, her hands splayed on the desktop before her. Her jaw was starting to ache from how hard she clenched it. Giving her neck a long stretch, she tried to relax, telling herself she had to pick her battles. This battle was not one worth losing energy over, since she suspected there would be more to come.

"Fine. You want to buy a house so you can spend more time with our daughter. If she'll let you, that is. Sylvia can be quite stubborn." She raised an eyebrow to emphasize her point.

Pablo chuckled and smiled ruefully. "A trait she inherits from both of us, GinGin."

Deep breath. Calm. Restraint. "So what area did you have in mind?"

"Indian Creek? South Beach? Fisher Island? I'd like to be somewhere close."

Pricey locales, but he claimed to be able to afford anything she showed him. She knew just what to do to dissuade him from this decision. "If you'll come back in the morning, I'll have one of my agents—"

"No one but you."

She met his gaze and realized this was another point on which he would not budge. She reminded herself about picking the right battle and slowly nodded. "I have a meeting in the early morning, but we can get together in the afternoon."

He rose and held out his hand to seal the deal, and while she wasn't necessarily happy about it, she couldn't be rude. She might be white trailer trash under her polished veneer, but she was trailer trash with manners. She shook his hand, but he held on to it when she would have let go.

"Would it be so bad if I stayed in Miami?"

"I'm not sure," she said. If he was staying, she wanted there to be total honesty between them this time around. Not like before.

He looked down at their joined hands and finally released hers before meeting her gaze once again. "Honesty. That's a surprising start. Is one o'clock good? We could have lunch and then—"

"Three would be better." As would avoiding lunch with him.

With a curt nod, because there was no doubt he knew what she was doing, he walked out of her office, leaving her to wonder how she would ever deal with this unexpected turn of events.

Pablo arrived promptly at three. Virginia had a list of properties in the areas he had indicated the day before, plus a home on Key Biscayne that was her personal favorite and not all that far from the others. After running through the listings, they selected four to visit that day, including the Key Biscayne location.

Since she was the one more familiar with the area, Pablo deferred to her offer to drive. Together they walked to the underground parking lot.

Pablo raised an eyebrow as she strolled to the convertible and pushed a button to put the top down. She opened the doors and was stepping into the car when she noticed he was still just standing there.

"Is something wrong?" she asked and shot a quick peek at herself just to make sure. The Versace suit she had chosen was elegant and modern and showed off her figure perfectly. Not that she had worn it for that reason or for Pablo, she told herself.

"Just pausing to admire perfection. A beautiful car and an even more beautiful woman."

Surprised, she found herself blushing and yes, even pleased by his comment. Not that she would admit to it.

"Pablo, *amor*. I've been schmoozed by the best, so could we please just cut the crap."

Her words did nothing to dissuade him. On the contrary, he walked right up to her as she stood by the car door and cupped her cheek. "Methinks the lady doth protest too much. But I will try to restrain myself." With that, he quickly walked around to the passenger side.

She doubted he would abide by her request, but it had been worth a shot. Especially if he was going to be staying in Miami. The last thing she needed was a constant barrage of unwanted attention from him. Better he should lavish all that on Tiffany or another of the groupies at the polo grounds, despite his protests that he had no interest in any of those women.

She sat behind the wheel, started up the car, and they pulled out of the garage and onto Brickell Avenue. The first location in South Beach was a short trip from her company's building. It was a gorgeous winter day, with the temperature hovering in the high sixties and the sun shining brightly. As she weaved from one lane to the next and finally onto the highway, the wind whipped through her hair, and Virginia smiled. She shot a glance over at Pablo.

A bit of a grimace marred the lines of his face, and as she honked and then quickly zipped around a slow-moving car in front of her, she noticed the tightening of his jaw out of the corner of her eye. "What's the matter?"

He looked at her and said, "GinGin, this car is a dream, unlike your driving, which is truly a nightmare."

She chuckled. "Mr. Big Bad Polo Player can't handle a little speed? Or is it that you would rather be in control?"

"Ño, Virginia," he mumbled under his breath as she passed yet another car, earning a loud wailing honk from that driver. "Speed is fine and as for control . . ."

He hesitated, which drew her attention for a moment. "Well?" she prompted him to continue.

"Control is one thing I've always seemed to lack around you," he admitted, and as she swerved around a slow-moving Hummer and increased her speed, he added, "a little control on your part, however, would be appreciated."

She laughed out loud at his comment, but seeing that he was holding on to his door and seat nearly in a death grip, she relented and slowed the car. "See? Control is my first, last, and middle name."

"Really?" he questioned as they came to the end of the causeway and the light before them turned red.

"Yes. I am so totally in control that there isn't anything you could do that would faze me."

He said nothing, just bided his time as the light turned green and she gave the car some gas. As she guided the XLR down Fifth Street, Pablo placed his hand on her thigh at the sharpness of the turn, but then kept it there, his palm firm.

Heat grew inside her with that touch, and even though she liked the feel of it, she swatted his hand away.

"If you want me to show you anything besides my foot on your ass, you will keep your hands to yourself," she said, which earned a chuckle from him.

When she turned to glare at him at the next traffic light and this time actually poked him in that rock hard chest, he finally seemed to realize she was deadly serious.

"*Ay*, GinGin. You have become one of these hard-hearted American businesswomen."

She wanted to argue that to be hard-hearted you had to have a heart, which she didn't, since he had ripped it out of her thirty years earlier. But instead she calmly replied, "This is *just* business, Pablo. Business has nothing to do with the heart."

"And our daughter? Is she just business as well?"

Touché. "What happens between you and Sylvia is between you and Sylvia."

The light turned green, but she didn't move as she waited for his answer until finally, the driver behind them gave an impatient honk. She began to drive but watched Pablo out of the corner of her eye. He finally nodded, as if confirming a decision to himself and said, "Whatever you want, GinGin."

"I want it to be *just* business. So no more compliments. No touchy, and absolutely no feely of any kind. Got it?" She arched her eyebrow to emphasize the point.

Pablo nodded once again, but she thought she heard him mumble something under his breath. Something in Spanish that she couldn't quite catch, although from his tone it was obvious.

Pablo might be saying *Sí, Sí* on the surface, but inside it was a big *Ño, Ño*.

The scary part was that she might actually be looking forward to having him break his promise.

12

Sylvia had skipped her usual Sunday lunch with her mother, since, witch that she was, Virginia would know something major was up. Sylvia wasn't up to discussing the fact that Carlos had moved out, or worse, that someone had accused him of being a dirty cop. She didn't know which of the two was worse.

She had also unfortunately had to miss her regular Monday night with her friends, since a last-minute re-scheduling of the opening of a new dance club had forced her to attend that gathering. To make matters worse, Sylvia hadn't gotten home until well after 2 A.M. since the hottest of the celebrity guests paid to attend hadn't shown up until nearly one in the morning. The promoters had been steaming about what had essentially been a no-show.

So instead of bonding with her mother or her friends, she had used what free time she had to spread out her notes and the copy of the police file on her kitchen table. She reviewed them time and time again when she wasn't working on another of the magazine's After Dark and Gossip assignments. During the day on Monday, she spent hours trying to track down the one eyewitness to the event, but with little success. The phone numbers in the police file had all been disconnected, and she'd had no luck tracking the witness down in any of the databases to which she had access.

Aware that she still needed more information, Sylvia checked in with Harry on late Tuesday morning to make sure he didn't need anything else on any of the other stories she had turned in recently. She dreaded reporting to Harry, certain he would ask about the Davis story. Which he did.

"Make any progress?" After he asked, Harry grabbed the large pastrami sandwich from on top of the paper bag he was using as a place mat in the middle of his desk and took a big bite, making an assortment of nauseating sounds as he chewed.

"I spoke to Phyllis Davis. I have some details, but . . ."

While still chewing, he asked, "'Fraid you were wrong about your earlier article?"

"Nope, just not sure what we'll do if it turns out Simon Davis was the one who was dirty. He's dead. What good will it do—"

"Imagine the buzz we'll get if we show that a hero cop—"

"A dead cop who has young sons who think he died a hero," she reminded, guilt awakening at the thought of the pain she would cause Phyllis and her sons.

Finally swallowing down a mouthful so big she worried he would choke on it and she might have to do the Heimlich—only she didn't think she could get her arms around his broad girth—Harry said, "Getting soft on me, Sylvia?"

Maybe she was. Maybe she actually had a heart, which some people doubted was possible. "Maybe I am."

Harry harrumphed and picked up the sandwich again. "Bring me a story. I'll decide whether we run it or not."

"Going soft on me, Harry?"

"That'll be the day," he said. He opened his mouth wide, but before he could take another bite of the heart-congesting pastrami, Sylvia whirled and walked out of his office.

When she was done with the one assignment Harry had given her for that morning—a late afternoon fashion show on the beach to raise money for AIDs—Sylvia decided to check out the bar Phyllis Davis had mentioned a few days earlier. Before heading there, however, Sylvia went home and pored over her notes again, just to see if a fresh look might make something new jump out at her. No matter how many times she perused the materials, the likely scenario for what had happened that night remained the same.

Simon shoots dealer one.

Dealer two opens fire.

One cop dead.

Two other cops wounded.

Second dealer dead.

By the time she finished, her head was pounding from the tension and her stomach growled from hunger. The doughnut she had scarfed down that morning had done nothing but increase her appetite.

She had at least an hour to go before the shift ended at the police station, and the cops were likely to visit the Port O'Call bar for a break before going home, so she decided to kill two birds with one stone.

Changing into what she assumed would pass for

acceptable attire for the bar—black leather jacket, low-rise faded jeans, and a simple cropped T-shirt in an emerald color that made her hazel-green eyes seem greener—she hurried from her apartment and down Thirteenth to Ocean on her way to Juli and Adriana's restaurant.

There was a sizeable late lunch crowd at the tables on the sidewalk, as well as under the open-air veranda. Sylvia stopped at the hostess podium and noted that the tables inside were likewise filled, which made her reconsider whether her friends would have time for a bite.

Teresa, the hostess for the day shift, approached Sylvia with a broad smile on her face. "*Hola,* Sylvia. Would you like a table?"

"Actually, I was wondering whether Adriana and Juli were busy?"

"They're both in the kitchen. Why don't you go on back."

She nodded, walked to the back of the restaurant, and paused at the door of the kitchen. Activity filled the space as the waitstaff flitted from one place to the other, picking up orders and prepping salads and bread baskets.

Juli's mother stood by one sous chef, instructing the young woman while the other three chefs were hard at work at the stoves and prep tables. Juli was at the far end of the kitchen, putting the finishing touches on a cake. In the open space in front of the refrigerators, Adriana and her mom were busy setting a table.

As Adriana looked up, she noticed Sylvia and waved her over.

Guilt rose up inside of Sylvia when she met her friend's gaze, but tamped it down. If she could show that Riley wasn't corrupt, it would help Adriana. She didn't want to consider what would happen if her investigation proved something different.

"It's good to see you," Adriana said as she hugged Sylvia.

Sylvia returned the embrace. "Good to see you too. I was hoping to grab a bite with the two of you if you weren't busy."

"We were just about to sit down before the dinner rush begins. Why don't you join us?"

"I'd love to," she said and walked over to the table set for four—Juli, Adriana, and their moms. Adriana quickly moved one setting over to make room and laid a place for her.

When the other women came to the table, Sylvia was once again surprised by the change that had occurred in the past few months.

Adriana and Juli had been at odds with their mothers for a long time, but now that seemed to be truly over. The four chatted and joked with one another easily. She sat back and enjoyed their camaraderie, but when Adriana's mom mentioned how happy her daughter was with Riley, a pang of not only guilt, but jealousy reared up.

"Are you okay?" Adriana asked, obviously sensing that something troubled her friend.

Sylvia noted the determined look on Adriana's face. She knew better than to try and avoid an answer, since Adriana was like a pit bull when she wanted something. "I'm just working on a tough project right now," Sylvia admitted.

"Are you sure? Nothing personal? Because if you need—"

"I know I can always count on both of you," she said.

Juli wrapped an arm around Sylvia's shoulders. "*Que pasa*, Sylvia? It's obvious something's wrong."

She wanted to be able to unload her concerns about

Randy Davis's allegations, but it was too soon, since she had nothing to either prove or disprove them. As she shot a surreptitious glance at Adriana, Sylvia didn't want to hurt her friend by making her doubt Riley.

So why are you doubting Carlos? the annoying voice in her head asked. Maybe because doubting him let her avoid the reality of her feelings toward him. Feelings she could not and did not want to think about.

"It's just that I haven't spoken to Carlos since he moved out," she admitted, hoping that would be enough to satisfy her friends for the moment and also hoping that they would help her figure out what to do about it.

The moms, as if sensing this was talk that the young women would rather they not hear, made a point of excusing themselves and leaving the younger women alone.

Juli leaned close and squeezed Sylvia's shoulder. "*No comprendo,* Sylvia. The last time we met you told us that you and Carlos had finally made some progress."

"Sure we did. But I guess that maybe it wasn't enough to make up for me pushing him away. He moved back to that damn sailboat."

Adriana shifted from her place across the table to sit beside her. In low tones, she said, "A very romantic place to make up. But you said the fight was before the boat. Now it seems as if—"

"We didn't fight again, it's just that . . . I'm confused about him. About what he is."

"What he is?" Juli asked, her brow furrowing as she tried to make sense of what Sylvia was saying.

Adriana was quick to question as well. "What, as in the Prince or the Frog?"

"Exactly." Sylvia emphasized the point with a wave of her hand. "I mean, he's Mr. Save the World Sensitive Guy one second and then . . . He's being all demanding and alpha. Unreasonable."

"Unreasonable because he wants what?" Juli asked, and at that a blush erupted across Sylvia's cheeks, because the reality of it was, Carlos didn't want anything that wasn't reasonable for two people in a committed relationship.

As she had before, Adriana picked up on it first, maybe because out of all of them, she and Sylvia were the most similar when it came to men. Hadn't it taken Adriana nearly twenty years to see that her Prince was right under her nose?

"I suspect that all he wants is to hear you say you want him."

"I do want him. Who wouldn't want him. Sweet Lord, the man could make a nun want him," Sylvia said with exasperation and dragged a hand through her hair.

"Want and love are two different things," Juli began, and then immediately added, "plus Carlos seems too nice to seduce a nun."

Sylvia groaned and buried her head in her hands, but not because Juli was wrong.

Carlos was too nice. Too steadfast. Too everything good in life.

"Sylvia?" Adriana asked. When Sylvia finally looked at her, Adriana said, "Sometimes the Prince and the Frog seem like the same thing at first. You just need to look deeper to find out their true nature."

Sylvia wanted to shout that she had seen his true nature. She had seen it and shoved it away because she was too afraid of all that goodness and love. In that instant, she hated that she had ever doubted him when Davis had first made his accusations.

"I know. I'll try, Adriana. I just need to work up the courage to face him again."

Adriana narrowed her gaze, as if considering whether Sylvia was telling the truth. She must have passed muster, since her friend nodded.

With the discussion seemingly resolved, the women cleaned up the table together. Juli left to instruct some of the sous chefs and Adriana walked Sylvia to the front of the restaurant.

Once there, Adriana hugged her hard. "You can't fool me, *chica.* I know there's more to this than you've told us. Just remember we're always here when you need us."

So much for thinking she had pulled it off without her friend noticing. "I will."

As she had before, Sylvia experienced remorse that what she had to do could possibly hurt her friend. She would hate that more than anything.

Even more than betraying Carlos? the voice in her head challenged.

As she walked away from Adriana and toward the policemen's bar on Eleventh, just a half dozen or so blocks away, it occurred to Sylvia that while men had come and gone in her life, her friends had always been there for her. Would always be there for her.

As for Carlos . . .

If Carlos was a dirty cop—something she truly did not want to believe—who had betrayed who first?

13

Unlike the crisp white station house just up the block, the exterior of the bar had faded gray cedar planks and the remnants of what had likely been someone's idea of a nautical theme. Bits of a tattered net clung to the weathered wood along with a few nearly fossilized starfish and the fragile remains of some seashells. Two crossed oars nailed to the wall bore the name of the bar—The Port O'Call.

Sylvia hoped the inside of the bar wouldn't be as bad as the exterior decor.

She pushed past the door, and to her surprise discovered that the nautical theme inside, while dated, was certainly more shipshape. It actually looked like the inside of a captain's quarters from one of those old pirate movies. Lots of dark woods, whitewashed walls, and wood beams. Scattered here and there on the walls were framed nautical maps and travel posters. Gleaming brass sconces and chandeliers provided golden light for the booths and tables filling the main portion of the bar. At the very back of the place, two pool tables and a foosball unit were in use. Directly behind them was another section of booths, definitely intended for more private discussions, due to their distance from most of the activity in the bar.

In the front section of the space a long wooden bar with a gleaming brass railing flanked one wall. Matching wooden stools with leather seats lined the bar, the leather matching that in the assorted booths and chairs in the rest of the place.

She must have timed her appearance just right because the bar was quite full, with nearly thirty or so men and women inside. Mostly men, and from the look of them, mostly cops.

Walking to the end of the bar, Sylvia slipped onto an empty stool close to a swinging door and realized that the bar also boasted a small kitchen.

"What can I get you?" the bartender asked, but the tone of his voice was less than friendly. Strangers were certainly not welcome in here, she decided.

Sylvia was sure any of her standard fare of drinks would raise one or both of the bartender's hairy eyebrows, so after a very quick glimpse around, she asked, "What do you have on tap?"

He seemed taken aback by her question but then quickly recited a list of all their draft beers. Knowing what he expected her to choose—the Corona with a twist of lime—she decided to shake him up yet again. "Make it a Guinness."

"A Guinness?"

"A Guinness," she confirmed, and he walked away, pulled a pint of the stout, and returned with it. As he placed it before her, he said, "Thought you were a tourist, only you don't smell like a snowbird. Don't drink like one either."

She chuckled. "I am definitely not a snowbird."

"But you're not a cop, so what are you doing here?" he asked, one eyebrow raised to stress his question.

"I'm hoping Carlos will show up."

"Ramirez?" the bartender said, and when she nodded, he continued. "He used to come around off and on. Mostly off lately."

"Doesn't come here as often as he used to?" Sylvia asked, knowing she had to play it cool if she was going to get any information.

"I wouldn't count on him showing up."

"And why is that?" she asked.

As the bartender—a gruff man in his mid-sixties and judging from the badge tattooed on his forearm, an ex-cop—leaned on the wood of the counter toward her to continue the conversation, she noticed a few heads at the bar turn her way, as if they had overheard the discussion.

"What do you want with Carlos?" an attractive Latino a few seats down called out, and even more people seemed to tune into the conversation.

Cool this is not, she thought, and so she decided to take a more direct approach. "Carlos and I . . . we had a fight."

"Thought you looked familiar," the man sitting next to her said while hunching over his mug of beer.

She picked up her own mug and took a sip. "Why's that?"

"You're the babe they interviewed on the TV. The reporter," a third man said as he came to stand beside her and leaned his arm on the shoulder of the man next to her.

No sense denying it, she thought. "Yes, that's me. I came to see how Carlos has been doing."

"Lady wants a piece of the hero," the cop standing beside her said and nudged the man sitting next to her, who glared at the younger man.

"Shut yer face, Billy. Carlos wouldn't want his shit out in public."

Billy straightened up, obviously put off by the command and clearly deciding whether to do as he was told. Which made him a perfect candidate.

She grabbed her beer and slipped from the stool. "Do you play pool, Billy? Care to play with me?"

The innuendo was not lost on the young cop. Of course, anyone with a smidgen more common sense or less beer in his system would realize he was the one being played, but not Billy. As she strolled toward the back, adding a sexy sway to her hips, it occurred to her that as young as Billy was, he might not have been around at the time that Simon Davis had been killed. Still, it was worth a try.

Billy did what she expected, following her to an empty pool table. Once they were there, she laid her beer on a small table at the edge of the room, took off her leather jacket, and hung it on a peg in the wall.

Billy obviously approved of the tight baby tee and low-rise pants. She could tell from the way he gulped and fixed his gaze on the inches of bare midriff the top exposed.

Men are sometimes too easy, she thought.

She walked over to a rack holding a number of cues, selected one, and grabbed a piece of chalk. Sashaying to the table, she bent over to sight the set of balls that someone had already racked up. She almost didn't need to look to know that her ass had Billy's complete attention, but she shot a glance over her shoulder anyway.

Bingo! She smoothly stroked the stick against the cue ball, which sped into the rack and sent the other balls flying. One dropped into a pocket, earning her the right to continue shooting.

She sauntered around the table, lining up her next shot and while she did so, peppered Billy with questions.

He hadn't been at the station long. Just a little over four years, but long enough to have known Simon Davis.

"It's a shame, isn't it?" she questioned, but didn't get an answer as another cop came over, grabbed Billy's stick, and leaned his hip against the edge of the table.

"*Niña,* you seem to have a lot of questions."

She stood upright and examined the man who had joined them. Early forties, but in tip-top shape. Dark brown hair was ruthlessly buzzed around his ears, but slightly longer up top with nary a hint of gray. His stance screamed ex-military as did the alert way his eyes traveled over her, as if sizing up an enemy.

"I'd like to learn more about what Carlos does for a living."

"Because you and he are like this?" He crossed his fingers to indicate they were together.

"Yes, we are." She approached him and laid the butt end of her cue stick on the ground. "And you are—"

"Andres Lopez. Carlos's brother-in-law. You must be Sylvia."

"And if I wasn't, Carlos would be in a lot of trouble, wouldn't he?" she teased the other man, trying to establish a rapport with him.

"So is Carlos in trouble? Is Ronnie going to want my hide when I get home?" He smiled, displaying perfect white teeth in a boyish grin. She could see how Carlos's sister had fallen for him. He was gorgeous, although not as drop-dead dangerous as Carlos.

"You're not in trouble. But Carlos has been in trouble a couple of times on the job."

Andres shrugged. "It's his job and he loves it."

"Must suck to have people shooting at you. Didn't he lose a partner a few years back?" She rounded up all the balls on the table, racked them up again, and motioned for him to take the shot.

Andres bent, lined up the shot, and with a swift sure stroke, broke the rack, sinking one ball to begin a run. As he walked over to line up his next shot, he said, "His partner Riley got shot, but he wasn't killed."

"What about Simon Davis? Wasn't he Carlos's partner?"

Andres paused and then picked up his cue stick and pointed at the wall behind her. She turned and finally realized it was a wall of honor as she noted Simon's face among the many others. Too many others. Her stomach clenched and she pressed her hand there.

"You okay?" Andres asked and steadied her with a gentle hand.

"Carlos could be up there one day."

Andres's face hardened, but not with anger. With fear. "Carlos can take care of himself. Seems to me he took care of you as well."

Andres obviously knew a great deal about her and Carlos. "He did take care of me. Which is why I'm trying to understand why he risks his life. For this?" she said, motioning to the wall of photos.

"For the people he helps. For himself. For you. Why else would he do it?"

"For the fame and the glory. For the money maybe." Less than subtle, and this time, Andres did lose a little bit of his cool.

"Maybe these are things you should ask Carlos."

"Maybe," she admitted, but as she looked at the wall again, something turned in her stomach, making her mumble, "I think I need to sit and have some more of my beer."

He grabbed her cue and his, and angrily tossed them at Billy. After, he snagged her glass from where she had placed it earlier and, with a hand at the small of her back, urged her to a table where another three men and a woman sat.

The men greeted her approach with guarded smiles, but the woman was immediately hostile until Andres announced that Sylvia was a friend of Carlos. That seemed to provide instant entry into their little group, but whether that was good or not, Sylvia didn't know.

She needed unbiased information and doubted she would get it here from Carlos's friends. She had hoped someone with an axe to grind might be able to tell her more. Cautious, because she didn't want to make them think that anything was wrong, she asked them questions under the guise that she was continuing her story, but this time focusing on hero cops who had lost their lives. That elicited tale after tale about some of the men on the wall. Eventually she was able to work in some questions about Simon Davis, but unlike the congenial tales about the others, the mention of Simon's name seemed to yield generally cold and distant responses.

Nothing at all like the convivial carrying-on that Carlos's name garnered. After only a couple of hours, it was clear that Carlos was well liked and well respected. Even as one man left the table and was replaced by another, each new man seemed to echo the good comments she had heard before.

No one had anything bad to say about Carlos, not even the female cop who had continued to linger at the table well after most others came and went.

Sensing that the other woman might respond better if

they were alone, Sylvia said, "I don't know about you, but I need to use the facilities."

"Women only travel in pairs," one of the male officers at the table groused when the other woman rose and followed her to the bathroom.

Sylvia really did have to go, and after she emerged from the stall, the other woman was leaning against one of the sinks, waiting for her, arms crossed.

The officer narrowed her eyes as Sylvia walked to one of the other sinks to wash her hands. "Why don't you tell me what you really want to know about Simon."

"Alicia, right? You knew him?" she asked.

"You might say that. We were . . . friends."

Sylvia faced Alicia, an attractive Latina who looked nothing like Phyllis Davis. Slim, trim, and sexy. Bright, she thought as she met the other woman's gaze and realized Alicia was no fool.

"His wife thinks he was having an affair. That he was ready to leave her," Sylvia advised.

Alicia uncrossed and then recrossed her arms, and shifted her gaze away from Sylvia's. "Why would she think that?"

"She found something that she thought meant he was getting ready to go out on his own."

Alicia laughed harshly and dragged a hand through the short strands of her dark brown hair. "Simon would never have left her. Especially not with her being pregnant."

Alicia's knowledge of that fact confirmed to Sylvia that this woman had been involved with the other cop. But it also clearly hinted at the fact that Simon had not known that the baby wasn't his. "What happened the night he was shot four years ago?"

Alicia shook her head and looked down at the ground,

in major avoidance mode. "I'm sure that by now you've read the reports."

"Someone says they're not true. That Carlos and his partner had something to do with Simon's death."

The movement of Alicia's head became more emphatic. "No way. If anything, Simon was the one who had been acting weird for days."

"So you think—"

Alicia finally picked up her head and raised her hands, as if in surrender. "I don't know. If Simon was into something, he wasn't telling me."

"Who was he telling?" Sylvia asked, but as another woman stepped into the room, Alicia clammed up and walked out of the bathroom.

Sylvia muttered a curse beneath her breath and followed Alicia back to the table, but instead of sitting down, Alicia merely grabbed her jacket and offered her good nights to everyone.

Sylvia watched her go, but at the door, Alicia paused for a moment and looked back her way. She didn't know why until a second later, when Carlos slipped past Alicia and met her gaze.

Busted, she thought, which was so not good.

14

She sat back down, trying to make believe that nothing out of the ordinary was happening. Of course, that lasted only until Carlos came over. The man next to her immediately popped up, offering Carlos his seat.

"Thanks, Ray, but I'd like to spend some time alone with Sylvia," he said and held his hand out to her.

Having no choice, she slipped her hand into his and rose, trailing after him as he went to a booth in the far back corner of the bar. The light there was more dim. The noise muted, given the distance from the bulk of the tables and other booths. In fact, as she had noted earlier, it was a very private part of the bar.

Sylvia eased into the booth, expecting Carlos to take a spot across from her, but he surprised her by slipping in beside her.

"Well, this is . . . close."

Carlos grinned and fixed his gaze on her. "All the better to see you."

"See me?"

"And hear you," he added, leaning even closer.

His cheek brushed the side of her face as he whispered, "And touch you."

She gulped and glanced at him out of the corner of her eye. Her stomach did a flip-flop at the promise of pleasure blazing in his gaze.

"Touch?" she barely managed to say.

"*Sí*, touch." As if to prove his point, he laid the tips of his fingers on the line of her cheek, and then trailed them downward until he cupped her jaw in his work-rough palm.

"You haven't called or come by in well over a week," he said and brushed his thumb over her lips.

"I was . . . busy." *Lame, Sylvia. Really really lame.*

He nuzzled the side of her face with his nose. Took a sniff and with his tongue, licked the shell of her ear. After, he tugged on her earlobe with his teeth. "Hmm. You smell like . . . beer."

The tones of his voice were low and rumbly, creating a sympathetic vibration within her that made her tense her neck to keep from letting the resonation grow into something she couldn't control.

When she did that, he leaned away, and she took the opportunity to squeeze back into the corner of the booth, giving her some needed distance, since all she could think about was having him touch her in lots of places that would land them both in jail if they did it in this booth.

But then again, maybe not. These were his friends here. Fellow officers who would stick up for him, as they had for most of the night so far. Which reminded her of why she was here.

"You seem to know a lot of people," she said and

motioned with her head to the various cops across the room.

Carlos raised his hand, and a young waitress immediately came over. After placing an order for another round of Guinnesses, he answered, "These are my friends."

She motioned to the wall of honor. "Were any of those your friends?"

He glanced uneasily in the direction of the wall. His full lips tightened into a thin harsh line, and along his jaw a muscle jumped with anger. "Too many."

If not for the fact that he was alternately stubborn and lucky, he might have been there as well, she thought and cupped his jaw, tried to soothe the tension she noted there by caressing the fine line of it.

The waitress came over and plopped the beers onto the table. When Carlos would have handed her some money, she waved him off. "It's on the house. Patrick says it's good to see you here again."

Carlos picked up the glass and raised it in the direction of the bar, in thanks. But Patrick's words prompted a question.

"Have you not been coming by since—"

He leaned back against the booth, breaking visual contact with her. Avoiding her glance he said, "Four years ago one of the undercover officers working with me was killed during a stakeout."

Simon, she realized. "So why did you come here tonight?"

He sipped his stout, and the foam left a mustache for a moment before he quickly licked it away. After, he said, "A little birdie told me someone was in here asking lots of questions about me."

"Oh." She picked up her own beer and feeling like she needed the fortification, took a long drag. After she put the glass down, she could feel the foam against her lips and was about to lick it away when he said, "Don't."

"What?"

He closed the distance between them and licked the edges of her lips, removing any remnants of the stout. Igniting want in her with just that touch.

She laid her hands on his shoulders and opened her mouth when he deepened the kiss. Accepted the slide of his tongue, imagining as she did so the slide of something else moving deep into her. She slipped her own tongue into his mouth to taste him. He tasted like the yeasty stout and Carlos.

When he reached between their bodies and cupped her breast, she moaned into his mouth, unable to deny the pleasure of the caress.

Even while he continued to fondle her breast, stoking the ache growing between her legs, he whispered against her lips, "Why are you here?"

"Here?" She was confused by his question, then lost all train of thought when he grasped her nipple between his fingers and tweaked it. Gulping in another breath, she looked down in time to see him snake his hand under her T-shirt.

"Carlos," she protested in a low whisper.

"Sssh. No one can see," he said, and as she looked past him, she realized his big body blocked whatever was going on from view. Not to mention that this back section of the bar was totally empty.

Which was why she didn't protest too much as he reached his destination and cradled her breast, the skin of his palm rough against her nipple. The roughness enticed it into a tighter peak, and he didn't hesitate to rotate that hard tip with his fingers. Between her legs, an aching emptiness rose up, demanding satisfaction.

"Sweet Lord, Carlos. What do you think you're doing?" she said, because she was certain that this was insanity, given the current state of their relationship and their present location in a public place.

"*Amorcito,* if you can't tell, I must be doing it way wrong," he teased. With that, he kissed her again, sucking on her lip. He gave her a quick love bite on her lower lip before soothing it with a lick of his tongue. After, he asked against her mouth, "Tell me what you're doing here."

Between kisses she said, "Is this how you interrogate all your prisoners?"

He chuckled, even as he playfully rubbed his nose along her jaw and moved toward her ear. With another tug on her earlobe with his teeth, he said, "Are you going to claim police brutality?"

He slipped his hand to her other breast, caressed it as he bent his head a little more and licked a spot at the crook of her neck and shoulder. As he gave her a gentle bite, sucked on it, she cradled the back of his head and pulled him near.

"I will file a complaint if you don't take me somewhere else and finish this," she said, because she needed his body closer. On her. In her. Surrounding her until she could forget about everything except how good it felt to be with him.

Carlos became all action as she moaned after another tweak of her breast. Scooting out of the booth and standing, he held his hand out to her. "You're sure about this?"

Sure she was sure, she thought as she eased her hand into his. She was sure that she was certifiable. That she was probably making yet another mistake when it came to this very complicated but sexy man. But as she shot a look over her shoulder at him and saw the look in his eye, she was even more sure that to not go ahead with this would be an even bigger mistake.

Sylvia wasn't quite certain how they made it back from the bar to her apartment. The four-block walk was a blur, as was what happened after they got through the door.

What she did recall was how their hands fumbled and collided in their haste to get rid of clothes. How they hadn't made it past her living room, and that her leather sofa had creaked and groaned in a symphony of noise as Carlos had made love to her there.

She lay there now, his big body pressing her into the firm cushions of the couch. His softening erection was still nestled between her legs, which were shaking from the force of the orgasm that had rocked her body just moments earlier.

He laid an elbow on the sofa and leaned upward, giving her some breathing room, but the loss of his body heat caused her to shiver.

"Cold?" he asked and cupped her breast. Rubbed his thumb over the still taut tip. The action created an immediate pull between her legs.

Carlos sucked in a breath as he felt it. "*Dios,* you're going to be the death of me."

"A nice slow death for both of . . ." She moaned and cupped the back of his head as his mouth replaced his hand.

Her body was headed half off the couch, when he rose above her again and moved his hips with a newly energized erection. Her mind . . . she had lost that a long time ago.

As he felt them slipping over the edge of the couch, he braced one arm on the coffee table to keep them from tumbling onto the floor.

"Do you think we could take this somewhere more stable?" he said.

Stable. A funny word to apply to their precarious state.

"My bed."

Sylvia wasn't certain just how he did it, only that with a surge of power, he was standing and she had her legs wrapped tight around his waist. The position forced her down onto him and she gasped, shocked by the feel of him penetrating her again.

He laid his forehead against hers and took a shaky breath, as if gathering himself. He took a dozen or so steps into her bedroom, his arms supporting her, and they tumbled onto the silk comforter on her bed.

"Feeling stronger, I see," she teased, but then any and all other thoughts fled her mind as he made love to her again, his movements sure. Almost rough. His body strong and full of life above her. Around her. In her.

After, when she could somehow breathe again and her body had stopped shaking, she slipped beneath the covers with him. Spooning against his warm body, she took comfort from his presence.

As she lay there, Sylvia could now better understand why her mama still had an itch for Pablo. If he had been anything like the Latino Bad Boy nestled behind her, her mama had been a goner from the beginning.

Looking up over her shoulder, Sylvia examined his face. The sharp lines of it were tempered by the fullness of his lips, which slowly spread into a sexy grin. He glanced down at her.

"*Amorcito,* I'm not really ready for a repeat performance yet."

She chuckled because amazingly, she was, despite how well he had pleasured her just moments before.

The itch, she realized. The one that not even sex could scratch. But maybe something else might help salve that need.

"Did you really go to the bar just because I was asking questions?"

His grin faded a bit. "It was part of the reason."

"What was the other part?"

"I missed you. And I wanted to tell you something important."

Something personally important, which made her feel guilty. The man sure knew how to make things difficult. "What did you want to tell me?"

"I'm leaving the force."

She bolted upright and faced him. "You're what?"

"Leaving the force. Riley offered me—"

"But you love being a cop. Why would you—"

"It's time to settle down. Think about doing something else with my life," he said and cupped the side of her face. As his gaze met hers, Sylvia realized that she might be a part of that something else he was considering.

"Don't do this on account of me. On account of what you *think* we have."

She hadn't meant the words to be cruel or cold, but once uttered, their chill was immediate.

Carlos dropped his hand from her face and sat up, the lines of his big body tense. "Don't flatter yourself. Maybe I'm just tired of being used for target practice."

With that, he slipped from her bed and began gathering his things, his movements brusque and filled with anger.

She jumped from the bed and grabbed his hand as he snared his jeans from the floor. For a moment, they both just stood there, staring at each other, breathing heavily from the force of the emotions driving them, but then she said, "What I want more than anything is for you to be safe. To not end up like Simon Davis."

His hands fisted on the fabric of his jeans. "What do you know about Simon Davis? Is he the reason you were at the bar?"

She couldn't keep the investigation from him any longer. Not when she wanted to believe that he had nothing to do with what had happened. "Yes. Someone came to me and said something wasn't right about his death. That there was more to the story that needed to be told."

Carlos took a step toward her, his blue-green eyes displaying a wealth of emotion. Anger. Sorrow. Despair. He fumbled with the jeans in his hands, gathering himself before he finally said, "Simon died a hero. He was protecting Riley and me. What more do you need to know?"

She cradled his jaw, trying to offer him comfort. "I've read the reports. Something doesn't ring true with that story. Tell me what really happened that night. Please."

He met her gaze squarely, with not a hint of evasion. "Is this Sylvia the woman asking or Sylvia the reporter?"

"Is there a difference?" In her mind, those two aspects were irrevocably intertwined, much as his being a cop and a man were impossibly joined in him despite his earlier announcement.

"If you don't know the difference, I feel sorry for you."

With those words, he finished gathering his clothes and left.

15

Virginia had shown Pablo several homes over the weekend and didn't know what to make of his request that he wished to visit one of the homes again because he needed more information before making an offer. The home had been her favorite, the one on Key Biscayne.

Because of Pablo's insistence that she be the one to go with him to the various locations, he had been forced to wait until Wednesday when she was free all day to go back and see the Hitchens villa. She had loved the property from the moment she had listed it nearly two years earlier after an assortment of other Realtors had given up on working with the difficult owners.

In a way, she was both intrigued and worried by his choice of that particular location. Intrigued because it spoke of how much they had in common even after thirty years apart. Worried because if he did purchase the run-down old villa that was the equivalent of a millionaire's fixer-upper, it meant that Pablo was well and truly serious about remaining in Miami for at least part of the year. You didn't invest that kind of money and go through the labor of the renovations necessary to make the place habitable just to say you owned it. That is, not unless you were incredibly wealthy and collected homes the way other people collected stamps.

Of course, the thought of Pablo staying beyond April brought a bit of anticipation. The sexual kind that she almost didn't want to acknowledge because of the risks.

As for being able to afford the villa and necessary renovations, the people in her financial department would have advised her if they had a problem with Pablo's possible funding for the deal. So far, they hadn't mentioned a thing.

Of course, there was another niggling little worry at the back of her brain—that Pablo might plan on tearing down the existing villa. The current owners had refused countless offers where the buyers had indicated that was their intent—hence the reputation they had obtained for being difficult.

Virginia had taken them on because she understood their concerns. Even though the villa needed work, it would be a shame to level the nearly century-old structure.

Which made her wonder about what Pablo planned. If it was to tear it down, he would be just another in a long line of potential buyers that the owners refused.

As she exited her condo building, Pablo was waiting at the curb for her in a bright, metallic red Chevy SSR, which surprised her. He hadn't struck her as the type to own a pickup, even if it was souped-up like this one.

In the back bed of the SSR was a collection of boards and sails, explaining his choice of vehicle. Of course with the SSR's speed and styling, it wasn't just a pickup, and she had to confess to liking the way he looked behind the wheel.

Even though Pablo had mentioned that she should wear a bathing suit and be prepared to spend part of their day at the beach, she still hadn't expected this.

She leaned on the hot jamb of the open window and shot him a confused look. "What's that in the back?"

Pablo smiled, his teeth brilliant white against his tanned face. His green eyes glittered with juvenile glee. "Windsurfing equipment. It's a new hobby, and I hear there's some wonderful locations near the villa."

There were some great beaches in the park right near the home as well as golf and tennis areas. *I could have handled the golf and tennis, but windsurfing?* Virginia thought. Despite that, she climbed into the cab of the SSR and buckled up, but as she did so, she said, "I'll just watch from the beach if you don't mind."

Pablo shook his head as he pulled away from the curb, out of the parking lot, and onto Brickell Avenue. As he drove, he teased, "What happened to try anything once, GinGin?"

She lowered her sunglasses with one finger and perused him carefully. "I got burned, *amor*. You of all people should know that."

The smile on his face faded, and as they came to a red light, he uneasily looked her way. "If you'd rather not do this—"

"I would like to understand what this has to do with buying the house? Is this really going to make—"

"That much of a difference? Maybe," he said and shrugged. "I like the outdoors. I want to know what I'll be able to do in the area before I make such a big investment."

A honk came from behind them. She motioned for

him to go and offered directions to get them on the Rickenbacker Causeway. As they were driving over the long span, the deep blue of the Atlantic was off to one side and downtown Miami to the other. When they hit the land for Virginia Key, she said, "You don't need me to check out the area."

"You're right, only you're probably far more familiar with the village, the surfing and the beaches, and whatever else I'm interested in. Although I guess I could have called Tiffany to show me around."

A twinge of jealousy rose up at the mention of his nubile groupie, but she tamped it down. He was trying to rile her, but she wasn't about to let him push her buttons. "You're right. Tiffany would have jumped at the chance, and after, she would have jumped your bones."

His smirk confirmed that he was pleased by her pique. "Well, GinGin. The truth of it is that I have no interest in having my bones jumped. I just want to spend a nice relaxing day exploring my possible new home."

"Home for the few months during the polo season, you mean," she corrected, and he shook his head.

"Are you always this contrary? *Home!* GinGin. Maybe for just the season, maybe for longer. It all depends," he said and followed a road sign for the state park.

She didn't want to ask him what it depended on, and so she tried to change the subject.

"So, windsurfing and relaxing are two words that don't seem to go hand in hand."

Pablo shrugged. "*No se.* There's just something . . . exhilarating about it. The motion beneath you. The pull at your muscles and the feel of the ocean. Soft. Hard. Enveloping you when you sink beneath its surface."

Okay, definitely not relaxing, she thought. If anything, his description had her thinking of things she shouldn't be considering with him. She remained silent until they were on the park grounds.

Pablo pulled into a spot close to where another group of windsurfers had collected. He reached behind her seat and slipped out a blanket and picnic basket, which he handed to her.

"Would you mind taking these while I get the rest of the gear?"

"Sure," she answered, certain that she was not about to help him lug the board and sails. Especially when she had absolutely no intention of joining him out on the water.

She stepped out of the SSR and waited for him to collect the equipment. She trailed behind him as he walked onto the beach and moved down a ways from a group of young windsurfers prepping to head into the water, where another wave of windsurfers was already skimming across the glasslike surface of the ocean.

As he placed his gear beneath a small palm tree, Pablo motioned for her to set her things down. "Let me get you comfortable."

He helped Virginia lay out the blanket in the shade of the palm tree. He placed the picnic basket in the shade next to the tree.

Virginia sat on the blanket and leaned back against the trunk of the palm. She watched as Pablo stripped off his clothes—a polo shirt and casual khaki shorts—to reveal a small Speedo beneath. No American boxers for her Argentine male.

Suddenly warm, she reached into her bag and fanned her face with the floppy hat she had brought to protect her from the sun.

"Hot already?" he asked but didn't wait for her answer as he grabbed the assorted parts of the windsurfer and walked to the water's edge. He handily hauled the sail up and into the board and carried the entire contraption into the shallow waters.

Hot? she thought. Yes, he was totally hot. Way hotter than a man his age should be and way more dangerous to her emotions than she had expected.

In the short time they had spent together at the polo match, dinner, and searching for homes, he had been difficult at times, but more often than not, he had been caring, solicitous, and clearly still attracted to her.

Or maybe that was wishful thinking on her part. She hoped that her man-radar wasn't so off that she was misinterpreting the signals.

Just to make sure, Virginia waited until he had finished assembling the windsurfer and had taken it out for a few spins. She had to confess that it looked like fun as he skimmed along the surface of the water, moving as gracefully on the sea as he did on the polo fields.

Damn him, she thought as he turned the windsurfer and jumped up and over the wave created by the wake of a passing boat. The muscles of his back and arms bunched with the effort, but Pablo seemed oblivious to it.

And oblivious to her, so maybe she had misread the signals he had been broadcasting.

After about an hour, she was starting to sweat, even beneath the shade of the palm tree. Since it seemed like break time for Pablo as well, who had turned the windsurfer toward land, she slipped off her wrap and walked toward the water.

Her suit was nothing like what any of the twenty-somethings were wearing, both because she wasn't twenty-something and because her size ten curves just wouldn't be contained by so little string and fabric. Still, she liked to think she could turn a head, which she did as she sashayed toward where Pablo had beached the windsurfer.

Pablo reacted immediately. A kind of slow-motion jerk of the head and his delicious perusal of her from toe to head, since Pablo had always been a breast man. Some things hadn't changed, she thought with a smile as he focused on that part of her anatomy for a bit longer before trailing his gaze up to meet hers.

"How's the water?" she asked coyly as she dipped in a toe, and he rose from where he had crouched to remove the runaway strap on the windsurfer.

"Tantalizing," he replied, the tones of his voice low and sexy. The signals were totally clear, she decided, which started an immediate response within her.

Hands held behind her back, she shot him a sly look from the corner of her eye. "Really? Sounds . . . dangerous."

Okay, so maybe she was laying it on a little thick, but hell, this man had been hounding her dreams for nearly thirty years, so payback was possibly in order.

Pablo stepped right up to her and whispered in her ear, "You can't even begin to guess how dangerous," he said, and before she could respond, he picked her up in his arms and tossed her into the water.

The chill enveloped her as she hit the surface and sank down. She jumped up, sputtering. Dragging back her hair from her face, she snagged her Chanel sunglasses from the sand where they had sunk beneath the clear waters. "That was—"

"Just to cool you off, *amorcito.* You seemed a little—"

He didn't get to finish as she launched herself at him, tackling him in the shallow surf.

They sank beneath the cool waves together, limbs and arms intertwined, but Pablo quickly brought them back to the surface. He laughed and slipped an arm around her waist.

"Now that's the GinGin I remember. Not that prim and proper power broker with a heart of ice."

Virginia wanted to lash out at him yet again, but she wasn't the little hellion she had been at sixteen nor the Ice Queen of the last few days. She was somewhere right in between, at least, with him she was.

Taking a deep breath to control not only her anger, but also the realization that their bodies still fit together perfectly, she reached up and plucked off the Oakley sunglasses he wore. Against the backdrop of the sea, his eyes were more of a teal than green. Startling with their intensity as he swept his gaze over her face.

"You know there can't ever be anything between us again. I'm not the same woman I was thirty years ago."

"And I'm not the same man I was. I'm not sure I was even a man back then. Maybe I was just a scared young boy trying to prove something," he confessed.

Just as she had been a scared young girl, wanting so much more out of life than living in a trailer and mucking out other people's horse stalls just to put food on the table.

With a nod, she handed him back his sunglasses and slipped out of his embrace, regretting the loss of the contact more quickly than she cared to admit.

"Hungry?" she asked and motioned in the direction of their blanket and the picnic basket.

"Most definitely," he replied, but even with the glasses back in place, she knew that his hunger wasn't for food.

Inside of her, excitement grew as she considered giving in to that hunger.

But first, there was Sylvia to deal with.

She wasn't quite sure how Sylvia would handle this new development, but then again, her daughter really had no choice.

It was time for her to mend the rift between father and daughter, and if along the way something else happened . . .

Virginia had been alone for too long. Thirty years way too long.

16

It had been days since she had seen Carlos. Days since she had called her mother to find out about Virginia's mystery man. Her mother had returned her call but missed her, due to an unexpected whirlwind of activity. The sudden upsurge in events kept Sylvia running from one locale to the next, so they had done nothing but play telephone tag.

In the free time Sylvia had between assignments, she kept working on her investigative report, trying to find the sole eyewitness to the shooting or someone else who would give her more information. For the moment, she drafted the basic body of the report with the details she did know.

Those were few and they were contradictory, but if there was one thing she had come to believe was certain, it was that Carlos was innocent of the charges leveled against him and Riley by Randy Davis. Maybe she was trusting her heart instead of the facts, but she just knew.

Rolling over in bed—a spot decidedly too big and too

empty with Carlos's absence—she realized it was nearly eleven. Time to get going, run by the office to pick up any new assignments, and drop off the work she had completed on others.

Dragging herself out of bed, she sat there for a moment, feeling nearly overwhelmed by all that had been happening lately.

Carlos leaving.

Making love with Carlos.

Fighting with Carlos.

Trying to prove Carlos was not dirty.

That he was a man with honor.

Not a criminal.

Of course, his possibly illegal activities hadn't put any kind of damper on her attraction to him during their first few meetings. Her initial concerns about his involvement in Simon Davis's death hadn't put an end to the itch she had for him physically either, but maybe that was because she had known in her heart all along that what Randy Davis had said wasn't true.

Now she had scratched and scratched and scratched that itch the other night, but with no relief.

She realized that now. Carlos was still there under her skin, despite everything.

Wrapping her arms around herself, she rose, thinking as she did so that there had to be something she could do to not only protect herself from getting hurt if she was wrong about Carlos, but also to safeguard what would happen to her friend Adriana, and to Phyllis Davis and her boys.

As she stepped into the shower, it occurred to Sylvia that there was one person who was always levelheaded and logical. Who could always be counted on to know what was the right thing to do.

Tori.

Ever logical and dependable Tori.

It was time to pay Tori a visit.

Tori's sister, Angie, was at the receptionist's station as Sylvia walked into Tori and Gil's law offices. The young woman smiled and slipped around the station to hug her.

"It's good to see you. Does Tori know you were coming?" Angie asked, a puzzled look on her face as she swung back around the receptionist's station and flipped through an appointment book.

Arms wrapped tight around herself again, Sylvia shook her head. "Is she busy? I could come back," she said, but Angie was busily shaking her head *no* and phoning Tori.

A moment later, Tori emerged from her office at the far side of the space. The broad smile on Tori's face slowly faded as she observed Sylvia's expression.

Sylvia examined herself quickly, making sure nothing was out of kilter with her clothes—a stylish dark blue Michael Kors suit, coupled with dark blue Prada pumps and a matching Prada bag. Satisfied, she glanced up at her friend and pasted a smile on her face, but Tori was never one to be fooled.

Her friend embraced her but didn't let go. Instead, she placed an arm around Sylvia's waist and guided her toward her office.

"Are you okay, Sylvita?" Tori asked as they walked to her office.

"It's complicated."

Once Sylvia had entered her office, Tori closed the door behind them and sat in the chair next to Sylvia.

"I get the sense that this is about more than man trouble."

Sylvia crossed her legs and arms, then realizing how defensive a posture it was, forced herself to place her elbows on the arms of the chair and relax. "I guess that's why I came to you. You always seem to see everything. Know everything."

Tori chuckled, raised her hands, and waved off that comment. "Remember the nuclear fallout from my elopement?"

"But it all worked out fine. Better than fine actually. Look at you and Juli and Adriana. You're all *locas* in love."

Tori leaned toward her. "I notice you're not including yourself in that happy picture."

Sylvia snorted and gestured with her hands, mimicking a frame around her face, and forced a frown that would make Eeyore jealous. It made Tori laugh out loud and burst the bubble of tension Sylvia had been feeling all day.

"You get the picture, right?" Sylvia said.

"It is indelibly ingrained on my retinas. So what's bothering you about Carlos?" Tori asked.

In a rush of words, Sylvia explained everything that had happened, including from the moment Carlos came home with her to the last few days when she had hit a stumbling block in her investigation.

"That is a truly monumental load of—"

"It's not guilt. Well, at least I don't think it is."

Tori held up one finger and began counting down. "One. You feel like you got him shot. Two. You're pushing him away so hard, it sends him running back to his boat before he's really ready to go. Three. You have sex on the boat and in your apartment, but worry that you've made a mistake."

Sylvia considered her friend carefully and realized that

much like her, Tori was still feeling her way with her new roles in life. Wife. Lover. Friend again. Business owner. Even sisterhood, since for a number of years Tori and Angie had been on the outs.

"I wanted sensible from you, but I also want . . ." Sylvia tapped a spot above her heart.

"What I really feel is going on? I think you care for Carlos more than I've ever seen you care about anyone, only you're afraid that if you trust what your heart is telling you, you'll get hurt," Tori said and laid a hand on Sylvia's arm.

"Trusting your heart can be wrong sometimes. Look at my—"

"Your *mami* made her choices. Maybe they weren't the right choices, but at least she took a chance with love."

Sylvia huffed with indignation. "Great. So now I'm a coward as well?"

"*Coward* and *Sylvia Amenabar* are three words I would never use together in the same sentence. Maybe . . . *cautious* would be a better word. Especially when it comes to matters of the heart." Tori rose and held out her hand. "Come on. Let's go get some lunch. Talk some more. Maybe even splurge and have a mojito. Or two."

"You think that'll make things better?" Sylvia said with a smile as she looped her arm around Tori's and they walked out of her office.

"Either that or some handcuffs."

Sylvia stopped short. "Handcuffs? You want me to put handcuffs on Carlos?"

Tori reached up and brushed back a lock of Sylvia's hair. "Silly girl. Carlos needs to put the handcuffs on you so you stop running. And as you know, a little bondage—"

"Can be a lot of fun. That is if he ever speaks to me

again," Sylvia said as they walked through the door of the law office and to the stairs.

"Don't worry, he'll speak to you again."

Sylvia stopped. "How do you know?"

Tori shook her head, admonishing her. "First, because in your heart you know he's innocent. Second, because no man can resist you when you set your sights on him."

Tori began to walk down the stairs, but Sylvia grabbed her arm, forcing Tori to face her. "But Carlos is not just *any* man."

A broad smile erupted across her friend's face.

"It's about time that you realized that."

Her lunch with Tori had helped somewhat in finding balance, Sylvia thought as she wheeled her BMW into the parking lot of her mother's condo. She was eager to talk about her mother's new mystery man. They had finally connected on Thursday, but her mother had been tight-lipped, refusing to say anything else, promising that she and Sylvia would discuss it on Sunday during their usual outing.

As always, Sylvia parked in a spot facing Biscayne Bay and took a moment to appreciate the eccentric lines of the building where her mother lived. The Atlantis, with its modern edges and funky red staircase and palm tree situated in a large square in the center of the building, suited her mother's free and eclectic spirit.

A line of sweat trickled down the side of her face. Sylvia wiped it away and realized it was time to get moving, since her mother would be waiting for her in the pool area by Biscayne Bay.

Her mother would normally have a small bevy of men surrounding her chaise lounge, and Sylvia looked for that crowd but discovered that only one man sat in the chaise lounge right next to the ones she and her mother normally shared.

A third chaise lounge was a first, as was the presence of only one man. *The mystery man?* she wondered and felt a bit of pique that her mother hadn't mentioned that he would be here.

As she approached, her mama noticed Sylvia and waved. The motion snagged the attention of the man next to her who gracefully rose to his feet but didn't move away like her mother's various male friends usually did when she arrived.

No, this one had spirit, and Sweet Lord, but he was quite a looker. Lean. Muscled. Tanned. Hair the color of rich caramel with not a sign of gray despite the fact that he was definitely into his forties.

This man had to be the hottie that her friends had been carrying on about the other night. The one who had taken her mother to dinner. The one who had made her mama go all googly-eyed.

Sylvia hadn't realized it, but she had stopped walking during her perusal of the handsome man. She forced herself to take a step and then another, slowly. Hesitantly, since her daughter-radar was telling her that this man's presence here was going to change things. Maybe even radically change things, and she wasn't sure she was ready for any more upset in her life at this moment.

As she finally arrived at their usual spot, her mother rose from the chaise lounge, stepped to the man's side, and shot him a look filled with intimacy. The kind of intimacy of longtime lovers.

Oh no, this is so not good, Sylvia thought, realizing that maybe her friends were right about her mama's feelings for this man.

The man reached up and removed the Oakley sunglasses he had been wearing up until that point.

His brilliant green gaze settled on her face, and in that second, Sylvia realized who he was.

"Sweet Jesus, Mama. What were you thinking?"

17

Sylvia bolted.

Virginia chased after her, her strides hurried as she rushed to keep up with her daughter's long legs. She finally had to lunge forward to grab hold of Sylvia's hand and stop her daughter's flight.

"Sylvia Lourdes Amenabar," Virginia said in that kind of parental tone that somehow became part of your speech pattern the second you gave birth.

Sylvia faced her square on. "You will not lay any kind of guilt trip on me, Mama. This was so wrong."

Virginia surprised Sylvia by acknowledging it. "You're right. I . . . *We* shouldn't have ambushed you like this. But, honey, if I had asked nicely, would you have come?"

"No."

Virginia picked up her shoulders a notch and tilted her head at a challenging angle. "It's time to meet your father. You've been running from this for far too long, Sylvia Lourdes."

"Just Sylvia, Mama. Remember?"

Virginia knew her daughter hated that middle name. A name Pablo had given to her. His mother's name, not that Sylvia knew anything at all about either of her grandparents. Her father's—correct that—Pablo's family had never contacted her, and as for her own family . . . Virginia had been disowned when her family discovered she was pregnant. So it had always been just the two of them—she and Sylvia—and her daughter obviously preferred to keep it that way.

"You made a mistake, Mama."

She dropped her hold on Sylvia's arm. "You're right. But if you walk away now, you will be making an even bigger mistake. Trust me on this, honey. It's time to put the past behind us."

Sylvia just stood there as Virginia walked away to join Pablo, who remained standing by the chaise lounge with a grim, almost pained expression on his too-handsome face. He glanced at Virginia, his look filled with understanding and yearning before he faced Sylvia once again and said, "I'm sorry. I didn't mean to cause problems."

Pablo made a move to place his hand over Virginia's, but then seemed to think better of it. His hand dropped down awkwardly, but the gesture had been telling. It hadn't been one of forced unity, but one of caring and concern. Of apology for all that had gone wrong in their lives.

Virginia hoped Sylvia found that telling gesture difficult to ignore.

She heard her daughter mutter, "Fine." Sylvia marched right up to Pablo and stuck out her hand with a crisp almost military snap. "Sylvia Amenabar."

The ghost of an admiring smile passed over Pablo's face as he released his hold on Virginia's hand, grasped Sylvia's, and shook it. "Pablo Amenabar."

Virginia stood there, anxious. She examined Pablo's

features, and then Sylvia's, noticing the familiar arch in both their brows. The green eyes, so nearly the same color except for the smudges of brown Sylvia had inherited from her own. There was no denying Pablo was her daddy, only . . .

While shooting a half glance at her, Sylvia said, "Let's get one thing straight, Mr. Amenabar. You're not my father. Well, maybe biologically you are, but it takes more than that to be a father. So don't expect me to call you daddy or *papi* or anything else."

He loosened his grip on her hand, and the hint of a smile broadened into a full one, which crinkled the laugh lines at the corners of those amazing eyes. "Agreed, *mi'ja.*"

Sylvia yanked her hand from his and waved it back and forth. "No *mi'ja* or anything else like that. Just Sylvia. Or if you prefer Ms. Amenabar."

He wrinkled his nose at the last, but nodded. With a gallant bob of his head, he swept his hand out in the direction of the chaise lounges. "Would you care to join us, Sylvia?"

"Actually, I was thinking we might go upstairs for lunch first, Pablo," Virginia said, reaching for her wrap and slipping it on.

"Of course, GinGin. Do you need me to carry anything?"

"We can leave the towels here to keep our spots. Come on, Sylvia," she said pointedly and slipped her arm through her daughter's.

After Pablo eased on a pale yellow guayabera, he followed them as they walked toward the entrance to the building.

Sylvia leaned close to her mother and mouthed, "Gin-Gin?"

"Just an old nickname," Virginia whispered.

A bemused look skipped across her daughter's face, as if Sylvia was wondering whether they had gone from the nickname phase to yet another more serious step in the relationship. She whispered, "When did you and Pablo decide—"

"I had wondered about him for some time and went to see him play polo. But after I met Carlos, I realized it was time to change some things in our lives," she said truthfully, wanting her daughter to understand. Maybe even trying to make herself understand why she had sought Pablo out again after so long.

As they entered Virginia's condo, Pablo asked, "Can I help with anything?"

Virginia shook her head. "No, *gracias*. Why don't you and Sylvia make yourselves comfortable at the table?"

The look and smile that Pablo gave her was filled with adoration, but when he glanced at Sylvia, that look turned to one of uncertainty.

"*Sí, como no,*" he said and held his hand out to Sylvia in the direction of the table, tucked against the windows that faced Biscayne Bay.

"Actually, Mama could probably use some help. Why don't you get settled and we'll be right out."

Sylvia snared her mother's arm and led her into the kitchen before Pablo could utter another word.

Virginia immediately chastised her. "Sylvia Lourdes—"

Her daughter raised her hand to stop her and reminded her yet again, "Just Sylvia, Mama. What do you think you're doing? And what do you mean that you thought of this after Carlos?"

Virginia crossed her arms. "I'd been wondering about Pablo for a while. Maybe forever, although I wouldn't admit it. Then I saw how Carlos looked at you. How you looked at him."

"Lust. Pure lust."

Virginia tapped her perfectly manicured fingers against Sylvia's arm. "See, honey. That's exactly what I'm talking about. You can't see the forest—"

"And you're seeing more to Carlos and me than there really is."

A long pause followed her comment. With a curt nod, Virginia said, "Fine. I'm sorry that I thought you could get over your commitment issues by meeting your father—"

"He's not my father, damn it!" Sylvia said with an angry slash of her hand and immediately regretted her anger. Virginia felt tears come to her eyes. Shaking her head, Sylvia gritted her teeth and closed her eyes. "I'm sorry, Mama. I just have a lot going on and I'm not ready . . . I'm not ready for anything more."

Virginia lifted a brow in question. "Not ready for Pablo or Carlos?"

Sylvia clenched and unclenched her hands, seemingly counting to ten before she answered. "Neither."

Virginia pointed toward the door of the kitchen. "You're a big girl. You go out there and tell him. I'm going to get brunch ready."

Her mother turned away from her, leaving Sylvia no choice but to march right out there and tell Pablo she was leaving.

Sylvia did just as Virginia instructed, striding back out into the main living area and over to the table where Pablo stood by the windows, staring out at the bay.

He faced her as she approached, and she was once again struck by the things that seemed familiar already. His eyes and the arch of his brow. His long lean build and the angular lines of his body. *He looks like me,* she realized, although nature had been kind enough to give her some womanly roundness.

"Does Gin . . . Sorry, does Virginia need any help?"

"Actually, no," Sylvia said and was about to tell him she was leaving, only the words caught in her throat with the expectant look in his eyes.

Coward. Tell him! the voice in her head screamed, but she couldn't. She might be a lot of things, but she wasn't cruel. She couldn't hurt him or her mother, since she had sensed that Pablo being here was important to her mother for reasons having nothing to do with her and Carlos.

"Would you like a drink?" she asked.

"I brought your mother a bottle of wine, only she says she doesn't drink alcohol anymore," he said as he followed her to the bar Virginia had at one side of the living room. The bar was a concession to the many parties her mama hosted for her friends and business colleagues.

Sylvia grabbed the bottle sitting on the top of the bar and glanced at the label—an unfamiliar wine from an Argentine vineyard. As she worked at opening the bottle, she said, "Mama blames one too many drinks for . . ."

She paused, and as her gaze met Pablo's, she realized she didn't need to finish. He understood all too well. "I'm not familiar with this winery," she said in an effort to get away from dangerous ground.

"It's not imported yet. I'm still working on clearing the brand and getting the necessary approvals." He began pouring the wine into two glasses.

"*You* are? This is—"

"A vineyard I started. Let me know what you think." He handed her a glass but then pulled it away. "That is if you drink. I wouldn't want—"

"I like wine."

He once again handed her the glass, and she took it, offered up a toast. "To my mother."

"To Virginia," he responded. They sipped the wine

and returned to the long narrow table tucked close to the floor-to-ceiling windows. Her mother had a formal dining room for larger occasions, but this smallish table afforded amazing views of the bay. As they sat at the table, Virginia entered, bearing a large serving tray with their lunches.

Pablo immediately jumped up, rushed over, and took the tray from Virginia. Her mother seemed taken aback by his gallantry, but shot him a grateful smile. "If you can just put that on the table, please. I have a few other things to bring in."

He did as she asked and once again settled himself across from Sylvia.

Sylvia glared at him from over the rim of her wineglass. "Think helping my mom will earn you brownie points?"

"Why do American women think that simply being polite is a ploy for getting into their pants?" He arched a brow as he took a sip.

"Isn't it?"

Pablo shrugged. "So if you provided similar assistance to a man, was it because you—"

"Wanted to get him out of his pants? Depends on the man."

His reaction was not what she expected. He laughed out loud. A sturdy, unabashed laugh accompanied by a broad smile that reached up into his amazing green eyes, crinkling the corners of them. "At least you're an honest woman."

Virginia came back with a smaller bowl in one hand and a pitcher of sweet iced tea in the other.

As before, Pablo rose and took the pitcher from her mother and placed it on the table. As he did so, he made a point of shooting a look Sylvia's way and she couldn't help chuckling at his audacity. She could better understand how her mother had developed feelings for this man. He had charm as well as looks.

"Did I miss something, honey?" Virginia asked as she sat down at the chair between them.

"Pablo and I were just discussing . . . our American customs." Sylvia picked up her glass and took a sip.

"Customs? As in—"

"The differences in cultures. How one thing in one culture means something different in another," Pablo clarified.

"Or how it means the same thing," Sylvia said, hoping to make it clear that she wouldn't let him bullshit either her or her mother.

With a nod, Pablo said, "Very true."

Virginia glanced between the two of them, her gaze uneasy, but then motioned to the food sitting before them. "Please help yourselves."

Pablo waited for both women to take some of the salad and panini before he helped himself. The salad was a mix of greens with goat cheese, spicy sweet pecans, pears and dried cranberries with a perfectly seasoned balsamic vinaigrette.

"Delicious. Did you make this, Mama?" Sylvia asked.

"Actually, I asked Juli to whip up something special for this morning," Virginia answered.

"Juli? My friend Juli?"

"Yes. Is that a problem? She had someone from the restaurant deliver the food earlier," her mother explained.

So Juli had known about this little gathering and not said a word?

"Was that the restaurant where we had dinner the other night?" Pablo asked as he picked up one of the sandwiches.

Virginia confirming it also verified to Sylvia that the

hottie her two friends had been talking about—the one her mother was supposedly all googly-eyed about—was none other than Pablo.

Which was so not good. Pablo had already done enough to mess with her mother's life.

She once again eyed him over the rim of her quickly diminishing glass of wine. "So, Pablo. You're here for the winter polo season?"

Pablo nodded and seeing that her glass was nearly empty, poured her some more wine. "Actually, your mother is helping me look for a house."

"A house? Here? In Miami?" she asked and shot a questioning glance at her mother. "I thought you didn't show homes anymore, Mama?"

Reaching out, Pablo laid a hand over her mother's as it rested on the table. "GinGin was kind enough to make an exception."

This was definitely more serious than Sylvia had initially thought. She slugged down a healthy portion of her wine. Her mama wasn't making a mistake—again—with the too handsome and too smooth man sitting across the table from her. Sylvia would not let her do that.

"So, Pablo," she began, putting undue emphasis on his name. "It sounds like you made a decision already." She glared at where he still had his hand on her mother's and he understood, pulling his hand away slowly before he answered.

"I did, Sylvia. I put in a bid on the Hitchens estate."

Sylvia nearly choked on the bit of sandwich in her mouth. "The Hitchens estate? The one on Key Biscayne?" Her mama's favorite place. A place she had longed to buy for longer than Sylvia could remember.

"That's the one, honey. The Mediterranean Revival mansion—"

"On the water and facing the Atlantic. Beautiful, but run-down. It'll take a lot of money to restore it. Money and patience," Sylvia said pointedly and looked Pablo's way to measure his response.

Pablo gave a careless shrug. "The money's not a problem, and as for patience . . ." He glanced at her mother for a second before facing her again. "I'm a patient man, especially when it's something that I truly want."

Sylvia had no doubt what Pablo wanted—Virginia. Again. The Hitchens estate and everything else connected to it was just the means to the end.

An unhappy end, Sylvia worried but said nothing. Her mother and she would have plenty of time to discuss this when they were alone. As they had been for the last thirty years. Alone and managing just fine without the too handsome and too smooth man sitting across from her.

A man she definitely intended to keep her eye on, because the last thing she wanted was for mother to be hurt again.

Just as she didn't want to be hurt by another too attractive and too charming operator.

She suspected that Carlos and Pablo were cut from the same cloth, but this was definitely not going to be a case of like mother, like daughter. Sylvia had thirty years of loneliness to show her the consequences of making that mistake.

18

That Sylvia was pissed and worried was apparent during the *chicas'* entire workout as she hefted heavier stacks of weights and pushed herself in the hope that it would help her dispel the emotions that had been churning through her mind since meeting Pablo the day before.

But all that her exertions accomplished was to make her immediately sore and tired. But not too sore or tired to pick up and toss back the first few mojitos until she was finally feeling a little looser.

Tori—ever perceptive Tori—was the first one to notice that Sylvia was ready to talk.

"Rough day?" Tori asked.

"Rough week would be more like it. Do you know who my mother had over for our Sunday get-together?" she asked and narrowed her eyes as she looked at Juli.

With a shrug, her friend replied, "Your *mami* asked me to make something simple for lunch. Something that would keep, because she wasn't certain when her guests would be eating."

"Or maybe not eating."

"*Chicas,* did I do anything wrong just by making lunch?" Juli asked, hands raised in supplication as she glanced around the table at her friends.

Sylvia couldn't deal with the wounded puppy look on her friend's face. "No, you didn't do anything wrong. The food was delicious. It was the company that was . . . unexpected."

"The hottie from dinner the other night?" Adriana asked and sipped on her mojito.

Sylvia placed her hands on either side of her plate, tensing her fingers on the linen tablecloth. "That hottie . . . He's Pablo."

"*Quien es Pablo?*" Juli wondered out loud.

"Pablo Amenabar. My father," she explained.

Adriana was the first one to speak after a long silence. "Your *papi?* We were—"

"Lusting over your *papi?*" Juli said, a slight squeak in her voice.

"You were lusting?" Sylvia said with her own little squeal of disbelief.

A guilty look crossed over Juli's and Adriana's faces before Adriana asked, "Are you sure the man with your *mami* at dinner was your father?"

"One and the same. Pablo Amenabar. Playboy polo player. Absentee father."

"But there's more isn't there?" Tori asked.

Sylvia picked at an imaginary speck of dirt on the tablecloth and said, "Pablo is buying a house. Here. In Miami."

Adriana asked, "What prompted—"

"He wants to get into my mother's pants again. What

other reason could there be?" she said, snagging her glass and taking a big gulp of her mojito.

"Maybe your *papi* feels bad about what happened before," Juli said.

"Is that why it took him thirty years to do something about it?" Sylvia said. She picked up her fork and attacked a ripe plantain on her plate with a vengeance. The fork squeaked against the china.

"Not that I'm any kind of expert on what men are thinking, because hello, it took me forever to figure out that Riley was interested." At Adriana's mention of Riley, Sylvia squirmed but said nothing as her friend immediately continued. "But let's assume that I'm a little smarter about things like that now. If I am, I would have to say that the way Pablo was looking at your *mami*—"

Sylvia slashed the air. "Please do not go there, because the Eww Factor would be major."

"What if there's really more to the reason he's staying?" Tori blurted out.

"You mean like he suddenly wants quality time with me?" Sylvia asked. Fanning her hands wide before her, she said, "Picture it. Pablo and me going to the park. Pablo buying me an ice cream to make me feel better when I fall off the swing and scrape my knee."

"Maybe it's too late for that, but it's not too late for other things," Tori pointed out.

"Like what?" Sylvia said with an annoyed huff.

"Being there when you have a *problema*. Walking you down the aisle. Buying *tus niños* an ice cream," Juli said softly, clearly fearful of how Sylvia would react.

She considered what her friend said, and in the *telenovela*-laden world in which Juli liked to indulge, forgiveness and living happily ever after were possible.

But not in Sylvia's world. Tapping the tablecloth with her finger, Sylvia said, "To have all of that, you need a guy. Something which I am lacking right at this moment."

"*No lo creo*," Juli began. "Did you break up with—"

"Breaking up requires that there be a relationship to begin with."

"Harsh, Sylvita. Way harsh," Tori immediately responded.

"Riley told me he thought something was wrong," Adriana added.

"Riley, Riley, Riley. Can you at least try to formulate a sentence that doesn't include the name Riley?"

Adriana would have normally been quick to respond with anger, but this was a kinder, gentler Adriana. She reached over and placed her hand over Sylvia's. "I know how hard it is to admit you might actually care for Carlos."

"You can't even begin to know," she said and shot an uneasy glance at Tori, before continuing. "Look, it's complicated at the moment. With my dad . . . I mean Pablo."

"Pablo *is* your *papi*," Juli reminded.

"Right. Listen, could we just drop this? I'm sure you all have lots of fun happenings in your lives, so please spill," Sylvia said. Picking up her glass and realizing it was empty, she signaled the waiter for another mojito.

Suitably shut down, her *amigas* did as she asked. For the rest of the night, she listened as they chatted about everything going on in their lives. The latest stuff with their businesses and, of course, their relationships.

Tori was still in the throes of marital bliss. Adriana and Riley—well, they seemed to be making up quite well for twenty years of lusting after each other. Even Juli had recently started up with a man—Vince, the cooking professor she had met months earlier.

Only Sylvia was alone.

Not that she needed a man to complete her.

Men came and went.

Men served one purpose and one purpose alone because . . .

Men were dogs.

Well, at least, most men were.

If she kept to that philosophy, she would spare herself the heartache that was likely to hit her friends, unless they had discovered the rare and elusive species—*semper fi semper erectus homo sapiens,* she thought with a chuckle as she finished off her mojito and signaled for another.

Sylvia e-mailed the article she had just finished to Harry, along with a very brief rundown on where she stood on the story about Carlos and Riley.

Very brief because so far she didn't have enough information to verify or disprove Randy Davis's allegations. Someone knocked on her apartment door. Sylvia perked up in her chair, wondering if it could be Carlos.

She exited her e-mail, walked to the door, and quickly opened it, an expectant grin on her face.

Adriana stood there, hands plastered on her hips. She smiled as she perused the look on Sylvia's face. "You thought it was him, didn't you?"

"Him? Who?" she asked, although her smile faded as she realized it was her friend at the door, not Carlos.

"I get it. You don't want to hear about Riley from me, so I'm assuming you don't want to discuss Carlos either," Adriana said and stepped into the apartment.

"Speaking of Riley, aren't you normally busy with Riley at this hour?" Sylvia glanced at her watch to emphasize the question.

Adriana shrugged. "Riley had to meet with Carlos about his coming to work with him, so we rescheduled our regular volleyball date. Since you seemed a little angry last night—"

Sylvia waved her off. "Not angry. Just . . . concerned."

"About me and Riley?" Adriana said as she plopped down on the couch. It squeaked in protest, prompting Sylvia to remember her last time with Carlos on that couch.

If things don't work out with Carlos, I'm going to have to get rid of that damn couch, she thought. She walked over, sat down next to her friend, and motioned to the laptop on the coffee table. "Mind if I shut down while we talk?"

After Adriana's nod, Sylvia turned off the computer while saying, "How well do you really know Riley? I mean, you may have known him for twenty years, but do you *really*—"

"*Know* him? Can you really ever *know* someone, Sylvia? Even after a lifetime, there's bound to be things that surprise you."

As the screen on the laptop confirmed that the shutdown was proceeding, Sylvia sat back and faced her friend. "Has Riley ever surprised you? And I'm not talking about in a sex kind of way because that's just TMI."

With a careless shrug, Adriana said, "He surprised me when he admitted that he had cared for me since the first day he saw me."

Sylvia considered the statement but didn't see why it had come as such a revelation. "We all knew it. Why did it take you so long—"

"Because Riley is the kind of man who always wants to be in control of things. Admitting that he hadn't always been in control of what he felt for me—that admission gave me power over him," she said.

So Riley was always in control? If Randy Davis's allegations were true, had Riley been the one behind what had happened? Glancing at her friend, Sylvia said, "But what if there was something you didn't know about him? Something that . . . changed what you thought about him?"

Adriana's eyes narrowed. "Is this about Riley now or about Carlos?"

As guilty as she felt about keeping Randy Davis's accusations from Adriana, she would feel even worse if she caused problems between her friend and Riley without having anything more conclusive.

"It's about Carlos. I'm not sure about him. About what he really is," she lied, looking away.

Adriana, however, was quick to pick up on her language. "*What* he is? You mean *who* he is, don't you?"

Shit, Sylvia thought, but plowed on. "Yes. *Who* he is. Whether he's like Pablo, who couldn't be relied on, or—"

"Carlos isn't like your *papi*. For that matter, you don't really know what your *papi* is like, do you?"

Sylvia nodded. "I don't know. Maybe because Pablo has never been my father."

"But you don't know the reason for that, do you? Your *mami* doesn't seem too upset about his being around. On the contrary, she looked—"

"Positively happy. When we had lunch on Sunday and after, when we went back to the pool to hang, she seemed pleased that he was there and that he planned on buying a place in Miami," Sylvia said, laying her hands on her jeans and rubbing them there nervously.

"Would it be so bad if she finally found happiness?" Adriana asked. She cupped Sylvia's chin and applied gentle pressure until Sylvia met her gaze.

Sylvia wanted to shout out that it wasn't possible. Especially not with Pablo, but she realized her friend totally believed that Happily-Ever-After could happen.

And for the moment, Sylvia didn't want to ruin that belief.

"No, *amiga*. It wouldn't be bad if it was possible for all of us."

A loud, insistent beep came from Adriana's purse. Adriana slipped her PDA from her bag, and as she glanced at the screen, a sexy smile came to her face. "Can you give me just a moment?"

Sylvia nodded and watched as Adriana's fingers flew over the keys. She paused, apparently having sent the message, and then another loud beep came.

Adriana chuckled, texted something back, and then eased the PDA into her purse. "That was Riley. He'll be finished in time for us to do lunch later."

Sylvia noticed the gleam in Adriana's eyes. Doing lunch with Riley would be more about the doing than about the lunch. "Tell me that it's about more than just the sex, Adriana."

The gleam in Adriana's deep green eyes grew brilliant, and the smile on her face filled with adoration. "The sex? Do you think the sex is what will keep you—"

"Warm on a cold winter's day? Miami, remember? Doesn't take much to keep—"

"You warm," Adriana finished and playfully nudged her friend. "When you're lying there and the only thing you can feel is peace . . . That's what it's all about."

Sylvia nodded but couldn't imagine that kind of

contentment. That kind of . . . commitment with any man.

Only as it had occurred to her the other day during her conversation with Tori, Carlos wasn't just *any* man.

He might just be the man to prove her wrong.

19

With her visit to the Port O'Call having been a bust and no additional information on the eyewitness, Sylvia double-checked her info again in the hopes of finding someone who had worked at the club where the shooting occurred at the time of Simon's death. She was worried. Bartenders and waitresses were usually not the kind to linger in establishments like these. Especially not for four years.

However one interesting thing came from the police report. On the list of Simon's personal effects was a notation that one of the items in his locker had been lingerie. She recognized the name of the shop—Naughty and Naughtier—on the bag holding the lingerie.

Georgie—formerly Jorge in an earlier life—was the owner of the shop, located on Washington, just a few blocks away from Sylvia's apartment. She had met Georgie nearly seven years earlier on one of her first assignments for the magazine. She had been asked to do an article on the gender illusionists who worked at the revues in various Miami hot spots and hotels. She and Georgie had clicked. They had become friends, and Sylvia was a regular customer at the shop.

What kind of customer had Simon been? Had the lingerie been for his wife, Phyllis, his squeeze, Alicia, or maybe even for himself?

She would have to drop by Georgie's before she started running down additional leads at the places on her list. As she worked, Sylvia also included the names she had considered less noteworthy and those whom she hadn't been able to track down. The magazine had a subscription to a service that provided some pretty intensive background checks. She would have to confirm with Harry if she could proceed with them, but not until she had exhausted all her other possible avenues of information.

Her stomach did a little grumbling, reminding her that lunch had come and gone thanks to Adriana's earlier visit. It was as good a time as any to take a break and grab a sandwich on her way to Georgie's.

Sylvia left her condo and walked toward Collins. On the way, she intended to stop at David's and hit their corner stand for a Cuban sandwich, but as she neared, she caught a glimpse of a familiar profile—Carlos.

He was sitting inside at the luncheonette counter shoulder to shoulder with another familiar face—none other than Riley Evans. Adriana's Riley. They were busy chowing down on something while talking and laughing. Neither man seemed to have a care in the world.

Adriana had mentioned that Riley was meeting with Carlos to discuss having Carlos work for him. Sylvia wondered if that business had been completed and Riley would soon be on his way to Adriana's.

Sylvia didn't want to risk running into Carlos. At least,

not just yet. So she hurried past David's without saying hello and continued onward to the Eleventh Street Diner. There was a good-size crowd inside the eatery immortalized in a Gloria Estefan video.

Still too crowded, she thought, so she just kept on going until she got to a smoothie bar on Washington and decided to do her version of a liquid lunch. With an ice-cold strawberry mango smoothie in hand, she walked until she arrived at Naughty and Naughtier, Georgie's lingerie shop.

Glancing through the front window, Sylvia noticed Georgie at the register with a customer. As always, Sylvia's flamboyant friend was wearing a sample of one of the pieces of lingerie available for sale. The deep coral of the peignoir set Georgie wore was a perfect foil to Georgie's warm milk chocolate–colored skin.

Sylvia pushed open the door, drawing Georgie's attention. Georgie smiled to acknowledge her entry but returned to completing the sale for the customer.

Not one to pass up the opportunity to shop, Sylvia looked through the racks, thinking a new outfit might be just the thing for a little morale boost. As she drew aside one set after another, something finally caught her eye—a La Perla camisole with a matching thong. Made of emerald satin so deep in color it appeared almost black, the camisole was sinfully edged by matching lace and satin ribbons.

After the customer left, Georgie approached Sylvia with artificially arched brows shooting ever upward as she noticed what had caught Sylvia's attention.

Georgie leaned close. "Girl, that is certain to make your man sit up and take notice."

With a glance at the garment again, Sylvia set it aside quickly. "Not what I had hoped for, Georgie."

A disbelieving harrumph exploded from her friend. "Pu-leez, girl. Everyone has seen you around the Beach with that luscious Bad Boy."

"Been there, done that," Sylvia replied flippantly and snapped one of the hangers across the rack with some force.

"Ouch. And here I thought true love had finally bitten you." Georgie reached for a garment at the far end of the rack where Sylvia stood, extracted another camisole set, and placed it against her body so Sylvia might consider it.

Which she did for all of a second before returning to the emerald-colored set she had put aside. As she pulled it off the rack and held it up to her, Georgie nodded emphatically but then quickly added, "It would look luscious, even though that's not what you want."

Sylvia faced Georgie directly, thinking this might be the perfect time to start asking the questions that had been circling around in her mind since discovering Simon's purchase in the list of his personal effects. "There are three reasons people buy this stuff."

"Only three?" Georgie teased her in a sexy but playful purr.

Sylvia chuckled, but continued, counting down on her fingers while still holding on to the hanger with the La Perla set. "Well, three major reasons. Number one: Women buy it to entice a man."

"Definitely, although I will say that with a body like yours, the best enticement is nothing."

"Thanks for admitting that. It may make me reconsider this purchase. However—" she said and held up the hanger.

"But then, again, it would really bring out the green in your eyes, so let's go ring this up," Georgie added eagerly. Fearful about losing a potential sale, Georgie snared the hanger from Sylvia's hand and walked toward the counter.

As Georgie began to ring up the garment, Sylvia continued with her countdown. "Reason number two, which is, by the way, the reason I am buying this, is that lingerie makes a woman feel sexy and decadent even if she's the only one who knows what she's wearing."

With a snort, Georgie said, "Doesn't your friend Tori know all about that now? Ever since she met her lover boy she's been a regular here."

Score one for the Torster, Sylvia thought as Georgie waggled her fingers in what passed as her request for payment. After handing over her credit card, Sylvia continued with the countdown. "Last, but definitely not the least—it's a guilt gift. Guy gets his girl angry. Guy's been messing with someone else and is sorry."

"Or the same guy is still just messing with someone else and wants to buy that someone else a gift," Georgie added.

"Definitely. So do you get many guilty guys in here, Georgie? Especially guilty cop kinds of guys?"

Georgie paused as she was wrapping up Sylvia's purchase. She lightly laid her thick fingers, heavy with an assortment of rings, on the bright pink tissue paper she had been using to wrap the garment. "Are you thinking about one cop in particular or in general? You know how high the divorce rate is for law enforcement types."

"I'm thinking about one police officer in particular— Simon Davis. He was killed—"

"Several years ago. I remember seeing his picture in the paper the morning after he came in here," she said and returned to wrapping.

"So he was here the day he died? Had he been here—"

"Never before. He was one of those guilty types like you said. Wanted a gift for his wife to make it up to her, he said." Georgie shook her head and made a tsking sound. "Always wondered if he gave it to her before he died."

Sylvia reached out and laid a hand on Georgie's. "This is important. Did he say what he had done wrong?"

An inelegant snort erupted from her friend. "Not exactly, but it seemed to me like he had been messing with someone else. From what I could gather after he was killed—a fellow cop."

Alicia. The attractive female cop she had met in the bar the other day. Which meant that another visit to the police hangout and some talk with Alicia might be the thing to do. "Thanks, Georgie. That helped a lot."

Georgie held up the bag with Sylvia's purchase and looked at her oddly. When Sylvia reached for the bag, Georgie slowly pulled it back. "There's something you haven't asked."

"Like?"

"Like what was up with Simon and Carlos. There was definitely bad blood between them."

This was definitely not what she had expected to hear. But it was Sylvia's job to find out the truth and report on it, no matter how much she might not like it. Or at least that was what she reminded herself.

"What was up with them?"

Georgie finally handed her the bag, but motioned to the door to a small back room, which doubled as storage and an office. She slipped into that room, and Sylvia followed.

"When that cop came in here, I remembered seeing him around the Beach. Actually, seeing him with Carlos.

Rumor had it he was trying to nail your Bad Boy for all his illegal activities."

Georgie didn't appear to know Carlos was a cop. "Carlos is into lots of . . . shit. Simon was a cop. Natural clash," Sylvia admitted

"I guess that was part of it. But I heard that it was also the cop Simon was hooking up with. Rumor had it Carlos had been hooking up with her too."

Sylvia was left speechless for a moment. She tried not to let the thought of Carlos with someone else bother her. It was pre-Sylvia, and Carlos was a handsome man. He was bound to have had his share of women before her. And come to think of it, after her. *Has he turned to Alicia already?* she thought, but then forced herself back to the job she had to do.

"So, they both wanted the same woman? Is that enough reason to kill someone?"

"Honey, you know how stupid men can get," Georgie said.

"So, you think Carlos shot Simon—"

"Unh, unh, unh. Not like that at all, or at least, that's not what a friend told me."

"A friend? What friend?" Sylvia asked eagerly, surprised by just how much information Georgie seemed to have. But then again, Georgie moved in all kinds of circles.

"Remember Javier? Slim, slight build. Does the Christina Aguilera impersonation?"

Sylvia remembered him. He had been another of the gender illusionists she had interviewed when she first met Georgie.

"One night Javier had a problem, and apparently Carlos came to his rescue. Javier wouldn't say much about what happened, which is a miracle in and of itself, because you know how talky Javier is."

"Do you think Javier would talk to me about what happened?" Sylvia asked.

"He might. You could ask him. Do you want his number?"

"I'd love it," Sylvia said.

She scribbled down the number on her receipt for the camisole. Then she put the receipt in the bag with her purchase and left Naughty and Naughtier. Though she planned to stop by her magazine's offices to do some background checks and research, she decided to stop by the Port O'Call first, since it was only two blocks away. She hoped she would find Alicia there again so she could ask the woman more questions.

Sylvia wasn't disappointed. As she rounded the corner, she saw Alicia standing in front of the bar. But she wasn't alone. Carlos was there too. And he looked mad.

Carlos had his hand on Alicia's arm and seemed upset with her. The feeling was clearly mutual. Alicia yanked her arm away and jabbed Carlos in the chest a few times, stressing whatever point she was attempting to make.

Startled to see them together, especially after Georgie had insinuated they used to be a couple, Sylvia felt a rush of disappointment. She didn't want to think he had replaced her already. Gone back to familiar ground when things between them hadn't gone as he had hoped.

Deciding it was best to go before she was noticed or anger got the better of her and she did something she would later regret, Sylvia turned and headed over to her magazine offices on Española Way about half a dozen blocks away.

As she hurried down the street, she shot another quick look over her shoulder to make sure she had seen it right. There was no doubting that Alicia and Carlos were fighting and she couldn't help wondering what was going on between them. And whether it had any impact on her relationship with Carlos.

When she arrived at the magazine offices, Sylvia quickly ran several background checks on people she suspected might have been working at the club at the time of the shooting. Though most of her sources were too new at the club to be of any help, she got lucky with the last one on her list. A bartender who had worked there for several years answered Sylvia's phone call.

The bartender was familiar with the missing young woman who had been the sole eyewitness to the shooting.

"So you knew Sasha Winchell personally?" Sylvia asked, skimming through the police report to see if there was anything else that would help during the conversation.

A slight hesitation came across the line before the female bartender said, "We went to the same high school, but we weren't friends. Then she started hanging out around the club to do her business."

Sylvia frowned. "What kind of business? Drugs?"

"Men, men, and more men, even though she'd apparently been busted for solicitation a few years earlier. That's why she was using an alias."

"What's her real name?" Sylvia asked, and the bartender quickly said, "Natasha Wynn."

Sylvia jotted it down and continued. "Does she still come around the club?"

"Nah," the other woman said with a snort. "Money must not have been good here, and then there was the shooting. I heard she's got a job at the polo club. Better clientele there."

It was impossible to miss the sarcasm in the bartender's voice. Sylvia thanked her and hung up.

Her next call was to Javier, although she wasn't expecting him to actually answer his phone. He surprised her by picking up on the second ring and recognized her right away as the reporter who had interviewed him in the past. When she asked if he'd be willing to answer some questions she had, he seemed strangely delighted at the thought that he might appear in another one of her articles and immediately agreed to an interview following one of his performances at a revue in a Miami Beach hotel. Sylvia decided not to mention the nature of the article or the types of questions she intended to ask.

Finished with her research for the day, Sylvia left the building in better spirits but froze when she recognized a familiar figure standing at the curb, leaning against one of the parked cars.

Carlos. And from the look on his face, trouble was on the way.

20
***

Sylvia turned sharply, intent on avoiding him, but he snagged her arm as she would have walked away, giving her no choice but to face him.

"This makes three times today that you've chosen to avoid me, *amorcito.* Only this time, you can't run away."

"I'm not avoiding you—"

"Bullshit. I saw you at David's and then after, by the Port O'Call. What gives?"

His grip was gentle; his hand warm. Deliciously so. She battled the desire that he move that hand elsewhere on her body. "Nothing. I just decided against anything Cuban today."

He moved his hand up and down lazily, sending a shiver along her spine. He leaned toward her and pitched his voice in low intimate tones as he said, "Really? So if Cuban isn't your thing, why all the continued interest in me?"

She yanked her arm away and gave him a shove.

"Conceited, aren't you? Can't you imagine that maybe I'm interested in something else? Maybe even someone else?"

"Maybe Simon Davis?" he said and blocked her way again when she took a step to leave. She bumped into his hard chest but then quickly stepped back and raised her chin a notch, trying to be eye to eye with him. Since she was dressed casually, she had lost the few inches of height that her heels normally gave her.

"Would that be a problem?" she asked.

Carlos uneasily avoided her gaze and let out a tired sigh. He dragged his hand through the thick strands of his hair before facing her again. "Why can't you let Simon rest in peace? There's no story there, Sylvia."

She cupped his cheek, his beard rough beneath her palm. Applying gentle pressure, she urged him to face her. "That's a lie, and we both know it. Something happened that night that doesn't add up, and you're a part of it."

Sadness dulled his normally strong features. "What if you don't like what you find out?"

Although she didn't want to admit it, Sylvia had been hoping that he would deny her accusation. Argue for his honor and innocence. His question burst that hope like a pin against a balloon.

She pulled her hand away and grabbed hold of her purse strap to refrain from touching him again because the temptation was just too great. "I can't let personal feelings get in the way of my job. I have a story to write."

He let out a little snort of disbelief. "Feelings? Some days I doubt you even know what they are. If you even have a heart."

Before she could reply, Carlos stalked off with his

hands tucked deep into his pockets and his shoulders hunched beneath the lightweight track jacket he wore.

She wanted to chase after him. Make him convince her that he had done nothing wrong the night of Simon's death. Tell him she really did have a heart, contrary to his belief. Somewhere in the middle of her chest the sharp, unexpected pain said her heart might just be breaking.

On Friday night, Sylvia endured the noise and gaiety of Javier's revue, hoping for a chance to pull him to the side after the show and ask him some questions. When the show finished and the gender illusionists came out to mingle with the crowd, Sylvia bided her time until Javier came nearby, still impersonating Christina Aguilera, but in her current kind-of-scary state.

She waved and managed to snag Javier's attention. He smiled and sashayed over, slipping into the empty seat beside her. He air kissed her and said, "I'm so glad you came. Please tell me you're doing another article. The attendance after the last one was phenomenal."

Forcing a smile, Sylvia shook her head. "I am doing a story, but not about the show. Do you have a few minutes to talk with me?"

"Sure. What do you need to know?" Javier asked but looked away, smiling at a handsome man a few tables over, his attention clearly wandering now that he knew he wasn't going to be the focus of her story.

"Javier," she said, her tone stern, which immediately dragged his attention back to her.

"Oh, this is a serious thing, isn't it?" With artful guile, he covered his mouth with his hand, feigning surprise.

"Can we please go somewhere private?"

Javier nervously glanced around the room, where the

other illusionists were busy working the crowd. "But I may miss—"

"It's a big story. I think you might be an important part of it. Might get you some good coverage."

"*Sí*, but only for a few minutes." Javier popped out of the chair, plastered a false smile on his face, and hurried toward the stage door with Sylvia close behind him.

Once they were backstage, Javier rushed to a small narrow room off the main hall where a long vanity held makeup, brushes, and cosmetics of all kinds. A mirror ran the entire length of the vanity, and at various spots, photographs and papers had been taped to the mirror. A motley assortment of chairs and stools were placed along the vanity.

Javier picked up a tube of lipstick and reapplied it while glancing at Sylvia's reflection in the mirror.

"So what can I do for you?" he asked after he had done his lips and was reaching for some face powder.

"Simon Davis. Does the name mean anything to you?"

Javier's face paled a little, and the practiced smile he had been wearing faded from his lips, but he shook his head.

"How about Carlos Ramirez?"

Javier's growing uneasiness was apparent. A muscle twitched along his jaw. "What about Carlos?"

"Tell me how you know him."

Javier looked down toward the surface of the vanity and searched among the cosmetics there as he said, "Who said I knew him?"

"A reliable source. Four years ago, Carlos Ramirez and one of his associates were shot. An undercover officer was also killed. What do you know about that night?"

Javier shrugged and grabbed a tube of mascara. Facing the mirror, he began to reapply the mascara while he spoke. "I don't know anything about that night."

He's an exceptionally poor liar, Sylvia thought. From the tension in his face and body to the inflection in his voice, she knew there was more he wasn't saying. "So maybe you don't know anything about that night, but you know what was up with Ramirez and Davis."

Javier shot a glance at his watch. "I'm really missing the best tips out there and—"

Sylvia held up her hand. "What's a few tips compared to being included in a lead story in the magazine?"

Javier's eyes widened, and a sly grin came to his face. "You're serious? How much of a mention will it be?"

"Depends on what kind of info you provide."

Javier considered it. "What do you want to know?"

"I want to understand what happened the night Simon Davis was killed."

He tossed down the tube of mascara and turned. Leaning his scrawny ass on the edge of the vanity, he crossed his arms and said, "A few months before Simon was killed, Carlos saved my life."

"How?"

"Someone arranged a meeting for me with a man. I thought the man knew what he was buying, but when things started to get a little intense out in the alley—"

"He realized he was getting something he hadn't bargained for."

Javier nodded. "Redneck Okie started beating the shit out of me. I think he would have killed me if Carlos hadn't stepped in."

The Prince comes to the rescue again, she thought. "So, Carlos stopped him. What does this have to do with—"

"Simon Davis? Who do you think set me up with the Mr. Brawny who was not into some ball action?"

Simon Davis had been pimping Javier? "What did Simon get out of this whole thing?"

Javier rubbed his thumb and forefinger together and she said, "Money? And what did you get out of it?"

"Simon gave me blow in exchange for the money."

"Where did Simon get the cocaine?" she asked, although it didn't take a rocket scientist to figure out that the evidence locker at the police department probably had its fair share of drugs, and if not, as an undercover cop, Simon knew just where to get the drugs.

"Never knew and didn't care. But after that night I went cold turkey. Decided I didn't want to press my luck."

"What about Carlos? Did he know that Simon—"

"Was my pimp and dealer? No, he didn't."

"So how did he figure it out?" she asked.

"Simon came out of the club to check what was going on. Carlos was still there, and I guess he put two and two together. Got real angry. I figured he didn't like Simon cutting in on his territory," Javier said, standing up to indicate the interview was over.

"Thanks, Javier," she said, her mind already racing as Javier walked away. What would she do with this latest information? It clearly implicated Simon as a dirty cop, but how was Carlos involved?

As she left the hotel, Sylvia thought that there had to be something else that would explain what had happened. She refused to believe that Carlos had wanted Simon dead for being a dirty cop, or for screwing his girl. She recalled the way the other officers seemingly idolized Carlos and how he had saved Riley's life. How he had saved her life too.

Carlos was a hero to everyone. Her article might implicate him. Could she ruin Carlos's reputation? Could she subject him to possible jail time if it turned out that he was somehow responsible for Simon's death? Could she hurt him when on some level, she still cared about him?

21

Hot.
Humid.
Horsey.

Sylvia was at the polo club, trying to track down Natasha Wynn. She wrinkled her nose as she passed by one of the polo players as he stood by the edge of the crowd, signing autographs for people. He didn't seem familiar at all, so she assumed his celebrity status must be limited to the polo groupies gathered around him.

Sylvia continued onward, past the stands where people were getting set for the first match and back to the large tented area where Natasha was rumored to be working as a cocktail waitress.

She walked through the lobby and past the terracotta-lined steps leading up to the grandstand. Beyond the central lobby was a pool area and a tented space where a local luxury car dealership had organized an owner appreciation day.

The hostess at the entrance to the tented area gave

SOUTH BEACH CHICAS CATCH THEIR MAN   193

Sylvia some flack at first, since she wasn't on the list, but when she mentioned her mother's name, the hostess immediately allowed her to pass and even directed her to the young woman Sylvia wanted to question. The tent was already starting to clear out as patrons began returning to the stands for the start of the match.

Blond, pretty, and young in a California surfer girl way, Natasha efficiently poured champagne, mixed mimosas, and handled the customers in a way sure to earn her a nice tip, especially considering that the alcohol was free. Sylvia could understand why the young woman had left the club for this job.

She got in line, ordered a champagne, and as Natasha handed her the glass, she said, "You're Natasha, right?"

The girl nodded and the blond hair she had swept up into a ponytail bounced with the movement. Natasha returned to serving drinks to the next customer in line.

"I need to talk to you," Sylvia said as she stepped to the side so the young woman could serve the next person in line.

"I'm working. I don't have time to talk," the young woman snapped, although the practiced smile on her face never wavered.

Sylvia downed her champagne, handed Natasha the glass to refill. "You do take breaks, don't you, Sasha?"

At the mention of her old name, Natasha froze. She glanced out of the corner of her eye at Sylvia and said, "In fifteen minutes. Who are you?"

Sylvia pointed to the side exit of the tent. "I'll be waiting outside to the left of the entrance," she said and walked away.

The spot Sylvia had chosen was just to the right of the stands and gave her a ground-level view of the polo field, as well as the players and horses along the one side. Curiosity got the better of her and she opened the program she had been handed as she entered the polo club. She checked the names of the players on the various teams to see if Pablo might be out on the field somewhere.

Sure enough, the team wearing red and black was her father's team. He wore the number twenty-seven, the same date as her birthday. Weird coincidence. Beside his name were a bunch of stats, including a special notation that Pablo was one of the few players ranked with a ten. She had no clue what that meant, but seeing that the bulk of the players listed had sevens and eights, she assumed being a ten was a big deal.

As she waited for Natasha, Sylvia watched the game. She had to admire the speed and agility of both the horses and the players, but one in particular stood out from all the rest. She tracked his run up and down the field, his body close to the horse's neck, arm held high as he brought his mallet around and struck the ball. As the player to whom he had shot the ball faltered, allowing the ball to be picked off by the opposing team, the man immediately stopped, turned his horse, and raced back upfield to defend.

It was then, in that moment where both horse and rider seemed suspended in motion before they took off upfield, that she caught the number on the player's back— 27. Pablo.

Sylvia couldn't pull her attention away, unable to deny the beautiful way he handled his mount. She admired his grace as he spurred his horse onward and with a facility that made it seem as if he and the horse were one.

"He is something to see, isn't he?" Natasha asked as she slipped out of the tent next to Sylvia. She took a long draw on her cigarette.

"Do you know him at all?" Sylvia asked, intrigued despite herself.

Natasha gave a snort of disbelief. "Everyone knows Pablo Amenabar. He's one of the few tens who comes to play."

"Must make him quite popular with the women," Sylvia said, imagining that his celebrity status provided a wealth of choices for female companionship other than her mother.

"This is my third season here and I've yet to hear any tales about him and any of the groupies hanging around. So either he's real discreet or truly not interested," the young woman said as she dropped her cigarette and stomped it into the ground. She glanced at Sylvia intently and said, "Why do you want to talk to me?"

"I'm a reporter. I'm doing a story and need to ask you some important questions," she said.

"But not about the stud muffin on the pony."

"You were the only eyewitness to a shooting four years ago," Sylvia stated, ignoring Natasha's insinuation.

"I'm trying not to revisit that me. That was another life and I was another person."

"'Sasha Winchell,' according to the police report and the rap sheet I finally found. I guess the police didn't need to reach you after the initial investigation?"

Natasha shrugged her fine-boned shoulders beneath the utilitarian white shirt she wore. "I told the police everything I knew. As for the woman I was then—we all make mistakes. I've left that life behind. I don't want it coming back to haunt me." She glared at Sylvia.

"It won't if you answer some questions for me. Where were you that night?"

"I was with a john, but he split the moment the shooting started."

"A john? So you were . . ."

"In the alley across the street. We were busy. I needed the cash."

Natasha's movements were jumpy, filled with nervous tension as she continued. "I heard something and looked toward the street. Saw this one guy pulling a gun."

"What about the other people with him?"

Natasha pulled a pack of Marlboros from her apron pocket and lit up another cigarette before she continued. "There were two men. They seemed kind of surprised, especially when their friend started shooting."

Sylvia reached into her blazer pocket and pulled out photos of Carlos, Riley, and Simon that she'd copied from the police file. With a curt motion of the hand holding the cigarette, Natasha identified Simon. "He's the one who started it."

A rush of relief washed through Syvlia. *Carlos didn't start the shooting.* "So what happened next?"

"Besides the guy inside of me nearly crapping his pants? He pulled out and ran, barely zipping up as he went. The police never found out who he was and I sure didn't know his name."

"And you . . ."

"Bullets were flying everywhere. I hid behind one of the cars on our side of the street. I couldn't see much after the first few shots, but when it got quiet, I went over to see if anyone needed help," Natasha said. She took a drag and then wrapped her arms around herself. She shivered as she continued. "I'd never seen a dead guy before. And there was so much blood."

Sylvia laid a hand on Natasha's shoulder, trying to comfort her. "I know, but it's important that you tell me exactly what you saw."

"The blond one—the shooter—he was on the ground.

Another man was holding him." She wiggled her fingers toward the photos Sylvia had in her hand, and when Natasha examined them, she pointed at Carlos.

"This guy. He was saying something like, 'Why? Why'd you do it?', but the blond guy just kept on mumbling 'Sorry' over and over again until he just sort of . . . stopped."

Simon had died in Carlos's arms, asking for forgiveness. Sylvia thought about the new scenario, that of Simon being the one who had set up Carlos and Riley. Natasha's account seemed to support that scenario. She gestured to Riley's photo. "What about this man?"

Natasha hesitated, her pale eyebrows drawing together as she concentrated on the photo. "What is that expression cops use? You know, the one when a cop gets shot?"

"Officer down," Sylvia said, and Natasha's confusion evaporated.

"That's it. He was sitting up against a wall in a small alley. Seemed to be hurt pretty bad. The front of his shirt was covered in blood, and he had something in his hand. Don't remember if it was a cell phone or radio, but he just kept repeating 'Officers down.'"

"You're sure about this?" Sylvia pressed Natasha, and the young woman nodded emphatically.

"There's just some things you never forget and that's one of them. I gotta get back to work now." She took a final drag before walking back into the tent.

Sylvia lingered for a moment, digesting all the information Natasha had provided. The young woman's version of what happened and her description of where each of the men had been discovered was perfectly in sync with the assorted police reports. There were just a few things missing from the police reports—the exchange between Carlos and Simon and the reason why Simon had fired first.

By the time the first uniforms had arrived on the scene in response to Riley's call, Simon was dead and both Riley and Carlos were unconscious from their wounds. Both had nearly died. The two drug dealers had been dead on arrival.

But why had Simon fired first? Did it have something to do with his being dirty or had he fired because he expected that Carlos and Riley had set him up?

Natasha's account hinted at the fact that Carlos and Riley had been surprised when Simon opened fire, so they might not have known what would happen that night. And if they hadn't known—it would prove they were innocent, contrary to Randy Davis's assertions.

A roar from the crowd snagged Sylvia's attention, and she caught the tail end of a battle for possession between two riders. The two horses impacted with a dull thud, jostling their riders. After the collision, one of the horses reared up on its hind legs, pawing the air and the horse and rider beside it.

Pablo, she realized with sickened fascination.

22

Pablo reined in his horse, directing it away from the dangerous hooves, and somehow ducked aside in the saddle, but a moment later, his horse angrily tossed its head, throwing him from his precarious seat.

He landed on the ground heavily and appeared stunned for a moment, vulnerable to being trampled by the unnerved horses who pranced way too close for comfort, hooves kicking up thick divots of turf.

Members of his team streamed from the sidelines toward him, but before they could reach him, Pablo recovered and rolled out of harm's way. While one of his teammates grabbed his horse and another shooed the second away, yet a third teammate assisted Pablo to his feet. His movements were measured, as if he was in pain.

Before she could stop herself, Sylvia was running around the corner of the playing field and over to where Pablo's team was positioned.

She arrived at the area at roughly the same time that

Pablo did. He stopped short when he saw her by the side-line. The movement ripped a grimace from him, but he waved off his teammate's attentions and gingerly walked her way.

"Sylvia."

"Pablo. Are you okay?"

He nodded, but his lips were pulled into a thin line and white from tension. Deep grooves bracketed his mouth.

"I guess I should go, then," she said and started to walk away, but he gently grabbed hold of her arm.

"Please don't tell your mother."

"My mother? Why would I . . . You want to be involved with my mother again, don't you?"

He released his hold on her arm, and a tired sigh escaped him. "Would that be so bad?"

"Only if you hurt her again."

Pablo eyed her up and down, as if taking stock of her before he said, "I didn't want to hurt her the first time, but . . . sometimes things are not in your control."

"That's hard to believe."

"I tried to do the right thing, Sylvia. I tried to make us a family," he said, his green eyes blazing with emotion.

His demeanor was so intense, she almost believed him for a moment. But then she remembered all the birthdays and holidays when he hadn't been there. When he hadn't called or bothered to do anything besides send money. As if that was enough when no check, no matter how large, could ever make up for his absence in her life.

Stepping up to him, she realized they were almost the same height. They were more similar than she cared to admit. "Please don't hurt her again."

"I won't," he promised solemnly, and surprisingly, she wanted to believe him.

*   *   *

Virginia didn't know what to make of her daughter's sudden interest in having dinner on a Saturday night. Weekend nights were always busy for Sylvia, so it was unusual—no make that inconceivable—that her daughter suddenly wanted to have dinner on Saturday night.

Virginia hadn't really been in the mood to go out, especially since so many restaurants had long waits on such a big date night, so she had suggested takeout and a girl's videofest so they could just spend some time and talk. She sensed Sylvia needed to talk more than anything else.

A DVD sat on the coffee table beside the bucket of fried chicken, coleslaw, and french fries from a local eatery that she loved. Sylvia would probably complain about all the calories and grease, but if you asked Virginia, her daughter could stand to gain a few pounds and give poor Carlos a little more cushion.

Virginia was just laying out some plates and cutlery when the buzzer on the intercom sounded, announcing Sylvia's arrival. Virginia buzzed her in, and a few minutes later, Sylvia knocked. She was dressed casually in low-rise jeans and a cropped T-shirt, her long blond hair pulled up into a ponytail.

"Hi, honey," Virginia said and opened her arms. Sylvia immediately stepped into them and hugged her tightly.

"Hi, Mama. I'm glad we could do this."

"So am I, sweetie. Come sit down. Tell me what's up with you?"

A flicker of apprehension drifted over Sylvia's features before she walked to the couch in front of the coffee table and sat down. Almost mechanically, she grabbed a plate and helped herself to the fried chicken, fries, and coleslaw, not uttering one word of complaint.

This is very bad, Virginia thought, missing the diatribe

that Sylvia usually released about the unhealthiness of Virginia's comfort food choices.

As she sat beside her daughter, she helped herself to some of the food.

"Rough week?" she said as she scooped up some coleslaw onto her plate.

Sylvia crossed her legs, balanced her plate on one knee, and began to pick at the chicken. As she did so, and without looking up at Virginia, her daughter said, "You might say that."

"Problems with—"

"Mama, let's skip the twenty questions, okay?"

A record. Sylvia had cracked faster than she had ever expected. She held out her hand, motioning for Sylvia to continue.

"I broke up with Carlos, who, by the way, I am currently investigating because someone accused him and Riley of being dirty cops. But that isn't the worst part of the week."

Virginia arched her brows. "What could be any worse?"

Sylvia looked pointedly at her mother. "Is it official that you and Pablo are dating now? Maybe even doing Lord knows what else."

So there it was. Out in the open with no possibility of being avoided. "What we're doing? What do you think—"

"I don't want to think about it. Not now. Not ever."

Virginia chuckled at the outright prudish tone in her daughter's voice. "Very mature, honey. But I won't deny that we've been seeing each other and that I've enjoyed spending time with him."

"For starters," Sylvia said, ripping a piece of meat from the chicken breast on her plate and popping it into her mouth.

Was Sylvia right and dinner was only the beginning of something else? She thought back to their windsurfing interlude and how enjoyable the day had been. Pablo had even managed to get her up on the board, but of course, there had been the fringe benefit of having his arms around her for most of the lesson. So possibly it was the start of something else.

"Maybe it will lead to other things."

"What? No denial? No considering that this is absolutely, positively insane?" Sylvia was shaking her head, and each word had been higher in volume than the one before.

"Why is it insane?" Virginia replied calmly as she forked up a bit of the coleslaw and chewed it slowly. Thoughtfully.

"Because he's my father. Because he left you—"

"Sometimes things aren't the way they seem," she said and braced herself for yet another eruption, only Sylvia surprised her.

"Pablo said pretty much the same thing—that sometimes things aren't in your control."

For so long, Virginia had avoided thinking about what had happened between her and Pablo. Had buried the memories of those first few years deep in a subconscious part of her brain because keeping them anywhere else was too painful. But as painful as it might be, it was now time for those memories to resurface from the abyss to which she had banished them.

"When I first found out I was pregnant, it was like the end of the world until . . ." Virginia paused. Sylvia leaned forward, searching her mother's face intently while she waited for her to continue. With a shrug, Virginia went on. "Until Pablo promised me the world."

"And gave you nothing," Sylvia said sharply.

Virginia shook her head in denial. "He gave me a new

life. One which may have been hard at first, but . . . It wasn't what we wanted, but like Pablo said, sometimes things are out of your control."

Sylvia looked upward and placed a finger on her lips, as if contemplating something. "Control? Funny word coming from two people who seem to lack it around each other."

Virginia let out a forced laugh and couldn't deny her daughter's accusation. "You're so right. But if you can't lose control with the one you love . . ." She locked her gaze with her daughter's, daring her to face her own truths.

"I don't love Carlos." Delivered calmly. Maybe too calmly.

Virginia examined Sylvia's face carefully, noting the tense lines around her mouth, and the way her eyes seemed to have gone dead with the statement she had just made. If Sylvia didn't have any emotion, she might have actually believed her.

"That's good, honey. It'll save you the kind of heartache I had with Pablo."

"Because he's a dog. Because all men are dogs."

"Pablo and I were married." There. She had said it. She had finally dug up the most painful and hurtful of all the secrets she had kept for so long.

"You were *married*?" Sylvia blurted out and waved her hands in the air. "When? How? Why didn't you ever tell me?"

"I was sixteen and pregnant in a small backwater Virginia town. As for the when and how—simple really. We went to the justice of the peace, and he married us."

"Are you still . . . Is he legally your . . ."

"Husband? No. We divorced a few years later, not that marriage was enough to satisfy my daddy. When he found out we had gotten married . . ." Memories raced back of that night. Of how her father had gone after Pablo, who had stood there, taking the beating. Never raising a fist or his voice as her father had whupped him down to the ground. "My daddy was always fast and loose with his fists. He hurt Pablo, but Pablo just took it because he didn't want Papa to hurt me. After, he got to his feet and stood before my papa. Told Papa that he wouldn't have to worry about me because he would take care of me, and he did."

"He left you—"

"After people in town found out, it got bad," Virginia jumped in, wanting to finish her explanation.

"And Pablo's family? How did they feel about it?" Sylvia asked.

Virginia shrugged, and much as Sylvia had done before, picked at the chicken on her plate. Then she met Sylvia's gaze and softly said, "Pablo's father never approved of the whole idea of his one and only son being a polo player. He always worried Pablo would get hurt, but then again, I worried too."

At her words, a guilty expression flashed across Sylvia's face.

"Is there something I should know?" Virginia asked, eyeing Sylvia's expression.

"Pablo took a spill today, but don't worry. He's okay. Only he asked me not to say anything to you."

"What? When did you see him?" The Palm Beach polo grounds were not generally in her daughter's social sphere.

"I had to interview someone at the polo grounds. I stuck around to watch the game," Sylvia said. She motioned for her mother to continue with her story.

"Pablo's father disowned him for playing. He hoped that the lack of money would help Pablo change his mind about the game. But Pablo . . ." Virginia chuckled, remembering the determined young man who had not been above mucking stalls in order to follow his dream. "Pablo defied his father and found a job training horses and instructing polo at the horse ranch where I was working. That's how we met. The owners of the ranch fired him when they found out about us. So we did the only thing we could—we came to Florida so Pablo could look for a job around the polo grounds."

"And he found one?" Sylvia asked. Virginia nodded. "So why no happily ever after?"

"Pablo's father got sick. He was needed at home, but I was too pregnant to go." She forked up some coleslaw, chewed it, and tried to swallow, but it was hard to do with the knot in her throat from all the emotions she was suppressing.

"Mama? What happened next?"

"He stayed until you were born. He was so happy. I was so happy. But his daddy was getting worse, and so we went to Argentina."

"We? As in you and Pablo—"

"And you. It wasn't easy. I didn't speak a word of Spanish. The people there didn't really care for the blond *gringa* who had ruined their son. I wasn't happy, and he knew it, but there was nothing we could do with his daddy that sick."

"How long were you there?" Sylvia asked, and Virginia could see that her daughter was trying to recollect any memories of Argentina, but she had been too young for their time there to have made a lasting impression.

"You were seven months old when I left Argentina and came back to Florida. Pablo's daddy was hanging on, and they had reached some kind of peace about his polo."

Sylvia slashed the air with her hands. "I don't get it, Mama. If you loved him—"

"I *did* love him and he loved me," she said, the threat of tears nearly choking her, making her voice tight.

Her daughter laid her hands over hers, gave them a reassuring squeeze. "So why didn't you—"

"Stay together? Pablo's family depended on him. It killed me every time he left to go back to Argentina after the winter polo season ended. I think it killed him too. You were two when we finally realized that having an on-again-off-again marriage wasn't going to work. We went to the courthouse together to file the papers. It was probably the hardest thing we ever did together."

Sylvia patted her mother's hand and said nothing else. Virginia was thankful for that. She didn't think she could have handled Sylvia being her ballistic and sometimes harsh self.

Long moments passed before Sylvia softly asked, "Why didn't you tell me, Mama? Why?"

The pain was finally there in her daughter's voice, making it difficult for her to speak. Virginia fought the tightness in her own throat. "We thought it would be better to make a clean break. You were too young to remember and . . ." Virginia swallowed hard before continuing. "Maybe we couldn't accept the end of it. Accept that we couldn't make it work, even though we both loved each other so much."

"But all those years I thought—"

"I couldn't have handled you being like so many other children, hoping that their divorced parents would reconcile. I'm sorry I hurt you like that," Virginia admitted.

Amazingly, Sylvia seemed to understand. "Being the way I am, I probably would have asked all the time. But let me ask you something now. What makes this time around with Pablo different?"

"Different? Everything's different. I'm not that needy

little girl anymore and he's . . . changed, but still the same somehow," she said.

"The same in a good way?" Sylvia pressed.

"Yes, in a good way. He's honorable. Faithful and just too damned sexy for words," Virginia said, the latter in an effort to lift the maudlin tone the evening had taken.

Sylvia knew her well enough to understand. "My friends thought he was a certified hottie. Which is like, eewwww."

Virginia chuckled. "A hottie, huh? I definitely think so."

"You're going on a proper date with him, aren't you?" Sylvia asked.

"Yes. Does that bother you?" she said and shot a quick look at her daughter.

Sylvia chewed her food, almost pensive. "I just don't want you to get hurt again."

Virginia chuckled harshly. "Honey, that makes two of us."

"So you do know what to do, Mama? Right?"

"Do? As in—"

"Sex, Mama. I mean if it gets that far," Sylvia said.

Virginia sat back, considering her daughter. Sylvia was clearly conflicted. "And if it did get that far? What would you think about that?"

"I'd support whatever you decided to do because I love you, Mama. I want you to be happy."

"I want the same for you, Sylvia. You know that, don't you?"

"I do, Mama. I do."

Her mother and father on a date. Maybe even having sex. A scary thought and yet, as Sylvia gazed at her mother out of the corner of her eye, she realized it was what her mama had to do. She had to scratch that thirty-year itch so that she could either find satisfaction or decide that it was time to put an end to her suffering.

"So where is he taking you?" Sylvia asked.

"Excuse me?" Virginia paused with her fork halfway up to her mouth.

"A restaurant? A movie? Not a hotel, I hope. This is a *first* date, isn't it? You wouldn't want him to think you were loose."

"Loose? Honey, we've had a baby together. I'm not sure loose applies anymore . . . except maybe to parts of me that used to be tight," her mama said and chuckled sexily. "Besides, at our ages—"

"Mama. You are still a desirable woman," Sylvia said.

Her mother's eyes narrowed as she examined her daughter. "You're serious, aren't you?"

Sylvia nodded. "I truly am. You can't let lust rule your emotions," she said and was painfully reminded about how she had let her need for Carlos lead her wrong.

"Lust, huh? At my age—"

"Mama! You are only forty-six, and since sixty is like the new forty, then you are—"

"In the prime of my life. You know they say a woman in her forties is at her sexual peak?" she teased.

"Peak, huh? Just remember that after all those peaks are some pretty nasty drop-offs." She emphasized the point by making a diving motion with her hand.

Her mother smiled and shook her head. "It's not all negative with men. I had hoped meeting your daddy might show you that."

"Maybe that was the original reason you did it, but it's not the only reason now, is it?"

"No, it isn't. The moment I saw him, so many memories came racing back. Fond memories." Her mother's tone was wistful, and a faraway look came into her eyes. "When it was good, it was very good. But when it was bad—"

"It was awful."

They both started laughing and resumed eating, the talk turning to other things until her mother suggested they turn on the movie. Sylvia placed her plate on the coffee table and grabbed the DVD her mama had chosen—*Seabiscuit.*

Sylvia hesitated, turned, and looked at her mama while holding up the DVD case. "You've got to be kidding."

"There's nothing better than a man riding a horse," her mama teased and tossed her a wink.

"Mama. Can't you get your mind off him for one second?"

"No," Virginia playfully teased, and after Sylvia had gotten the DVD running, she returned to the couch, picked up her wine, and sat back down.

As the titles for the movie played, Sylvia said, "Pablo was rather amazing today. Even with the fall."

"Was it a bad one?" Virginia asked and winced in sympathy.

"Not too bad. He knew just what to do," Sylvia admitted, albeit reluctantly. She had thought badly of Pablo for so long, that anything different was . . . difficult.

"After so many years, that's not a surprise. He's a ten, you know. That's the highest rank—"

"A polo player can have. I know. Someone told me today." She paused for a second and wondered aloud, "Is that what he always wanted? To be a ten?"

"That was always his dream," her mother admitted.

"And yours? What was your dream?"

Virginia sighed sharply. "My dream? To leave that backwater town and make something of myself."

"So you did it. You fulfilled your dream."

"I just never expected that I would do it alone, you know?" Her mother leaned forward and examined Sylvia carefully before finally asking, "What's your dream?"

"Mine? To be a real reporter and not just do fluff," she said.

"And to do that—"

"I probably need to move to a different magazine. Or one of the bigger local papers. I want to have people take my work seriously, and I'm not sure that will happen where I am," she admitted.

"Is that why you're working on this new story—the one about Carlos and his . . ."

"Partner. Riley was his partner. The cop who was killed was working with them as well."

"Is that the only way Carlos fits into your dream—as a means to an end?"

Harsh, but Sylvia knew she might just deserve it. "Carlos and I . . . it's complicated right now."

"But what if it wasn't?"

She was so not sure of what it was . . . except difficult. There was even the possibility that she liked it that way because it kept her from thinking about how much she missed him. How in that short period they had been living together, she at times had dared to imagine if it could be a Happily-Ever-After with him because he brought her . . . peace, she thought. At night, in the morning. When she lay beside him, rest came to her heart.

"Sylvia?" her mother pressed when she delayed.

She gulped. "When you said you hadn't pictured achieving your success alone . . . Was Pablo the one you imagined by your side?"

"Yes," her mother answered quickly. "I imagined you and him. All of us as one big happy family."

"You and I were happy . . . *are* happy," Sylvia reminded her.

Her mother laid a hand on her leg and patted it. "We are happy. You're my best friend. I wouldn't change that for the world."

Sylvia smiled. "Have you thought about what you'll wear?" she said, wanting to be supportive, since for her entire life, her mother had been nothing but understanding.

"Wear?"

"Yes, for your big date. What are you going to wear?"

Virginia shrugged. "I haven't given it much thought."

"You haven't thought about it? It's your first real date with him and—"

"Not really a first date, since we've had lunch and did a few other things together. Besides, I don't want to make a big deal about it."

Sylvia snorted. "Mama. The man you have lusted after for nearly thirty years is now back in your life and you don't want to make a big deal about it?"

Virginia grabbed the remote for the DVD and paused the movie, not that they had really been watching it anyway. "Since you're clearly not going to leave this alone, would you like to help me pick something out?"

Sylvia jumped up off the couch and held out her hand. "I thought you'd never ask."

It was Monday night, and Pablo would be here any second to pick her up.

Virginia slowly did a twirl before the full-length mirror, inspecting the dark blue Michael Kors dress that she and Sylvia had selected on Saturday night. The front of the dress flattered the full curves of her breasts and hips, thanks to the graceful fall of the navy silk. Almost staid compared to the back of the dress, she thought as she turned once more and glanced over her shoulder at the back.

Or rather, the lack of a back. Except for the silk along her shoulders and the spill of silk below the small of her back and down her buttocks, the rest of her back was bare. Just creamy, pale skin against the darkness of the fabric.

Is it a trifle much? Virginia wondered.

Sylvia had said the dress showed off all her best features, but was that what she wanted? Did she want Pablo to look at her and lust? Want to touch? Want to do more than just touch?

They weren't youngsters anymore with the impatience of youth. They were adults who'd had their share of experiences and knew just what sex was all about. Who were painfully aware of what happened when you let sex overtake common sense.

And this dress . . .

She twirled again and imagined the look in his eyes as he saw her. Saw the back. Put his hands there.

Screw sensible, she thought.

23

Just another Monday, Sylvia thought as Tori raised her mojito and said, "To life, love, and always being *amigas.*"

They clinked their glasses together and immediately launched into a discussion about the news that Adriana and Riley were thinking of making their living together a permanent arrangement.

"So this thing with Riley and you . . . it's been good?" Sylvia asked as she snagged a skewer of beef satay from the platter of appetizers they had ordered.

"Duh, of course it has," Adriana admitted with a broad smile.

Sylvia winced, thinking that Riley still might be a dirty cop, and risked a glance at Tori, who met her gaze and forced a smile, aware of Sylvia's predicament. "Well, I'm happy for you."

Adriana's head snapped back. "Wait a second. You're happy that I'm happy with a man? What happened to 'Men are dogs'? What about—"

"Maybe I've had a change of heart," Sylvia confessed, because in part, it was true. Ever since her discussion with her mother on Saturday night, she had reconsidered a lot of what she had previously thought about her father. Lain awake at night in her big empty bed, wishing that it wasn't empty. That Carlos was there beside her, his big body spooning against hers while they talked.

Maybe there, in the dark of the night, she could forget all the problems in her life and could admit to him that she believed in him, no matter what.

"*Cuidado, chicas.* This must be some kind of pod person talking and not Sylvia," Juliana teased.

"No pod person. It's just that Mama and I . . . We had a talk on Saturday night. I learned a lot of interesting things." She gulped down a good part of her mojito and experienced a moment of brain freeze from the chill of the drink.

"Must have been pretty major stuff, Sylvita. Care to spill?" Tori said and snared a small egg roll from the appetizer platter.

With a shrug, she said, "Mama and Pablo were married for a few years."

Knives and forks clattered to plates as her statement registered. It was Adriana who spoke first.

"You're rather calm about this revelation."

Sylvia picked up the satay skewer and took a bite before saying, "What am I supposed to do?"

"Rant," Adriana retorted.

"Rave," Juli added.

"Reconsider?" Tori asked, eyeing her with concern.

"Definitely the latter. As for the first two, maybe I've mellowed," she said to her friends.

"*Sin duda.* A pod person," Juliana muttered and picked up her mojito.

As Sylvia examined all her friends, she met Adriana's gaze, but was unable to hold it, guilt rising up faster than anything else.

"Does that mean that you're maybe reconsidering your relationship with Carlos?" Adriana asked.

Time to get it over with. "You know we broke up and nothing that's happened will change that."

Raising a glass, as if in a toast, Juliana said, "Now this is the Sylvia we know and love."

Tori shook her head. "We do love you, which is why we want the best for you."

"What if Carlos is what's best for you?" Adriana chimed in.

"Maybe he is," Sylvia finally admitted, bringing shock to the faces of her friends. "Maybe there could be something more there eventually, but right now . . . We need some time to think things through."

"I guess you've got a lot going on," Tori immediately said, trying to defuse the situation.

Sylvia picked up on Tori's cue to shift the topic away from Carlos, and since she needed to keep the discussion away from Riley as well, it left just one topic to discuss.

"Mama and Pablo have a date tonight."

"A date?" Juli asked. "As in a business date or a date date?"

"They were looking at papers when they came by on Friday night," Adriana explained.

Sylvia nodded. "Probably real estate stuff. Pablo bought a place out on Key Biscayne—one of my mama's favorite properties. But no, this one's a date date."

"Did he buy the property for her, you think?" Tori said. She finished her mojito and as she realized all their glasses were almost empty, waved at the waiter to bring another round.

Sylvia thought about Tori's question, but then shook her head. "I don't think so. Just dumb luck."

"So, let me get this," Adriana began, counting down each item on a perfectly manicured finger. "One. He decides to linger in Miami. Two. He buys the house of her dreams and . . . Three. He's taking her on a date date."

"A maybe-we'll-like-each-other-so-much-we'll-go-home-and-have-sex date?" Juli suggested.

Sylvia waved her hands in the air. "Mama is a sensible woman. She knows what to do on her first date with a man."

"And you're just fine with that?" Adriana teased.

"I guess I am mature enough to deal with the thought that my mama may become sexually active once again," Sylvia said.

Adriana arched an eyebrow. "Really? You are truly okay with this?"

"Of course not. But I love my mama and want her to be happy."

"That's very . . . mature, *sabes*," Juli said and spooned some shrimp and cashews onto her plate.

"Right. Mature. That must explain why I feel like a mama on the night of her daughter's first date," Sylvia said and motioned to the center of the table. "And on that note, pass the moo shu, please."

"I sense something else there," Adriana said and handed Sylvia the platter.

Sylvia paused for a moment. "Maybe there is. Maybe I'm a little jealous that Mama may have found someone to love. Maybe I wish it were me."

"It could be," Adriana immediately shot back.

Sylvia could have argued, only she knew her friend was right. It could be, but not until she proved Carlos was innocent.

Pablo arrived at the door to Virginia's condo right on time, looking decidedly too handsome in a dark gray silk suit. The gray had just a tinge of olive in it, as did the lighter gray cotton shirt he wore. That slightest hint of green brought out the intense color of his eyes. His caramel hair was ruthlessly brushed back from his face, exposing the chiseled lines of his jaw and cheeks.

"GinGin? Is something wrong?" he asked at her too long perusal.

"I'm sorry. I was just . . . admiring," she admitted.

He laughed and shook his head. "You always were direct, *amor*. And may I say that you look wonderful?"

Bending at the waist, he placed a rather chaste kiss on her cheek and held his arm out. She looped her arm through his, and they rode the elevator down to the lobby. In front of the building, a limo waited for them.

"I thought it might be nicer if I didn't let driving distract me from talking with you," he explained

The driver opened the door for her, and she slipped in. Pablo walked around and got in on the other side of the car. Once they were seated and the car was moving, Pablo popped open the bar. "Would you care for—"

"I don't drink. I like to keep my wits about me," she reminded him, but he just grinned.

"I was about to say, 'Would you like some sparkling cider?' Nonalcoholic?" As he said it, he poured the cider into a champagne glass and offered it to her.

She took the glass, waited for him to pour himself one, and they raised their glasses. "To a new start."

Virginia scrutinized him. "Is that what you think this is? A new start?"

He shrugged, his broad shoulders stretching the fine fabric of the suit. "If you're willing to give it another try. Sylvia says—"

"Sweet Lord, please do not get into what Sylvia says. I don't know where that girl gets her ideas," Virginia said, picking up her glass and offering up a new toast. "To our daughter. May she find someone to keep her occupied so that she stops meddling in our lives."

"Here, here," he said and clinked his glass with hers. After a sip, he said, "She warned me about hurting you."

Virginia took a big gulp of her drink and motioned to him with the glass. "You had better watch out then. She is probably strong enough to kick some ass. I pity poor Carlos when she's mad."

Pablo considered her over the rim of his glass. "Is Carlos her . . . *novio?*"

"She and Carlos have an on-again-off-again relationship. I think they're going through an off phase right now."

Pablo paused for the longest moment before asking, "Are we on again?"

"Maybe."

Pablo chuckled. "Beats a no."

The motion of the car slowed, but as the driver eased into the turn, she slipped on the seat toward Pablo, bumping into his arm and spilling some of his cider onto his pants. She quickly brushed at the liquid to keep it from penetrating, but she couldn't fail to notice the hard muscles beneath the fabric. Her strokes slowed, until her hand rested on his thigh.

Pablo leaned forward and put down his glass, then cradled her cheek. Lightly he ran his thumb along her skin there, his green eyes alive with emotion. Bending his head, he finally kissed her, and she let herself savor the kiss. She opened her mouth to the possessive thrust of his tongue and returned the caress by running her tongue along his lips.

The car rocked back and forth for a moment as they went over a large bump, shattering the moment. They both pulled away, seemingly surprised by how quickly passion had risen.

Virginia wondered where he was taking her as bump after bump jostled them in the back of the car.

"Sorry. The road needs more work than I thought," he said and braced one hand on the frame of the privacy window and another around her shoulders to steady her.

Virginia looked out the window and realized they were at the estate that Pablo had just purchased from her. She wrinkled her brows and asked, "What are we—"

"I thought you might like to see the plans I had for this place."

"Plans?" she said, worried that he would want to demolish the nearly century-old structure.

The car pulled up to the front door of the building with one last bone-jarring thud.

"Note to self. Have them lay more gravel in the road," Pablo teased as he stepped from the car.

The driver opened her door, but Pablo was immediately there, holding out his hand. She slipped her hand into his, and he then tucked it into the crook of his arm and guided her up the broad steps of the Mediterranean Revival villa. The limestone steps were still in good shape, but the rest of the home needed an assortment of repairs, many of them major, for the building to be habitable again. It was the reason why so many people had planned on tearing it down.

Virginia hoped Pablo's plans were different because she loved the old building and at the owner's behest, had steered away more than one prospective buyer whose plans involved demolishing the property. Pablo's offer, however, had been too much for the owners to refuse, no matter what his intentions.

Pablo pushed open the large front wooden door. The Florida weather and insects had eaten away at its former glory, making it appear almost like balsa wood. Pablo hit a switch, and lights flared to life within the interior court-yard of the building. Bare bulbs were strung all along the perimeter. A large table covered in blueprints sat next to the fountain in the center of the courtyard.

Pablo led Virginia toward the fountain. At the table, Pablo dropped her hand and flipped a few of the large blueprint pages until he arrived at the architect's rendering of the final structure—the villa lovingly restored to its former grandeur. She breathed a heavy sigh of relief, which grabbed Pablo's attention.

"You don't like it?" he said, a worried look on his face.

"No, I like it. Very much. For a moment I was worried that you planned on taking it down," she confessed, walking up to the table and lovingly running her fingers along the drawing.

"Just because a lady is a little older and possibly difficult doesn't mean you discard her," he said, the tone in his voice playful.

She jabbed him in the ribs. "A gentleman wouldn't bring up a lady's age."

"I see that you're not denying the difficult part." He raised an eyebrow while rubbing at his ribs.

Virginia smiled. "Difficult is my middle name, Pablo. Don't forget it."

"How could I?" Pablo placed his hand at the small of her back. His hand was warm, his palm rough, as he applied gentle pressure and turned her in the direction of the door leading to the back of the home, where a large limestone patio opened onto the Atlantic.

She followed his lead—feeling a little too much like one of his polo ponies—and walked out the door and onto the patio.

Surprisingly, someone had already leveled the large limestone slabs, which had at one time been all out of kilter. Toward the seawall, matching new slabs edged the top of it, and the decaying wood pilings of the Venetian-style dock had been replaced with brand-new ones. But what caught her attention more than anything was the candlelit table set for two at the center of the patio. Off to the side was a serving cart where low blue flames burned beneath silver serving platters.

She looked up at him. "This is . . . romantic."

"I hoped you would approve," he said with a wide smile.

Virginia faced him, alternately pleased and annoyed by his actions. "You understand that while the candlelight and the moon, the dinner and all these romantic things might sway one of your twenty-somethings—"

"GinGin, contrary to what you believe, girls—"

"Women, Pablo," she warned.

With a nod, he continued. "*Women* my daughter's age don't interest me. I prefer my ladies older and well . . . more difficult. Infinitely more complex. So, are you staying or going?"

Damned if she did and damned if she didn't. But better to take the risk than never love at all, right?

She slipped her hand from his, and a disappointed

look swept across his face. The look vanished as she said, "So what's for dinner?"

He gallantly bent at the waist and invited her to join him at the painted wrought iron table and chairs. The chairs were placed close together and faced the dark blue waters. Across the way in the distance were the lights from downtown Miami and the Rickenbacker Causeway. To the left, a few scattered lights from homes twinkled beside the natural darkness of the park.

It was quiet on this part of the key, with only the slap-slap sounds of the water against the stone seawall and the distant hum of a boat's motor.

Virginia shot a peek at the night sky, a velvety black satin studded with sparkling stars. "It's a beautiful night," she said, and sat as he pulled out one of the chairs for her.

"It is now," he replied with a smile. He walked to the serving cart and began dishing out food.

"What? No waiter? That's highly domestic of you," she teased.

Pablo returned to the table with two plates piled high with a salad. "Nothing domestic at all, *amorcito*. I just didn't want anyone around to interrupt us."

Interrupt, huh? she thought to herself. Pablo clearly had ideas about where the night would lead. She glanced at him out of the corner of her eye, observed him as he ate, but he caught her perusal and met her gaze.

"Something wrong?" He put his fork down and wiped his mouth with a napkin.

"What are we doing here?" she wondered aloud.

"I suspect 'having dinner' is not the answer you want to hear."

She nodded, and he grabbed a bottle of wine from the center of the table and poured himself a glass. After a sip, he bobbed his head in approval. "Excellent vintage. It's one of the first batches from my vineyard."

"Your vineyard? I don't recall that your family—"

"Owned one? They didn't. Many years ago I decided to diversify, and this was one of those ventures." He again picked up the glass and took a sip.

Virginia reached out, grabbed her empty wineglass and held it out to him. "May I?"

"Really? I thought you didn't—"

"One glass isn't enough to get me in trouble. Besides, I get the sense this vineyard is important to you." Once he had filled the glass about halfway, Pablo stopped and waited for her to take a sip.

She swirled the wine around in the glass and then took a moment to smell the bouquet. Fruity, but full-bodied. She sampled the wine. Robust with hints of berries and maybe even a touch of vanilla. Definitely hearty and complex.

"Very good. Is it available in the States?" she asked and placed the glass down.

"This is from the first shipment. We have to wait and see how it does with the critics."

Virginia forked up some more salad but paused with the fork halfway to her mouth. She faced him and said, "Do you know how to make a millionaire?"

Pablo's brows knitted together as he considered her question. "No. How?"

"Start with a billionaire and have him invest in a vineyard," she said with a devilish grin.

Pablo laughed out loud. "Very true. But some things are worth taking a risk."

Despite the humorous tone in his voice, she understood that the risk he spoke of wasn't just the vineyard.

The night progressed leisurely, with the two of them

talking, mostly about the villa and the renovations, and sharing the delicious meal and, of course, Pablo's wine. She was almost sorry when Pablo took away the dishes for the dessert, since she hated for the interlude to end.

"This has been lovely," she said, fiddling with her napkin as it sat on the tabletop.

He covered her hand with his. "Who says the night is over?"

As he twined his fingers with hers, he stood and led her to the lower landing of the patio near the water. She realized there was a small boom box on the side railing of the veranda.

Pablo turned it on, and the low melodious tones of the music drifted through the night. With an impatient tug on her hand, he led her to the center of the landing.

Virginia stumbled on one of the slabs, but Pablo caught her in his arms.

"I must have that fixed," he said as he wrapped his arms around her waist and brought her close.

She laid her head against his chest and swayed with him to the nearly indistinct sounds of the music. The low bass beats carried through the night air. Or maybe it was the beat of her heart. Of his. Low and steady. Close against her breast.

He moved one hand up and placed it in the middle of her back. The skin of his hand felt hot. The roughness of it was enticing.

She raised her head and met his gaze. His eyes seemed an even darker green in the dim light, but his smile was brilliant as he asked, "Are you having a nice time?"

With a nod, she said, "Very nice. There's only one thing that might make it even nicer."

His smile broadened and he dipped his head until his

lips were only an inch from hers. "*De verdad?* And what would that be?"

She raised herself on tiptoe, and with a whisper against his lips, she said, "This."

The kiss began innocently enough, with the simple meeting of their lips. Followed by another kiss and then another until they were straining toward each other, hungry for more.

"Maybe it's time we went somewhere—"

"More private?" she offered. Without missing a beat, Virginia snagged his hand and led him back toward the limo. Pablo asked the driver to take them for a ride around town.

He helped her into the backseat, slipped in beside her, and immediately put up the privacy screen. Then he reached for her and eased her onto his lap where once again, they resumed the kiss.

Virginia opened her mouth to his, accepted the thrust of his tongue. He tasted like his wine and the sweet berries they had shared for dessert. In between kisses, she said, "Sylvia warned me about this. That you would be a scoundrel on this date."

"Really? But who kissed who first, *amorcito?*" he teased and worked his way to the edge of her mouth and then down to the crook of her neck and shoulder.

She held his head to her, shuddered as he sucked there, and then soothed the spot with a kiss. "That feels good."

"Hmm. I'd like to feel that too," he confessed, and with clumsy fingers, she undid his tie and shirt collar, bent her head, and sucked on him.

His skin was salty. Undeniably masculine. The muscles of his upper shoulder firm. She bit down and he groaned, slipped his hand to the middle of her back, and urged her closer.

But the only way to accomplish that was to straddle his legs, which she did, bringing the hard length of his erection to nestle between her legs.

She paused at the pressure of him there and looked down at him. "You do have protection, don't you? I promised Sylvia I'd be responsible."

Pablo chuckled and laid his hands at her waist, keeping her hips immobile. "I've heard it said that children get in the way of romance. I just never thought it would happen quite like this."

Virginia laughed and cradled his face in her hands. "Is this a romance or are we two sad, old people grasping at our youth?"

The mirth on Pablo's face softened but didn't completely recede. With care and patience, he slipped his hand beneath the edge of her dress and slowly moved it upward, until he was cupping her naked breast in his hand. Her nipple beaded immediately, and he smiled at that.

"Old? I've always heard that a woman in her forties is at her prime sexual peak." As if to emphasize his point, he grasped the tip of her nipple and gently caressed it, drawing a gasp from her.

He reached up with his other hand, undid the single button at her neck that held up the front of her dress. As he did so, the fabric spilled downward, baring her breasts to him. He cupped both of them and ran his thumbs over the tips.

She sucked in another breath and bit her lip. When he bent his head and kissed one breast and then the other, she cradled his head to her, but she nearly fell off his lap when the car swerved to one side.

Pablo reached out and braced a hand on the door to keep them on the seat. As their position steadied, he looked up at her. "Sorry."

She urged him to kiss her once again, needy of his mouth on hers. But as another bounce had them holding on to each other for balance, she said, "This is insane, you know."

Pablo pulled away and reached for the front of the dress to put it back on, but she stopped him. When he looked at her quizzically, she clarified, "It's insane to be getting bounced around in the back of this limo when we have a perfectly comfortable bed waiting for us back at my house."

 *Sylvia lay in bed,* running through every-thing she had to do that day.

Give Harry a report on the progress of the article.

Try to track down Carlos and get his side of the story. Again.

Call her mama and find out how her "date" with Pablo had gone.

The first one would be easy to do, since she now actually had enough information for the beginnings of a story. Knowing Harry, however, he would want more. He would want definitive proof of the guilt and innocence of everyone involved. Which was in part the reason for item number two on her list, namely seeing Carlos. With the information she already had in hand, he might finally be willing to speak with her about the case. Confirm what she had come to suspect—that Simon Davis had wanted him and Riley dead. Maybe he would even tell her what it was that Simon had said in his last few minutes of life.

But she wasn't sure Carlos would be willing to speak with her, heartless bitch that he thought her to be.

In some ways, Sylvia didn't really blame him. She knew she'd been distant and driven him away. She finally forced herself out of bed.

She walked to the kitchen and put up a pot of coffee. While she waited, she stared at the phone, wondering whether to call her mother. It was nearly ten o'clock. Not too early. Her mama would have already been at work for a few hours, early riser that she was.

Picking up the phone, Sylvia dialed her mother's number. Her mother's secretary answered.

"Hi, Celeste. Is my mother around?" Sylvia asked.

A pregnant pause followed her question. Finally, Celeste said, "Your mother called and said she was taking the day off. You may want to try her cell phone."

Sylvia thanked the woman and hung up. Her mother never took the day off. As she was about to dial her mother's cell phone, it occurred to Sylvia that Virginia might be otherwise occupied on her atypical day off.

Sylvia placed the phone back in its cradle quickly, deciding that the call to her mama could wait until later.

At the magazine office an hour later, Harry reviewed the proposal for the article Sylvia had done. The way he held the papers up to his face precluded any observations on what he thought, but the occasional harrumph or grunt didn't inspire confidence.

Sylvia fidgeted in her chair, waiting for his decision.

With a surge of action, Harry slapped the papers on the desk, making her jump.

"You've got the makings of a great story, Sylvia. More than what I expected from you. Only . . ." He picked up the papers once more and buried his face in them. After a few more grunts, he once again lowered the draft of her story but motioned with the papers in her direction. "We need more."

She clasped her hands in her lap and nodded. "I know that, Harry. I still need to interview a few more people. But there's something else."

"You're sleeping with this Carlos character, aren't you? That's not good for either you or the story."

Never let it be said that Harry is thoughtful and compassionate, she thought.

Inclining her head deferentially, she said, "We were . . . involved, but we're not involved anymore."

"Your journalistic integrity demands that—"

"I be impartial. I understand that, believe me. Which is why I'm going to ask a favor."

Harry's bushy gray eyebrows shot up. "A favor? You? Well this is a first."

Anger surged through her at the delight in his tone. For years the two of them had battled for control over her articles, with Sylvia somehow managing to get her way. She hated having to ask but knew it was what she had to do.

"It's what's right for this story, Harry. And the story is what's important, isn't it?"

After his nod, she continued. "Facts are subjective, contrary to what most people believe. They can be skewed to make the story what you want. So I need someone to check over all the facts I've got there and make sure that I haven't let my personal feelings twist the story into something it shouldn't be."

Harry ran a pudgy finger across the words on the page before finally looking up at her. "Doable, but we still don't have enough information."

"I know we don't. I'm going to try and meet with—"

"Your ex? Will he cooperate?"

Sylvia shook her head. "I don't know, but whether he does or doesn't, I will find someone to corroborate this story."

Harry's eyes narrowed as he examined her, making her uncomfortable with his perusal. She squirmed in her chair and finally said, "I'm a journalist. I know what's expected of me."

To her surprise, Harry chuckled and tossed the papers back in her direction. "I never doubted you would get to the bottom of this story, no matter what."

"Thanks, Harry," she said. She scooped the papers off his desk, but as she turned to walk away, she stopped and looked back at her editor. "Why didn't you doubt me?"

"Because only someone with a heart would let her emotions get in the way of the story." He laughed.

Sylvia raced out of his office. As she hurried down the hall to her cubicle, the heels of her Jimmy Choos beat a rhythm that echoed Harry's sentiments.

Heart-less-bitch. Heart-less-bitch. Heart-less-bitch.

Virginia didn't want to move. She was just too sore.

Maybe Sylvia had been right, that she was too old for this kind of thing.

Until Pablo reached around and laid his hand in the middle of her stomach, pressing her back into his morning erection.

"Umm, Pablo?" she said, but that turned into a moan as he reached down, parted her lips, and found the still-sensitive center of her. He caressed her slowly.

"*Amorcito?* This is what you had in mind when you called to take the day off," he said as he trailed a line of kisses along the top of her shoulder.

Virginia laid her hand on his as it rested between her legs, intending to stop him, only . . .

Passion flared to life, making her legs quiver. Dragging a gasp from her that made it impossible for her to deny the pleasure he could give her. She managed a weak protest when he switched places, urging her hand downward so she could touch herself, but then he said, "I think you'd like me to be doing something else."

He moved his now free hand up to tease the tip of her breast. That yanked another moan from her.

"Pablo, love. I'm not sure—"

"Don't stop this, Virginia. *Por favor.*"

She turned her head, looked up at him, and met his gaze. An intense gaze filled with so much need, she realized she couldn't say no, but not just because of him. Because she saw her own need reflected back in the dark emerald green of his eyes.

Virginia shifted her hips, and his erection slipped between her thighs. Lowering her hand, she stroked him. Held him to the wetness and heat between her legs, and he groaned, dropped his head, and kissed the side of her face.

"You are beautiful, GinGin. I want—"

His breath exploded from his lips as she guided him into her. He filled her and the pressure of him inside nearly undid her. But Virginia needed more. So much more.

"Finish it, Pablo. Finish what you were going to say."

"I want forever, Virginia," he said, sending them both over the edge again with a forceful thrust of his hips.

25

Sylvia dialed Carlos's cell phone for what seemed like the hundredth time that week. Days had gone by without his answering and without her getting any new information for her story.

Well, if Carlos wouldn't answer his cell phone, she would go straight to him. Shooting a glance at her watch, she realized it was early enough that he still might be at home. She didn't even bother with a shower, knowing that with Carlos being an early riser, he might not linger at his boat for long. Quickly, she slipped into jeans and a T-shirt, grabbed a jacket, and headed out the door.

Traffic heading toward Coconut Grove was blessedly light, as most were headed in the opposite direction toward Miami during the morning rush. But as she pulled into the lot for the marina, she didn't notice Carlos's distinctive and classic baby blue Corvette anywhere. Still, she parked and headed to the boat. It was all locked up.

He was gone already, but she took a guess at where he would be and headed back to South Beach, this time experiencing the bottleneck due to the toll and construction along the roadway. When she hit Fifth Street, she headed straight to David's on the corner, certain Carlos would have gone there for some coffee and the flattened Cuban bread toasts.

He had, but again, she had just missed him. A waitress informed her he'd left a few minutes ago. *Damn.* Glancing at her watch, Sylvia realized that with the traffic she had encountered, it was now just past nine.

But it was Wednesday, which meant that Adriana and Riley would be playing beach volleyball in about half an hour. It also meant that Carlos might drop by to watch the match, as Adriana had indicated he'd been doing ever since his release from the hospital.

Sylvia left her car parked by David's and walked down toward the beach.

Lummus Park is as busy as ever, she thought as she crossed Ocean Drive and walked down one of the trails through the park leading to the wider path near the low seashell-covered beach wall. In the grassy areas beside the smaller trail, people lay on blankets, enjoying a light ocean breeze and the shade of the palm and sea grape trees.

At the beach wall, Sylvia stopped to sit and peruse the path, hoping she would catch sight of Carlos down at the volleyball courts. Disappointment filled her as she realized that though Adriana and Riley were playing on the sand, Carlos was nowhere nearby.

Nevertheless she lingered on the seawall, appreciating the sunny morning and lack of humidity. Besides, if she maybe waited long enough, Carlos might show before the end of the match.

She watched from afar, appreciating the skill that Adriana and Riley exhibited on the court. Adriana wasn't tall, but she was athletic and determined. She dove into the sand, executing a perfect dig that allowed Riley to send the ball back deep into the other team's court.

As the two teams approached the net, Sylvia realized that it must have been the match point she had just seen, ending the game. She walked the twenty or so feet down to the wall by the court, just in time to meet Adriana and Riley as they came up off the sand.

Sylvia hugged her friend. "That was some great play."

"Have you been here for long?" Adriana asked.

"Not too long. Just came down to see—"

"He hasn't been here today," Riley said, and she sensed a chill coming from him.

"Oh. I was hoping—"

"There's a party for him this afternoon. At the Port O'Call," Riley added. She wondered why he was so forthcoming with information, when he clearly seemed to have an issue with her.

Adriana placed a hand on Riley's arm and asked, "Is everything okay?"

Riley glanced at her and smiled. "It is, Adriana. The guys are giving Carlos a farewell party. You know, since he decided to leave the force."

So he really went through with it, Sylvia thought.

"I'm glad that Carlos decided to settle down, even though it couldn't have been an easy choice," Adriana said and stroked her hand down Riley's muscled arm in a loving gesture.

Her words and actions caused a funny twist to Sylvia's stomach, which only became an even tighter knot when Riley glared her way and said, "Not an easy thing for him to do, but he thought he had something better waiting for him in civilian life."

Somehow she managed to ask past the lump in her throat, "What time is the party?"

"Planning to drop by?" Riley asked and raised one sandy eyebrow in challenge.

"Maybe."

She was prepared for Riley to out her, since he obviously knew she was investigating the shooting. She had kept from approaching him all this time because of his relationship with Adriana and her fear that once he knew, Adriana would become aware of what was happening, and it would harm their friendship.

Plus, Sylvia had suspected that interrogating Riley wouldn't have helped at all. As Carlos's best friend and a cop, he would have likely protected Carlos no matter what.

She was ready for him to tell her that she might not be welcome at the party, which she suspected she wasn't. But if he did so, there was no way she could help explaining to Adriana what was up. That would only cause a world of grief between the two of them that she had been trying to avoid all along by not approaching Riley.

She braced herself for those words. For the explosion that would follow, but instead Riley surprised her by saying, "He might like to see you there. Four o'clock."

"Four it is. Will you be there?"

"We'll *both* be there. Carlos is our friend," Adriana jumped in.

Sylvia forced a smile and hugged her friend. "I never forgot that, Adriana. I'll see you later."

Adriana whispered into her ear, "I'm always here for you, Sylvia. Don't forget that."

Her friend's words brought a glimmer of tears to her eyes, but Sylvia wouldn't acknowledge them. She stepped away from Adriana and with a curt nod to Riley, walked down the path and back toward her apartment. She had an afternoon assignment—a beach dance marathon being sponsored by a local community organization—but she would stop by the party for a little while first.

Of course, that was assuming they would even let her into Carlos's party. She was probably persona non grata if word had gotten around about her investigation.

But Riley had told her about the festivities. Riley had hinted at the fact that she should show her face. Would Riley set her up for a fall, especially since Adriana would be there?

In her gut Sylvia knew he wouldn't. While Riley was clearly not enamored of her because of everything that had gone on with Carlos, she sensed he loved Adriana too much to do anything to hurt her.

Which meant that she needed to get ready to face Carlos, even if he thought she didn't have a heart. Even if she had turned out to be a big disappointment.

But maybe it isn't too late to change that, she thought. *Maybe it isn't too late to let him know that I miss him.*

Hell, if her mother could seemingly make a go of it after nearly thirty years, why couldn't Sylvia after just a few short weeks?

On her way to the party, Sylvia spotted Carlos's vintage Corvette parked in front of the Port O'Call. Gathering herself, she paused, took a fortifying breath, and walked inside. As she did so, it seemed that everyone in the place turned to stare at her, stifling the merriment that had been going on within.

Carlos sat at the head of a long table to one side of the room. Adriana and Riley sat beside him. When Carlos saw Sylvia, he rose and walked toward her with a hesitant gait at first. But his gaze was trained on her, his eyes a dark, intense blue as he picked up his pace. Two large men came to stand before her, blocking her view.

She glanced upward and noticed that one of the men was Carlos's brother-in-law—Andres Lopez.

"*Niña*. What are you doing here?" Andres asked, but unlike last time, his tone lacked any humor or friendliness.

With a quick look at the man next to him, she noticed the hard lines of his face. They clearly didn't intend to move out of her way. It was, unfortunately, just the kind of welcoming committee she had been expecting.

"I came—"

"To see me," Carlos said as he slipped a hand between the two men and urged them to part. He held that hand out to her, and she took it. She walked with Carlos to a booth at the back of the bar. He gingerly eased onto the bench of the booth, his leg outstretched before him, as if it pained him today. She laid a hand on his thigh and felt the muscles bunched beneath. "Are you okay?"

"I've been better. And you?"

She wanted to say so much. That she had missed him in every way one could imagine. From his easy smile across a dinner table to the warmth of his body in bed. But pride kept her from it.

"You didn't return any of my calls."

He gave a negligent shrug. "I didn't think we had anything left to say to each other."

Inside of her, pain erupted squarely in the center of her chest. Smack in the middle of her heart, even though Carlos, like Harry, didn't think it existed.

Fighting the pain, she said, "What if there's more to say? What if . . . I don't want it to end."

"That all depends on you. What do you want?" With another grimace, he bent his leg, motioning for her to join him.

In a simple world, the answer might have been easy, but nothing between them had ever been easy. She slipped into the booth across from him, remembering how they had shared the space so intimately last time. "Are you asking Sylvia the woman—"

"Sylvia the reporter," he immediately answered, but as he noticed her pained reaction, he seemed to relent. Shaking his head, he laid his hand on the table, palm up, and she placed her hand there, offering a momentary truce.

"I don't think you had anything to do with Simon's death."

He ran his thumb over the back of her hand and in low tones, said, "I didn't. If I'd had the power to change things . . ." He lowered his gaze and shook his head.

Sylvia grasped his hand more tightly, trying to offer comfort. "Tell me what Simon said. What he did."

Carlos's head snapped up. His voice was rough with emotion when he spoke. "And ruin his reputation? Ruin what his boys think of him? He died a hero."

Sylvia cupped his cheek. The rasp of his beard was painfully familiar. "How can he be a hero? The witness I spoke to says Simon was the one who opened fire first."

Carlos's lips tightened into a harsh line. He moved his head away from her hand and eased his hand out from under hers. She immediately regretted the loss of the contact. "At the end, he made the right choice. He died because of it. Please let him lie in peace."

"I can't, nor can you. Randy Davis is accusing you of being dirty. Of killing his brother. He'll keep making that accusation until someone listens," she stressed, wanting him to understand that she was doing it for him. Trying to protect him.

"Worried about being scooped?"

The coldness in his voice shifted upward, creating a chill in his normally alive blue-green eyes that transferred itself to her heart. Killed whatever hope she had left that they could make a go of it.

"Think what you will, Carlos."

"What am I supposed to think? It seems to me that the only thing that's important to you is this story."

Had she really been so distant with him that he could think that? Couldn't he see that this story meant so much to her because of him?

"If you truly believe that, then I guess I'm done here."

She slipped from the booth, and without a backward glance or a look toward either Riley or Adriana, which was sure to earn her an inquisition sooner than she cared for, she fled the bar. If she hurried, she could make her afternoon assignment and after that, try to figure out what to do next.

The winners of the beach dance marathon were a fifty-something couple from Little Havana who managed to outlast the younger—and much more exuberant—competitors. Sylvia waited for the presentation of the prizes and took a moment to interview the winning couple, so she could add it to all the other notes and interviews she had conducted over the course of the last two hours. After the couple posed for a photo, and they snapped pictures of the check the organizers had received from a corporate sponsor, she told the photographer she was calling it a day. She tried hard not to think about her failed encounter with Carlos.

Nose buried in her notes, she walked off the sand and paused to sit on the beach wall, intending to at least get her opening line for the story set, when she noticed a cop pedaling toward her. A familiar female cop.

Alicia wheeled to a stop and dismounted from the bike. She unsnapped her helmet and whipped it off her head, let it dangle from her fingers as she approached.

"I heard that you crashed the party," Alicia said, eyes narrowed as she gazed at Sylvia.

Sylvia closed her notebook with a snap and slipped her pen into the spiral binding. "I didn't crash. I was invited."

Alicia guffawed at her comment. "Really? Carlos wasn't too happy when you got there and even less happy after."

"Which should please you." It annoyed her to think of Carlos and this attractive woman together. Even more, it hurt to imagine that Carlos would hook up with her again. Alicia would happily step in to fill the void, Sylvia realized.

With a sly smile, Alicia scrutinized her. Finally she said, "Carlos and you. Not that I like the idea, but . . . he likes you. Don't know why."

"But you do know about Simon, don't you? You've known all along."

Alicia's smile disappeared and she leaned forward until her nose almost bumped Sylvia's. "You've got *cojones, chica.* Maybe that's what's got Carlos so crazy about you." Alicia stepped back and crossed her arms. "What do you want to know about the night Simon died?"

Sylvia shook her head, unwilling to believe the other woman was suddenly being so accommodating. "Just like that?"

The other woman shrugged her shoulders and the skintight fabric of the bike police shirt rippled from the muscles beneath. "Carlos and I may be done—"

"Done as in over? As in you're finished?"

"Put in the proverbial fork if you'd like, but he's still a friend and you're hurting him." Her gloved hands clenched and unclenched on her arms, as if in warning about what she would do to Sylvia if Carlos continued to hurt.

But Alicia didn't need to warn her, since guilt and that inconvenient pain in the center of Sylvia's chest rose up again. She tamped both down and in a tone way calmer than what she was feeling, said, "What happened that night?"

Alicia looked away and her rough demeanor softened. "Simon had been freaked for days. We had been together the night before and . . ." She hesitated, and Sylvia could see what it was costing her to tell the story.

She laid a hand on Alicia's arm, wanting to offer her comfort. With a deep, shaky inhalation and a murmured "thanks," Alicia continued. "He broke it off with me. Told me he had made a lot of mistakes and wanted to make things right between him and his wife. He said he was sorry he had hurt me. That I should find someone who could make me happy.

"Carlos had nothing to do with Simon's death. Simon brought that all on himself."

Alicia slipped the helmet back on, and as she buckled it, she said, "There's a cop in IAD—"

"Internal Affairs? Why would they—"

"Carlos knew Simon was in trouble, but before he could do anything to help him, IAD got involved. Ask for Captain Morales. He'll give you what you're looking for."

Before Sylvia could ask anything else, Alicia hopped back onto her bike and pedaled away. Sylvia watched her go, feeling paranoid and wondering why the other woman had been helpful. Possibly too helpful. Was Alicia setting

Sylvia up for a bigger fall so she could fire up her old affair with Carlos again?

But if Morales was the man with the information that could clear Carlos . . .

Sylvia needed to put an end to the hurt, both Carlos's and hers.

26

The next day, Sylvia was in Morales's office, arguing with him about the release of the IAD file. "I've talked to the lawyers at the paper. The Freedom of Information—"

"Why do you want to do this?" Jesus Morales asked, his dark brown eyes boring holes into her with their intensity. His clasped hands rested on top of the file on his desk, fingers fisted tightly together. As he waited for her answer, he gave an impatient bounce of those hands against the papers.

"Someone has made some serious accusations against two police officers. Those accusations aren't going away."

"You think you're the best person to deal with these allegations?" Morales raised his thick eyebrows and glared at her again.

"Carlos and Riley are my friends. I want to see their names cleared."

"And what about Simon Davis? What will you do

about his name? About his family?" The tone of Morales's voice increased in intensity with each question.

She had asked herself the same questions dozens of times since beginning the investigation. She was no closer to knowing what she would do, basically because she didn't have the complete picture of what had happened that night.

"I will do what I can—"

"To protect his boys? To safeguard the memories of a father they will never get to know?" Morales was just shy of screaming as he continued to bounce his hands angrily on his desktop.

Sylvia raised her chin and met his gaze straight on. "Tell me what happened and I promise—"

"A reporter's promise? That's almost as good as a politician's," Morales said with a harsh laugh.

She wasn't about to be cowed by the police captain. "You can either tell me what happened or I can go see the magazine's lawyers."

She paused as Morales grudgingly slid the file across his desk toward her. She picked it up and as she opened it, he said, "You know that you can't reveal the identity of any officers on active undercover assignment."

She could have corrected him, since she knew Carlos and Riley were no longer on the force. But just as she had kept Carlos's identity secret for the last article, she intended to do the same this time with both of them. Simon Davis, however, was fair game.

Or was he? she thought as she began reading through the file.

The internal investigation filled in many of the gaps in what she knew about Simon's dealings with Javier and others like him. Simon had been pimping them out in exchange for a cut of the cash they paid for the drugs he provided them and their johns. When he wasn't pimping them, he was delivering shipments of drugs from the suppliers to the dealers in the clubs.

Carlos and Riley had been trying to uncover the source of the drugs when Carlos unwittingly discovered Simon's illicit activities the night he came to Javier's assistance as the drag queen was being pummeled by his surprised john. They had never expected that one of their own was the go-between for the drugs, nor did they know that Internal Affairs had already gotten wind of Simon's activities.

Or that IAD would ask them to help collar a fellow officer.

Sylvia paused and looked up at Captain Morales. "Why did you involve them in your internal investigation?"

Morales shrugged and leaned back in his chair, which creaked with the motion of his big body. He was at least six foot three inches of thick muscle. "Carlos and Riley are as straightforward as can be. No one would think of them as snitches."

"So Simon would trust them? Tell them what he was doing?"

"Carlos thought Simon would do the right thing if he knew that someone was onto him."

"But he didn't, did he?" Sylvia pressed. Morales merely gestured to the file in her hand.

Carefully, she read through Carlos's reports on his efforts to turn Simon back into one of the good guys. His frustration with Simon was obvious, as was his continued belief that the other cop would eventually do the right thing.

Which he had, she realized as she reviewed the transcript of Carlos's bedside interview. It had been taken with urgency, because no one had been sure whether or not Carlos would survive his injuries.

Captain Morales: Officer Davis returned fire?

Detective Ramirez: Davis fired first. Killed one suspect immediately.

Captain Morales: And after?

Detective Ramirez: Second suspect opened fire . . . hit Davis, Evans, and me . . . I returned fire.

Captain Morales: Officers Davis and Evans? Did they return fire?

Detective Ramirez: Davis . . . down. Riley still in line of fire . . . Pulled him to . . . safe location.

Captain Morales: What about the second suspect?

Detective Ramirez: Shooting. Don't know . . . hit him . . . or Riley . . .

Captain Morales: Detective Ramirez? Can you hear me? Detective?

Sylvia took a moment for a deep breath, needing to collect herself as she pictured Carlos wounded . . . again. As she imagined those moments for him and Riley. The fear. The pain. Their brotherhood even in a time of intense need.

Her hands shook as she continued onward, skimming through what some thought would be a deathbed interview. A cold sweat bathed her body until she got toward the end of the transcript, when Carlos provided the details of Simon Davis's last minutes of life.

Captain Morales: Davis regained consciousness?

Detective Ramirez: Said he . . . couldn't do it.

Captain Morales: Do what, Detective?

Detective Ramirez: Set up Riley and me. For a hit. Afraid we knew too much.

Captain Morales: He knew you were onto him?

Detective Ramirez: (Reporter's note: Detective nodded in response)

Captain Morales: Detective? Did Officer Davis—

Detective Ramirez: Hero . . . Saved me . . . Saved Riley . . .

Captain Morales: Are you saying Officer Davis fired to protect you and Officer Evans?

Detective Ramirez: (Reporter's note: Detective nodded in response)

Captain Morales: Are you sure, Detective Ramirez?

Detective Ramirez: Simon did . . . right thing. Saved us.

The next notes in the file reflected that further interrogation was impossible, as Detective Ramirez had become unconscious.

Her hands trembled as she closed the file, unable to read further, although she suspected there was likely a similar interrogation of Riley. Her gut was in a knot, and she struggled to draw yet another deep breath to control herself before facing Captain Morales again.

"Carlos and Riley were always clean."

Morales nodded, and she continued. "Simon Davis found out that they knew about him, but didn't know that IAD was already involved. He was instructed by his drug dealers to set up Carlos and Riley for a hit."

She wanted confirmation that she had the story straight. He nodded, but then said, "Officer Davis realized the error of his ways that night. Unfortunately, too late to save himself. He died a hero."

"A hero?" she asked, finding it hard to believe that any of the officers involved could think that.

Morales began his explanation. "We don't know why Davis did what he—"

"For the money. Why else?" Sylvia knew where the money had gone—to the account his wife had known nothing about.

Morales shrugged those thick shoulders again. "You're

probably right, but the important thing is—he could have let those two dealers kill Carlos and Riley. They had way more firepower and would have cut down the two men with little effort."

"Davis could have also stopped it well before that night."

"Maybe, but he was afraid of the consequences, until he realized what was about to happen to his fellow officers."

She tried to imagine what Simon must have been thinking in those last minutes as he walked toward the dealers, knowing that Carlos and Riley were behind him, aware that the two dealers were packing enough automatic weapons to take them down in the blink of an eye.

"He shot the first dealer to give Carlos and Riley a fighting chance."

Morales nodded, unclasped his hands, and laid them flat on his desk. "They barely managed to survive one perp with a Tec-9. Two? Highly unlikely. They weren't equipped to handle automatic weapons fire."

Simon had realized that. He must have been afraid of what would happen after he took down the first suspect. Afraid of the outcome, knowing that Carlos was aware of his activities.

"There's nothing in the file about what Simon Davis said, but the witness I spoke with . . . She said Simon was saying he was sorry."

"That's what the eyewitness said. Carlos didn't have much to add, even after he had stabilized and we continued the interrogation." Morales held out his hand for the file.

Sylvia passed it back, but as she did so, she asked, "You think there's more that Carlos isn't saying?"

"I think Detective Ramirez provided us with all the information necessary to complete our investigation. There may be other things—private things—that Officer Davis told him."

What did one dying man say to another? "Sorry" didn't seem like enough and yet, that's all the file indicated—that Simon had offered his remorse over and over again to his wounded companion. If he had said anything else, Carlos was clearly not revealing it.

Maybe it had been private things. Like a good-bye to Simon's wife and boys and maybe even Alicia. Private things she didn't need to know for the story she knew she could finally write.

She rose from the chair and offered her hand to the police officer. "Thank you, Captain Morales. You've helped clear up a lot of my questions."

The captain rose and shook her hand, but as he did so, he said, "Just remember that like the atom bomb, your report can cause mass destruction if unleashed improperly."

"I'll try to remember that, Captain Morales. I may need to have a fact-checker go over the file once my story is written. Will that—"

"Send them to me, Ms. Amenabar, along with a copy of the story you plan to run."

Sylvia yanked her hand out of his meaty one. "You can't censor what—"

He held up his hand to stop her. "I just want to prepare for the fallout."

27

As *Sylvia stared* at the empty screen on her laptop, she struggled with the consequences of her actions and their impact on those around her. She had done that all night long since speaking with Captain Morales. If the story was going to run in next month's magazine, she had less than a week to finish it.

No answers came to her.

No words.

After another half an hour of staring at the screen, she shut down the computer and changed into her running clothes. She wasn't really a fan of jogging, but when she was stuck, the physical exertion and fresh air helped to get her unstuck.

She walked out of her condo and headed down the block to Ocean Drive, where she crossed over to Lummus Park. In the park, she jogged beneath the palms and sea grape trees until she hit the wide winding path along the seawall. Once on the path, she turned toward Southpointe.

The late morning sun was strong and the humidity had already built to a level approaching uncomfortable. The only thing that kept it from becoming that way was a brisk breeze blowing off the ocean. It swept across the path and kept her cool.

Along the trail, she crossed other joggers, bikers, and inline skaters, together with people headed to the beach. Sometimes, however, a wind this strong blew in the Portuguese man-of-wars, making it impossible to swim and even walk along the edge of the water. The jellyfish, looking like discarded balloons, would litter the beach.

As she passed one of the playgrounds scattered every few blocks along the path, the delighted squeals and shouts of children at play on the swings and slides pushed her onward. They reminded her of Simon Davis's kids too much, so she quickened her pace, moving to the end of the park and back onto the sidewalk.

She kept on going, pacing herself as she neared Adriana's condo building across from Joe's Stone Crab. At the end of the street, she turned around and went back along the edge of Lummus Park until she was at the block for her condo, where she returned home.

Normally a jog helped her center herself, let her focus on what she had to do, but today it had accomplished little. As she showered, Sylvia considered the story, but as before, no answer came.

When she finished her shower, she dressed and walked to her office. She stopped on Washington Avenue to pick up a smoothie before going the last few blocks to Española Way and the magazine's offices. At her cubicle, she plopped into her chair and reviewed her snail mail, skimmed through the e-mails on her computer, listened to her phone messages, and finally, decided to see if Harry was available.

He might be a hard-ass, but his editorial senses were usually on the money.

The door to his office was closed. Never a good thing. She stopped by his secretary's desk.

"What's up, Carmela?" she asked as she leaned on the edge of the low cubicle.

"Mr. Davis is here. He called Harry yesterday and asked to come by," the older Latina said, not breaking away from her typing as she spoke.

"Davis? As in Randy Davis? As in *my* story?" She couldn't believe that Harry hadn't said anything to her about Randy Davis's visit. As she waited outside Harry's office, she paced, her steps measured at first, but as her anger intensified, so did her speed until Carmela called out, "*Niña, por favor.* The noise from those heels is like a bad conga band."

Sylvia whirled and leaned on the edge of the cubicle again. "Did Davis say what he wanted?"

Carmela finally raised her eyes from her computer screen. "Not a thing. Only that he wanted to see Harry."

Harry's door flew open and rebounded against the wall with a loud thud as Randy Davis rushed out, shaking his fist at Harry. "I'm calling a lawyer. You can't say those things about my brother."

Great. A lawsuit. If Harry killed the story . . .

Sylvia realized that maybe that wouldn't be a bad thing. It would certainly put an end to all the doubt and indecision that had kept her from sitting down to write the article.

Harry waddled to the door, clearly intending to follow Davis, but as he saw her, he stopped short and guiltily looked away, a bright red flush erupting across his cheeks.

"Isn't there something you want to tell me, Harry?"

"Get in here, Amenabar," he said with a toss of his balding head.

Sylvia followed him in, but when he motioned for her to take a seat, she remained standing before his desk. "Care to explain what Randy Davis was doing here and why you didn't see fit to include me in the conversation?"

"Not that I owe you any kind of explanation, but Davis called yesterday. He wanted to know how the story was going, and so I invited him to come by. I thought it was right to tell him in person." As he spoke, Harry shuffled various papers on his desk in an obvious attempt to avoid her.

Sylvia leaned forward, slapped her hand on those papers, forcing Harry to face her. "You should have let me sit in on this little meeting."

Harry tracked the line of her arm up until he met her gaze. "So you could have even more doubts?"

"Meaning?" she asked, although Harry was right on the money. She was having doubts about the story.

"You told me you had issues. So I had someone check the facts, and your draft was right on the money. But you knew that, didn't you?"

In her heart Sylvia had known, but she had needed someone else to confirm it because she was just too personally involved. She realized that clearing Carlos and Riley hadn't ended her involvement. Somewhere along the way, she had lost her objectivity when it came to Simon Davis as well. No matter how twisted his logic, he had saved the other two police officers from certain death.

"What do you want me to do?"

"I want you to finish the story. I've pulled you from all the assignments this weekend so you can stay focused. Take the draft and do what I know you can do with it."

Sylvia straightened and crossed her arms. "What if I can't?"

"If you're going to run every time the going gets tough, you may want to consider another job." With a self-satisfied smirk, Harry laced his hands behind his head and leaned backward in his chair. It groaned from his weight and teetered precariously for a moment, but then held fast.

Sylvia hated that he wanted her to go ahead with the article. But she hated one thing even more—that he was right. That she couldn't run away from doing what she knew she had to do.

"You'll have your story by Monday," she said, then turned on her heel and walked out. Harry's final words chased her out the door.

"I'd better have it if you want to keep your job."

"Lucy, you have some 'splaining to do about what happened the other day at the party," Adriana said as she dropped a stack of papers on her desk and then leaned against the edge of it with arms crossed.

Sylvia plopped herself into the chair and shifted nervously. "I know that I've been . . . secretive lately."

"Girlfriends can tell each other anything, right?" Adriana uncrossed her arms and leaned her hands on the edge of her desk.

Sylvia nodded. "I know, only . . . I didn't want to hurt you or interfere in what was going on with Riley. Especially since you were so happy with him."

"I *am* happy with him and I actually do understand why you might have held back."

Sylvia could read her friend well enough to know that Adriana already knew what was happening. "Riley told you, didn't he?"

Adriana confirmed it with a quick bob of her head. "After the party, Carlos told him what you were working on. He thought it best that I should hear about it from him first."

"I'm sorry that I didn't say anything, but—"

"You did the right thing, although I was a little pissed—"

"Only a little?" Sylvia teased, now that she knew her friend was handling it reasonably.

Adriana chuckled. "Okay, maybe more than a little."

"I didn't want to hurt you. If it turned out that Riley was dirty—"

"Riley could never do what that man said. I knew that in my heart when he told me."

Sylvia thought back to when she had first heard the accusation. To her initial thoughts about Carlos and Riley. She hadn't had the same depth of conviction at first. But after considering Randy Davis's charges and what she had come to know about Carlos, it hadn't taken her all that long to come around to believing in Carlos's innocence.

"Sylvia?" Adriana asked.

She looked up at her friend, regretting that she had even had that initial doubt. "I should have believed more."

"Carlos?"

Sylvia ran her hand through her hair. "It took me a little time to come around. To listen to what my heart was telling me."

"When it comes to men, you've got trust issues, and that's understandable," Adriana offered in her defense.

"Except that Carlos is nothing like my father," she said, and Adriana smiled.

"So he's your *papi* now and not just Pablo?"

Sylvia waved her hand. "No way. That was just a slip."

Adriana nodded and sat down in the chair beside her. "Your *papi* and *mami* were here last night for dinner."

"Again?" Sylvia challenged.

Adriana shrugged. "Can I help it if we're one of the best restaurants on the Beach?"

Sylvia chuckled. "Modest, aren't you? So spill. What was up with them?"

"Remember starry-eyed?" Sylvia nodded. "Well, make it mutually starry-eyed, hand-holding and—"

"Kissing? Touching?"

"Not to mention sharing their meals. Feeding each other their desserts," Adriana added.

"That can only mean one thing."

"Sex," they both said at the same time.

Sylvia dropped her head into her hands and said, "What am I going to do?"

"There's not much you can do about your parents. They've got to figure out what to do themselves. The bigger question is, 'What are you going to do about Carlos?'"

"I've really screwed it up, haven't I?"

"Do you care for him?"

Sylvia thought about all the emotional turmoil of the last few months. Of the conflicting thoughts and desires she'd had about Carlos, but there was one thing she had come to be certain about—she had an itch for him that she still had to scratch. An itch that as her wise mama had pointed out, she didn't think just sex could stop.

"I care for him," she admitted past the lump in her throat.

Adriana squeezed her hand. "As long as you still care, it's not too late."

28

I might be ready to run a marathon by the time I finish the story, Sylvia thought.

She had run on Friday night after seeing Adriana and before sitting down to write.

Now it was Saturday afternoon, and she was out running again since it was the one thing that seemed to help take her mind off the article.

But as her feet pounded the pavement in and around South Beach, the rhythm of her steps eerily began to echo his name.

Car-los. Car-los. Car-los.

Her investigations had absolved him of any wrongdoing in Simon Davis's death, and yet she sensed that there was something Carlos wasn't saying about the last few moments he had spent with his dying friend. Did it matter what Simon had said? Why did it bother her so much not to know?

Captain Morales had thought he had enough to close his file and maybe he was right. Since she had all the facts, there was not a single reason for her not to write the story—except maybe Simon's widow and sons. The memory of those boys weighed her down. Kept her fingers from working every time she sat down before her laptop.

But if she didn't finish the story . . .

Harry's words added themselves to the cadence of her jog.

Out-of-job. Out-of-job.

Not to mention that Harry would just have someone else finish the story. Someone who might not be as sensitive as she was to the fallout of destroying Simon Davis's reputation.

The sun stung against her skin and sweat trickled down the side of her face as well as the back of her neck. Her breath rasped heavily in and out of her chest. She needed a break.

As she hit the beginning of Lummus Park she paused, hands propped on her hips as she sucked in one hurried breath after another. When her breathing was a little steadier, she started a slow walk back to her apartment, pausing by one of the beachside showers to spritz some cool water on herself.

Sylvia slicked her hair away from her face, pulling it back and securing any loose strands. She sat on the beach wall, gazing out at the ocean as she considered what to do.

Before her, along the water's edge, a man and a woman played with two young children—a boy and a girl. The boy was dark like his father while the girl had her mother's blond hair and fair skin.

She tried superimposing her face and Carlos's on the man and woman. The images touched something within her. A spot right above her nonexistent heart ached as she thought about Carlos. If there was one thing she had come to realize, it was that she wanted another chance with Carlos. An opportunity to see if the chemistry between them could amount to something more . . . permanent.

Of course, the presumption that Carlos was even still interested or willing to give her another chance was a big one. Especially since Carlos might not ever want to speak to her again after the story about Simon Davis.

Surging up off the beach wall, Sylvia hurried back to her apartment, aware that she couldn't keep on avoiding the story.

After a quick shower, she dressed and forced herself to sit down at her laptop. Hands poised over the keys, she hesitated, but then she finally began.

Courage is not about the absence of fear. Courage is about doing what you know to be right, even though you are afraid to do it . . .

Sunday with *las familias,* Sylvia thought as she wheeled her BMW into the parking lot for the Atlantis and slipped into a spot beneath some palm trees close to the bay.

Juli and her mother were spending their day working up some new dessert together at the restaurant.

Tori and Gil were off to her parents' house in Little Havana.

Adriana and Riley were spending the day with both sets of parents at Riley's parents' place on Key Biscayne, which was not all that far from where Sylvia's *papi*—where Pablo—had bought his broken-down villa.

Before her, the bright blue of the bay stretched out as far as she could see, and she imagined that if she stared hard enough, she could pick out the place along the water that Pablo had bought. She wondered whether he would be here today for her usual Sunday visit with her mama. She hoped not. She wanted to talk to her mama about a

bunch of things. Mother/daughter kinds of things. Carlos/
Sylvia kinds of things.

Sylvia put the top up on the convertible, grabbed her
beach bag, and slowly strolled toward the pool nestled
at the back of the Atlantis by the bay. Normally it was
easy to spot her mother—she just had to look for the spot
where all the fifty-something men in the complex were
congregating. Her mother was usually somewhere in the
midst of the fold of flabby and gabby men.

But not today. Again. Last time it was because of Pablo's presence, but today he was nowhere in sight.

Her mother sat alone, her nose buried in a book. A
free chaise lounge beside her. Just one free chaise lounge
with a towel on it.

Which was both good and bad.

Bad because it meant that Pablo had staked his territory and the other men were respecting it.

Good because it meant she might have lucked out and
it would be just the two of them today.

As she approached, her mother raised her head,
slipped her Chanel sunglasses down a notch to look at
her, and smiled. She patted the chair beside her, and
Sylvia bent, dropped a kiss on her cheek. "Mama. You
look well."

Which wasn't just a meaningless pleasantry. Her mother's hazel eyes glittered happily, and a contented glow suffused her face. It wasn't color from the sun—her mother
put on enough SPF-45 to avoid the kiss of the sun's rays
during their brief time at the pool.

No, that shine . . . no, make that radiance, came from
something else—from contentment deep within.

"Things are good with you, Mama?" she asked and
eased off her wrap, exposing the black string bikini beneath, which earned a few surreptitious glances her way,

before she lay down on the chaise lounge beside her mother.

A hesitant pause came before her mama said, "Yes, things are . . . good."

Sylvia inched down her Escada sunglasses and trained her attention on her mama. "Business is good?"

"Great. I snagged that deal for the new condo development and—"

"The sale of the old villa? Pablo completed the sale, didn't he?"

Her mother marked her spot in the book she had been reading, slowly closed it, and shifted toward her. "Yes, Pablo bought the old Hitchens place. He's renovating it."

Sylvia nodded and reached for some sunscreen from her bag. "That must please you. It always was your favorite place."

With great care, Virginia placed the book down on the table between the two chaise lounges as she considered just what to tell her daughter. Too little and Sylvia would only keep on prying like the reporter that she was. Too much, and . . .

"It is my favorite place and the plans for it are wonderful."

Sylvia stopped in the middle of putting some suntan lotion on her legs. "You've seen the plans?"

"At our date the other night. Pablo and I—there's more going on now."

With a nod, Sylvia began to put on her lotion again, but her movements were short and almost brusque.

"Sylvia, honey. We need to discuss this," Virginia said, wanting everything out in the open with her daughter. Sylvia meant too much to her to ruin that relationship for any man, including Pablo.

With one last swipe of her hand, Sylvia finished, tossed

the bottle back into her bag, and slipped onto her side to face her. "Mama, I would think that you're smart enough to know when a man is trying—"

"To get on my good side? Is that what you think Pablo did by buying the villa?"

"Buying that run-down old place scored him major brownie points," Sylvia replied harshly, but then she immediately seemed to regret it. "I'm sorry. I just want to see you happy."

"Pablo didn't know how I felt—"

In a lighter tone obviously meant to smooth over her earlier pique, Sylvia said, "Mama, poker is not your game. One look at your face probably gave away how much you loved that place."

Virginia raised her hands to her face, wondering if what Sylvia said was true. Wondering if Sylvia could see everything else there, which became clear as her daughter surged up off her chaise lounge and said, "Oh no, Mama. You slept with him."

Heat suffused Virginia's cheeks as she recalled the many times she and Pablo had made love, but then she immediately berated herself about how stupid they had been the last time, when they hadn't used protection. Stupid, but incredibly satisfying. Her body still came to life just by remembering it.

Sylvia snapped her hand up, as if realizing where her mother's thoughts had gone, but even then there was something loose and playful about the action that made it clear she wasn't condemning, just teasing. "Okay, Mama, I get it. You're still a young woman with physical needs."

"I think I care for him. For Pablo. Your father—"

"Genetically only, Mama. And we've had this discussion to death."

Yes, they had. She had thought that after Sylvia's last

visit when Pablo had been here, some lines of communication had been opened between father and daughter, but maybe she had been wrong. Regardless, Sylvia had to understand and deal with Pablo.

"I want to see where this thing with Pablo goes. You were right when you said I had a thirty-year itch for him. I need to find out if I can get him out of my system, much like you have to decide what you want in your life."

With a harsh sigh, Sylvia said, "I want to be a better reporter. Be at a bigger place."

"Careers without anything else—"

"Can be lonely. It has been lonely," she finally admitted. "I hadn't realized how much until I met Carlos. He made me feel . . . different."

"So go after him," Virginia pressed, certain that it would be a big mistake for her daughter to not try and make things right with him.

Sylvia looked down and shrugged. This indecision was totally unlike her normally aggressive and take-charge daughter. With her free hand, Virginia cupped Sylvia's chin and applied gentle pressure until her daughter looked up at her. "Can you imagine a future with him?"

A furrow deepened along Sylvia's forehead. Virginia added, "Okay, maybe this one is easier to answer—Can you imagine him not being in your life right now?"

"No," was her daughter's immediate answer.

"So, what do you plan on doing about that?"

"What do you plan on doing about Pablo?" Sylvia parried.

Virginia didn't need to consider the answer to that question. She had already gone over it and over it, both before and after their very romantic night and morning together.

"I plan on taking a chance. How about you?"

Sylvia shook her head and let out a short little laugh. "You've always said the apple didn't fall far from the tree. I guess that means I'm going to take a chance as well."

Virginia leaned forward and embraced her daughter. As she did so, she said, "Let's just promise each other that we'll be here to pick up the pieces when it's all over."

"I promise, Mama. I love you," Sylvia said with a sniff.

"I love you too."

 "*To life, love,* and always being *amigas*, not to mention to Sylvia finishing the damned article," Tori said and held her mojito high up in the air.

Sylvia clinked her glass with her friends' and quickly downed a good portion of her drink, which only served to create a massive case of brain freeze, much like it had the last time. She winced as she added, "Not that Harry has acknowledged that I turned it in."

"The ol' bastard is keeping mum about it?" Adriana teased and peered at her over the rim of her glass.

Grimacing, Sylvia rubbed at her temples and said, "The ol' bastard hasn't said a word all day. I don't know if that's good or not."

"No news is good news," Juli said and forked up a shrimp from her plate.

"So Carlos not returning any of my calls is a good thing?" she said and took another big gulp of her mojito. Seeing that she had managed to almost drain it with those few gulps, she waved at the waiter to bring another.

"Maybe he's been busy settling into his new job," Adriana offered, clearly more aware of what was going on in Carlos's life than Sylvia was.

"He started work with Riley already?" she asked. When the waiter placed the second mojito before her, she finished off the first before he whisked the glass away and then quickly picked up the second.

"Aren't you rushing those a little?" Juli asked.

Sylvia glared at her friend as she took another big sip. "Just celebrating. My story is done. So is my relationship with Carlos apparently, but my mama . . . She and Pablo are having a grand ol' time."

Tori laid a hand on Sylvia's arm and applied gentle pressure. As she glanced at her friend, she noticed that Tori was looking toward the entrance of the restaurant. She tracked her friend's gaze.

Pablo stood at the hostess's podium along the open-air veranda. Alone. He was dressed casually, in khaki pants and a cream-colored guayabera that played up his dark good looks. More than one woman turned to peer his way, but he didn't acknowledge anyone other than her as their gazes locked across the distance of the room.

He inclined his head in a graceful move but made no motion toward her.

"Ask him to join us," Tori said from beside her.

"What? Are you crazy?" Sylvia whispered, but before she could do a thing, Juli rose and approached the hostess's podium. She introduced herself to Pablo and motioned to their table.

"I'm not sure I like this new self-assured Juli," Sylvia muttered as she came to her feet and grudgingly waved for Pablo to join them.

He looked behind him and then pointed to himself, as if to confirm it. When she nodded, he walked toward them, Juli following behind him.

Sylvia snagged a passing busboy and advised him that they needed another place setting and chair. In a flurry of activity, she introduced Pablo to all her friends, and he settled himself in a chair next to her.

"You two own that great restaurant on Ocean Drive," he said and motioned toward Juli and Adriana.

"Yes, we do. You've been there with Sylvia's *mami*," Adriana said, and Pablo nodded.

"We really like it. In fact, we plan on having dinner there tomorrow night."

"You're spending a lot of time together lately," Sylvia said and took a sip from her mojito.

From the corner of her eye, she detected Pablo's hesitation, but then he gathered himself and said, "I'm sure I don't have to tell you what an amazing woman your mother is."

"Sylvia's *mami* is quite an inspiration to all of us, Mr. Amenabar. She's a successful businesswoman," Tori said.

"And totally independent," Adriana added.

Juli finished up with "Amazingly beautiful."

Pablo picked up the menu the waiter had left for him, but before perusing it, he said, "I can see that Virginia has her share of admirers. That's good to know."

He only took a quick look at it before saying, "What would you recommend, Sylvia?"

"The *bistec empanizado* is always good here."

In deference to her recommendation, Pablo ordered the breaded steak. Once the waiter had left, he turned to Tori and said, "So what do you do for a living?"

Sylvia sat back, finishing her second drink and then a third, followed by a fourth as dinner progressed smoothly, even with her friends' less-than-subtle interrogation of her father.

She had to give it to him. He was smooth. Or maybe it was the alcohol she had consumed that made him appear so calm and composed as he fielded the assorted questions about the villa, his plans for it and staying in Miami, not to mention his polo playing and, of course, her mother. He even enlisted Tori to handle the contracts with the assorted contractors who were going to do all the renovations.

By the time dessert and coffees had been consumed, Pablo had charmed her friends completely. Sylvia, however, still needed additional convincing.

She stood and wavered a little on her high heels. Pablo's steadying hand came to the small of her back to offer support as they all walked out of the restaurant. They paused on the sidewalk.

"How about I walk you home?" he offered.

Sylvia was about to refuse, but Tori accepted the offer on her behalf. "That's so nice of you. Normally Sylvia and I walk home together, but I have to swing by the office to pick up Gil."

"At midnight?" Sylvia asked.

"He's been working overtime on a big case," Tori explained and quickly headed down Eighth toward Collins, where her law firm's office was located.

"Right," Sylvia said, disbelief dripping from her voice. She faced her other two friends. "And you two?"

"We're headed the opposite way," Adriana said and slipped her arm through Juli's.

"*Hasta mañana,*" Juli said as she and Adriana walked down Ocean toward their restaurant.

Pablo stood patiently beside her, his hands clasped before him as he waited.

"I'm a big girl. I don't need a bodyguard."

"You're right. But maybe this will give us some time to speak alone. About your mother and me."

Sylvia recalled her mother's face the day before. The happiness there as well as the uncertainty. She wasn't sure allowing Pablo to walk her home qualified as daughterly support, but then again, she needed to understand what was up with him to make sure her mother wouldn't get hurt.

She slipped her arm through Pablo's, and he smiled, laid his hand over hers. He inclined his head in the direction of Lummus Park. "Why don't we walk through the park. It's not as crowded or noisy."

They walked in silence for the longest time until Sylvia finally asked, "Do you love her?"

Pablo's answer came a little too quickly for her peace of mind. "Sí. I love her. I think I have always loved her."

"How do you know?"

Pablo stopped. She met his gaze, and as before, was amazed by the familiar green of his eyes and the arch of his brows, so similar to her own. With a shake of his head and a shrug, he said, "You just know."

She let out a rough sigh and started walking once again. "Right. You just see a person and you know—"

"That every moment you're not with them, a part of you seems empty. That when you're with them, you're at peace."

She gazed up at him, amazed that his words had echoed Adriana's. But even more important, she didn't doubt the sincerity of his feelings. He wore his emotions on his sleeve for her to see. "Is that how you've felt all this time? For thirty years?"

"That would be rather melodramatic of me to admit, wouldn't it?" he said with a lift of his brow.

She laughed. "But you did feel—"

"Dissatisfied. No matter what I did, nothing gave me true happiness . . . until I saw your mother again. Things seemed different after that."

"Different? And you think this difference—"

"Is on account of your *mami*? *Sí*, I think so," he said and began walking again, but remained silent.

She considered what he had said. Wondered if the confusion and unhappiness that had colored her world lately might have changed with Carlos in her life. Not that she had much choice about that, since he hadn't returned any of the calls she had made to him since Friday.

As they approached her block, she motioned to Pablo, and they strolled through the park, crossed back over Ocean and to her building. At the door to her home, Pablo stood before her, slightly anxious. "*Gracias* for letting me walk you home. A father—"

She held her hand up to silence him, and he winced as if he had been struck. "Pablo, it's still too soon, but . . . I'm glad we had this time to talk."

"I am too. We both love your *mami*—"

"We do. The last thing I want is for her to be hurt again, so . . . Please don't hurt her," she asked again and was unprepared for his actions.

He had her in a bear hug before she could protest, and somehow, she couldn't muster the fight to push him away. Instead, she awkwardly returned the hug, but as she stepped back from him, she caught a glimpse of a familiar light blue vintage Corvette zipping past, Carlos at the wheel.

"Damn." She followed the car as it jerked to a stop. Carlos looked over at them and then peeled away with a loud squeal of the car's tires.

"Was that someone you know?" Pablo asked and glanced down at her.

"Just someone who made my life . . . different for a little bit."

"I'm sorry. I didn't mean to cause any problems." He glanced back up the block to the Corvette, where Carlos waited for traffic to let up. "Do you want me to—"

"No, that's okay. This is something the two of us need to settle when we're calmer. But thanks, anyway."

With a nod and a quick kiss on her cheek, he walked away, and Sylvia wondered where he would go. Whether he would call her mother or whether he would head home alone to wherever he was staying.

Get into a cold bed alone.

Wake up alone.

Unfortunately much like she would do, she thought, and gazed wistfully at the taillights of Carlos's Corvette as he turned onto Ocean.

With that last glimpse, she walked into her building.

Alone.

30

Sylvia had expected that Carlos wouldn't bother answering her calls or coming by again after seeing her with Pablo on Monday night. He probably assumed the worst—that she had moved on with another man.

Wednesday came and Harry had still not said a word to her about whether he had appoved the article for publication, so she dropped by the magazine's offices to check for any new assignments. Once she had the schedule for that day's events, she popped by Harry's office, but he was busy and Carmela said that she doubted he would be done anytime soon.

With an event in just over an hour that she had to cover, Sylvia didn't have time to wait. In her cubicle, she reviewed her e-mails and messages.

Nothing from Carlos.

But that wouldn't stop her from contacting him. She needed closure.

Sylvia called Adriana and asked for Carlos's new

e-mail at M&E Imports, where he was now working for Riley. She assumed he was in the security section, although she had never really understood what it was that Riley and his people did at the import company.

Adriana happily provided the e-mail and wished Sylvia luck.

Sylvia hoped that by sending Carlos an advance copy of her article before it was published, there would be one less bone of contention between them.

Her e-mail didn't say much. Just that she hoped he would find the article accurate. She didn't dare hope that he would approve. Carlos probably wished that the article would never be published, and considering that Harry had yet to say a word to Sylvia about it, maybe it wouldn't.

Regardless, she felt she had done right by everyone involved while fulfilling her obligations as a journalist.

The event she was supposed to cover was down at the beach, the first of a series of jazz concerts. Both old and emerging artists were scheduled to perform for the rest of the week, culminating on Saturday with a daylong concert with multiple artists. After that concert, the event would end with a fashion show featuring the work of a number of local designers.

The photographer was already waiting for her when she arrived. The two of them quickly started working the crowd, Sylvia interviewing the organizers, artists, and attendees while the photographer snapped an assortment of pictures. They were there for close to two hours when she decided she had enough information for a short piece. She also picked up the press packet so they could include information on the remaining acts that would be appearing during the rest of the week.

As she headed off the beach toward the park, Sylvia

noticed Carlos standing by the low seashell-covered wall. She almost didn't notice him at first, since he looked so different. Dressed in an expensive dark blue suit, crisp white shirt, and striped tie, he screamed "corporate." Totally unlike his bad boy clothes or the suits he had worn when he had been undercover in the clubs.

His hands were propped on his lean hips and dark mirrored sunglasses hid his eyes from her, but his stance communicated just how awkward he felt. As she approached, he dropped his hands and shifted his weight from foot to foot.

"Hi," she said as she stopped before him and looked up, seeing nothing but the reflection of her face in the lenses of his glasses.

"*Hola.* I just came by to . . ."

She waited for him to go on, but instead he just looked away and shoved his hands in his pockets, jingled some change there.

"It's okay, Carlos. I know this is difficult and—"

"Does he make you happy?" he asked, whipping off his sunglasses.

"Happy? Who?" she said, but then it occurred to her. "You mean Pablo? The man you saw me with on Monday night?"

He nodded. "*Sí.* Does he—"

"Hopefully he's making my mother happy," she clarified and chuckled with a shake of her head.

"Your *mami?* Is this some kinky three-way—"

"He's my father," she explained, and a stunned look came to his face.

"Your father?" he said and gulped. "So what I saw that night—"

"Was a fatherly hug. Nothing more than that, but thanks for thinking otherwise. This sensitive, jealous guy thing is kind of sexy." She stepped up to him and cradled his cheek.

The ghost of a smile came to his lips. "Really? So this is a good thing?"

"Yes, it is, because that means that maybe you still care. Even if only a little," she said and passed her thumb across the defined edges of his mouth.

Carlos took a step toward her but made no move to touch her. "Actually, more than a little. I've been miserable thinking about everything that's been keeping us apart."

"*I've* been keeping us apart. My being afraid of any kind of relationship with you has kept us apart." She pointed to a spot above her heart. "But I think I might be ready now, if you're willing to give me another chance."

Carlos dragged a hand through his hair and stared past her, considering his words carefully. Finally he looked at her again. "The article . . . Simon was supposed to set Riley and me up for execution because we were causing his bosses too much trouble."

"Is that why he was sorry? Is that what he said to you—"

"Before he died. I tried to stop the bleeding, but he was hurt too bad. But he told me what he had done. He said he was sorry and to take care of his family. That's what I've tried to do. I've tried to keep his secrets."

"I understand that. I want you to understand that I tried to do the same when I wrote that piece."

"He was a hero at the end. You made that clear in your story," Carlos said. He picked up his hand and rubbed at a spot along his side, as if it still pained him. The side where he had been shot four years earlier.

Sylvia picked up on that cue, laid her hand over his, and stilled the nervous motion. "I'm glad that you're working with Riley."

"Why is that?" he asked and twined his fingers with hers.

"Because I don't think I can deal with people using you for target practice anymore."

Carlos smiled at her use of his own words. "Me too. So I guess the fact that you still care like that—"

"Is a good thing. Which means that if you care a little and I care a little, we can maybe give this another try."

His smile broadened, and he swung one arm around her shoulders and drew her close. "*Amor,* I suspect that as hardheaded as we both are, it may take several tries until we get this right."

Sylvia chuckled and wrapped her arms around him. "That's okay. As long as it doesn't take thirty years."

Carlos pulled away, a confused look on his face. "Thirty years? Why would it possibly take—"

"Do you have time for lunch? It's a long story."

"A long story? Does it begin like, 'Once upon a time . . .'?" he teased and slipped his arm around her waist.

"Actually it does. Once upon a time, there was a polo player named Pablo and a stable hand named Virginia," she began as they started walking toward Adriana and Juli's restaurant on Ocean.

"This story sounds promising, but maybe not as interesting as 'Once upon a time, there was a cop called Carlos and a reporter called Sylvia—'"

She held up her hand, but he snagged it. "What's the matter, *amorcito?* Not interested in a Happily-Ever-After?" he quipped and playfully nudged her.

"I think I can handle only one fairy tale at a time. So for now, I'm learning to deal with the possibility that my father and mother may actually make us one big happy family after so many years," she said and shot a look up at him to gauge his reaction.

Carlos stopped and met her gaze. "I know that it's hard for you to imagine that after so long they might still love each other."

"Nearly impossible. So you may need to be patient while I get used to the idea," she admitted.

Carlos laughed again. "*Querida*, if I wasn't a patient man, do you think I would be here now?"

As they waited at the corner for a break in traffic so they could cross the street, she faced him and asked, "Why are you here now?"

"Because I believe in fairy tales, why else?" He bent his head and kissed her in a way that left no doubt as to why he was there.

When he ended the kiss, she looked up at him and said, "You know what?"

"What?"

"Maybe it's time I believed in fairy tales too."

31

SIX MONTHS LATER

The heat of his body warmed her entire back as she lay beside him. She liked these mornings, when she could lie in bed next to him and for the first time in her life feel . . . peace. Happiness. Completeness.

Only her stomach started doing the funny rumbling thing that had started earlier in the week. The rumbling grew in intensity until she knew she couldn't just lie there anymore.

Sylvia bolted to the bathroom, knelt before the toilet, and lost the contents of her stomach. But that didn't bring any relief. For the next few minutes, she gagged over and over as waves of nausea racked her body.

She heard his footsteps behind her, and then Carlos passed a cool washcloth across the back of her neck as Sylvia held on to the chilled edges of the porcelain toilet bowl.

It helped, but only a little as another wave of nausea

washed over her. After the spasms had finally passed, she leaned back and took a deep breath.

"You okay?" he asked.

She shot a half glance at him over her shoulder and nodded. "I'll be okay. It must be a flu or something."

"For an entire week? And only in the morning?" Carlos said as he rubbed her back.

Unfortunately, he was right, which was why she had gone to the drugstore the night before and picked up a pregnancy test. Motioning to the medicine cabinet, she said, "There's a kit in there. If you could get it down . . ."

Carlos did as she asked, stood by as she read the instructions and after, gave her the privacy she needed to take the test. When she was done, she called him back in, and they waited together, hand in hand, counting down the minutes until it was time to check on the little plastic stick sitting on the edge of the deep maroon-colored bathroom sink.

"What does it say?" she asked, too nervous to reach for it.

Carlos grabbed the stick and held it up to the light. She knew even before he uttered a word from the self-satisfied smirk on his face.

She snatched the stick from his hand, confirmed what she had guessed, and tossed the pregnancy test into the garbage can.

Poking her finger into the hard muscles of his chest, she said, "Don't get all full of yourself now. Just 'cause one of your speedy little swimmers managed to get past—"

He covered her mouth with his hand, but she bit down on it.

"Ño, what was that for?"

"Because now we have no choice but to have you

make an honest woman of me," Sylvia said and stalked out of the bathroom.

Carlos immediately chased after her, and when she plopped down on the edge of the bed, he knelt before her, a broad grin on his face. "Why, Ms. Amenabar. Is this your rather unromantic way of saying you would like for me to marry you?"

She wasn't the kind of woman who had spent countless hours picturing just this moment, but she had to confess that she had imagined it would be a little bit more romantic than this. She realized that if it wasn't, it was because of her.

Taking hold of his hand, she urged him to rise and stood before him. "Carlos Ramirez. I love you. I can't imagine spending the rest of my life without you. So will you marry me? Be a father to our baby?"

"I thought you would never ask," he said, swept her up into his arms and twirled her around.

Her head whirled from the motion, however, and she tapped on his shoulder.

With a look at her face, which she suspected was a rather sickly shade of green, Carlos rushed with her to the bathroom once again.

Sylvia wanted to break the news to her mother alone, since for so long it had been just the two of them. Now, there was Carlos, and soon there would be yet another person who would be part of her life. Part of her mama's life.

She wanted this moment to be special for her mama. Not to mention that she wasn't sure how her mama would react to the fact that at barely forty-seven, she would soon be a grandmother.

When her mother opened the door to her condo, she

seemed a trifle nervous. The hand that held the door open gave a little shake.

"Are you okay?" Sylvia asked.

"I'm fine, honey. Just a little worried about you. You were rather cryptic on the phone."

Sylvia began to answer, but before she could utter a word, the rumble in her stomach threatened to erupt like Mount Vesuvius. A cold sweat swept across her as she controlled the urge, but before she lost it, she bolted from the entry and across the condo.

Virginia closed the door and quickly followed her to the bathroom, where she was leaning over the toilet, much as she had been doing for the better part of the morning. Her body shook from the force of her heaves.

Her mama whipped a small hand towel from the rack, dampened it with cool water, and placed it against the back of her neck, trying to offer comfort, much as Carlos had done earlier that day.

Eventually, Sylvia's iffy stomach settled down, and as she shot a glance at her mother, a glitter of something on her mother's ring finger caught her eye. Sylvia's concentration on that hand snared her mother's attention, and with a smile, her mama held up her hand to reveal the large emerald and diamond engagement ring on her finger.

"Mama, is this what I think it is?" Sylvia asked as she took hold of her mother's hand and peered at the elegant setting.

"It is, and is this bout of vomiting what I think it is?"

"It is," Sylvia said, but then she slowly picked up her left hand to reveal her ring finger as well. The one where barely an hour earlier, Carlos had placed his grandmother's prized engagement ring.

Her mother opened her arms, and Sylvia stepped into them. In that instant, Sylvia knew.

There really was such a thing as Happily-Ever-After.

But she also knew the story wasn't complete just yet.

It was never a good thing when one of the *chicas* called an emergency meeting. It was typically a very, very bad thing when that meeting couldn't even wait until the dinner hour.

Due to the urgency of her call, Juli and Adriana had set aside a table at the back of their restaurant, and when Sylvia arrived, her three friends were already sitting there, tall glasses filled with mojitos, waiting.

Juli was the first to comment. "*Amiga*, you look like hell."

Sylvia chuckled, too happy to be annoyed. "I feel like hell."

Tori laid a hand on her shoulder and urged her to sit. "Sylvita, tell us what's wrong. Did Harry kill the story?"

"No. It'll be in this month's magazine."

Adriana said, "So what's—"

Sylvia waved her index finger to motion for them to stop. Picking up the glass, she usurped Tori's usual role as the giver of the toast. "To life, love, and always being *amigas*," Sylvia said and held her mojito high up in the air.

Her three friends quickly drank from their mojitos, but Sylvia just put her glass back down, which prompted an immediate comment from ever-perceptive Adriana.

"You're not drinking?"

"No, I'm not," Sylvia said with a smile, eliciting an assortment of astonished outbursts.

Tori went first. "You're pregnant?"

"*Estas embarazada*," Juli said.

"Girl, you can't be telling the truth," finished Adriana.

"Yes, I am, so I hope you are all prepared to be fairy godmothers to this baby," she said and laid her hand over her still flat belly in a protective gesture, but as she did so, that immediately created a raucous series of near screams.

"*Dios mio, no lo creo.*"

"Sylvita, you're engaged!"

"No way. Is it true?"

"Way," she said, mimicking Adriana as she held up the hand with the ring. But then she plunged on. "So I hope you won't mind if before you become fairy godmothers, you have to be maids of honor at my wedding."

In a flurry of motion, Sylvia was surrounded by her friends. Embraced with their love and well wishes.

It was only then that she could finally say what was in her heart.

It had finally ended Happily-Ever-After.

Up Close and Personal
with the Author

What inspired you to write this second novel in your South Beach Chicas series?

When I finished writing the first novel, *Sex and the South Beach Chicas*, I just knew that I had to further explore not only what happened with Sylvia and Carlos after the shooting, but also what made Sylvia's mother, Virginia, into the woman she is today. Sylvia and Virginia were so totally alive for me that it was a pleasure giving you a further look into their lives and loves in *South Beach Chicas Catch Their Man*.

Sylvia has a hard time trusting men in her life because of her rocky past. Why do you think she finds Carlos so appealing when, on the exterior, he seems like such a bad boy?

I think women are suckers for bad boys. That explains Sylvia's initial attraction to the seemingly too-suave and too-handsome Carlos. But being a reporter, Sylvia knows people aren't always what they seem, so I think that from the beginning, in addition to finding him incredibly attractive, Sylvia also senses Carlos is different from the tough appearance he shows the world. Their encounters over the course of both South Beach Chicas books proves that her initial hunch about Carlos is correct!

What influenced you the most in creating Sylvia and Virginia's mother–daughter bond?

Definitely my relationship with my mother, Carmen. She was not only my mom, but also a mentor and a friend that I could always count on for anything. My mother laid the groundwork for me and her guidance made me strong and determined. I was able to work with my mom right after I graduated from college and every payday we would go out to lunch together and just chitchat about everything that was going in our lives, much like Sylvia and Virginia share their Sundays together. On Saturdays, my sister and I would help our mom take care of household shopping and that, too, was usually accompanied by a quick lunch where the chicas would all talk and have fun. Our bond was special and I have tried to create that same kind of bond with my daughter. Now my daughter and I are the best of friends—just like Sylvia and Virginia!

Virginia is a hoot! What made you focus on her character as a sexy, older woman?

They say forty is the new twenty and that's definitely the case with Virginia. Because I find that older women are not usually portrayed by the media as vibrant and sexual creatures, it was important for me to show that Virginia is not only successful at her career, but also a passionate, attractive woman with a responsible and compassionate soul. That's a blend that's hard to resist, and one that only gets better with age. Clearly Pablo couldn't resist her!

Your sensuously vivid descriptions of South Beach make it seem like an exotic paradise. Is South Beach really as sexy as you make it seem?

South Beach sizzles with sex and excitement. Maybe it's the tropical weather or the mojitos you sip while sitting on the veranda of one of the Art Deco hotels, but there is definitely a vibe that energizes the entire city as night falls and the beautiful people come out to play. Of course, South Beach is totally lovely by day as well, especially the section on Ocean Drive that includes Lummus Park. As kids, my family and friends used to stay at the hotels along this strip when we would visit the city (before they became so expensive!).

Sylvia wants to be taken seriously as a journalist, which causes her to temporarily put her friends, family, and boyfriend second to her career. Have you ever had to make a choice between your career and your loved ones?

As a working mom I am always pulled between my career and my loved ones because modern women must not only run a household, but earn a living as well. As an attorney, I sometimes work long hours and having a second career as a writer eats up even more of my time. Despite that, family comes first. It's important to me, and I've been lucky to have a supportive family. Also, I've included my daughter in as many of my writing-related activities as I can. She's now a budding writer as well, being a very creative individual.

Each of the chicas is so different. Where did you find your inspiration for each of their characters? Which of the chicas is most like you?

All of them! Actually, I'm most like Tori in that I'm the responsible one who hides her passion behind boring business suits. A bit of me is like Adriana, a little stubborn-yet-caring and always thinking about the next thing that has to be done. Juli is a part of my soul because of her passion for what she does—I love to cook and if I wasn't a lawyer and writer, I'd be a chef. And what about Sylvia, you ask? What I wouldn't give to have Sylvia's determination and daring! So, that's how the chicas came to life in my head—by taking a little bit of me and infusing it in each of them.

Your books have such an authentic South Beach flavor, including both American and Latin influences. Have you spent a lot of time in Miami? To what extent does being a Latina writer affect your characters' dialogue and motivations?

I had a grandmother who lived in Miami, along with many family friends. As kids we would go to Miami every summer to visit and for me, Miami replaced the Havana that I had not known and which I still do not know. As an adult, I've spent many vacations in South Beach and just love the energy along Ocean Drive. As for being a Latina writer, I think of myself more as a writer who just happens to be Latina. When I write, I treat Latino things as just part of the mainstream, which I think reflects the current status of Latinos in the United States. By doing so, I involve all kinds of readers in what I write and hopefully foster understanding of Latino culture by exposing more people to it with my novels.

Do you have a group of "South Beach Chicas" that you hang out with at home in New York? What do you do together for fun?

My chicas are unfortunately spread all over the United States so I don't get to see them as often as I'd like! We get together at writing conferences and hang out, talk, share some drinks, dance, and do all kinds of things just for the fun of it. Because we only see each other occasionally, it makes the time spent together special, but I definitely miss being with them when we're apart. It's a comfort that we all have Internet access because it makes the physical distance between us seem smaller when we can just shoot each other an e-mail.

What do you find to be the most difficult part about writing a book?

For me, the most difficult parts of writing a book are creating the synopsis and developing love scenes. A synopsis is torture for me because I am a seat-of-the-pants writer and hate to commit to a plot when I know I will end up wanting to change it! As for the love scenes, researching them can be stimulating, but actually it's tough to do them well because I want each encounter to be different and to be in sync with the personalities of the respective characters. It sometimes takes a few revisions before the love scene feels right for a particular story and pair of characters.

Where can we find out what's up with you or contact you?

I will be visiting a number of bookstores and conventions in the coming year to promote *South Beach Chicas Catch Their Man* as well as my other 2007 releases. For more information on this and other appearances, or to contact me, you can visit my website at www.caridad.com.

Whether you're a Good Girl or a Naughty Girl, Downtown Press has the books you love!

Look for these Good Girls...

The Ex-Wife's Survival Guide
DEBBY HOLT
Essential items: 1. Alcohol. 2. A sense of humor. 3. A sexy new love interest.

Suburbanistas
PAMELA REDMOND SATRAN
From A-list to Volvo in sixty seconds flat.

Un-Bridaled
EILEEN RENDAHL
She turned the walk down the aisle into the hundred-meter dash…in the other direction.

The Starter Wife
GIGI LEVANGIE GRAZER
She's done the starter home and starter job…but she never thought she'd be a starter wife.

The New York Times bestseller!

I Did (But I Wouldn't Now)
CARA LOCKWOOD
Hindsight is a girl's best friend.

Everyone Worth Knowing
LAUREN WEISBERGER
The devil wore Prada—but the bouncer wears Dolce.

The New York Times bestseller!

And don't miss these Naughty Girls...

The Manolo Matrix
JULIE KENNER
If you thought finding the perfect pair of shoes was hard—try staying alive in them.

Enslave Me Sweetly
An Alien Huntress Novel
GENA SHOWALTER
She has the body of a killer… and the heart of a killer.

Great storytelling just got a new address.

A Division of Simon & Schuster
A CBS COMPANY

Naughty Girls